Doc Voodoo: Crossfire

A novel by
DALE LUCAS

Published 2013 by Beating Windward Press LLC

For contact information, please visit:
www.BeatingWindward.com

First Edition
ISBN: 978-1-940761-02-2

For Gabriel

Haitian vodou, like organized crime, is a hierarchy: a complex system of patrons and clients; bosses, captains, and soldiers. Everything works on a basic quid pro quo principle as old as time: this for that; a favor for a favor; you scratch my back, I scratch yours. Collectively, the gods of vodou are known as the lwa.

At the top of the lwa pyramid are the Orishas: the movers and shakers; the matriarchs and patriarchs of a number of elemental clans whose powers bind all those beneath them: the cool, fluid Rada; the fierce and fiery Petro; and the Ghede, the house made up of the ancestors, the dead, and their chthonic keepers.

Doing the work of the Orishas and running their own stables of servants and soldiers are the caporegime of the vodou realms: the Barons.

And at the bottom of the heap—the minor spirits, dead souls, and lingering ancestors who do the grunt work of the Orishas and the Barons, along with everyday Joes like you and me: people of flesh and blood who give the Barons and Orishas offerings in exchange for blessings and curses; and who sometimes give their bodies over to possession as shuttles and mouthpieces for the lwa.

Small wonder that when we're saddled by the lwa, doing their dirty work, they call us horses...

1

The meeting was three hours old, and the Reverend Barnabus Farnes's patience was at an end.

"The answer is plain," the Reverend Adam Clayton Brown, Jr., was saying. "Harlem needs a moral re-awakening. A renaissance of the spirit."

Beside him, Ms. Lucille Walker cocked her head. "All well and good, but spiritual aims need practical application. We need community solidarity—and I'm not just talking about landlords and businessmen. I'm talking about trade unions, artists' cooperatives, and voter registration drives—"

"You're still missing the point," Jebediah Debbs, his self-styled majesty, argued. "There is no place for the Negro on this side of the ocean. The only answer is a return to the land that bore us. The establishment of a Negro empire, with Negro legislators, and a Negro population. Africa for the Africans, in the words of my esteemed colleague, Mr. Garvey. This land—these United States—are someone else's dream, and we'll never be welcome to share in it."

The Reverend Farnes sighed. "I think," he said, pinching the bridge of his nose, "this meeting is adjourned."

Reverend Brown studied his pocket watch. "Time does fly," he said wistfully. Farnes smiled a little at that. Adam had always been a master of polite understatement and irony.

"My honorable brothers and sister, this is a crisis. We can't adjourn with so little decided!"

Ms. Walker studied the notepad that she'd been recording the minutes on. "I've got pages and pages of motions and resolutions here, Mr. Debbs. How on earth can you call that 'so little'?" She began to read the many motions. "A trip to the mayor's office, an apprenticeship program linked to the Chamber of Commerce, an appeal to the temperance and truancy committees, a neighborhood vigilance association—"

"You see, *that's* the sort of motion I can stand behind," Debbs said. "A vigilance committee! The police are corrupt and City Hall completely indifferent—"

"Dear lady and gentlemen," the Reverend Farnes broke in, determined to nip another one of Debbs's harangues in the bud, "I think we've done more than enough for one night. I move we adjourn."

"Second," the Reverend Brown said.

"Motion carried," Ms. Walker said, closing her stenographer's book.

"This is just the sort of apathy I fight against, day after day after day," Debbs grumbled.

"Ms. Walker," Reverend Farnes said. "Make a note that at the next meeting, the first order of business is a discussion concerning just this sort of apathy."

"Note made, reverend."

Debbs glared at the Reverend Farnes. "I don't appreciate humor at my expense," he said.

The Reverend Farnes stared him down. It would take more than a two-hundred-twenty pound West Indian demagogue to bully him in his own church. "Mr. Debbs," he said, "I don't much appreciate your constant attempts to hijack these meetings and shape them to your personal agenda. But we can discuss that at the next meeting, if you like. This night's business is done. Now, if you'll excuse me," he rose, "I need to close this place up and be on my way."

The others rose in answer to his prompt. Debbs still fumed. Reverend Farnes hated to be uncharitable, but it was late, he was tired, and he still had to walk home in a cold April rain. He hadn't eaten since lunchtime, either. His niece, Fralene, would give him what-for about that.

As the Reverend Farnes slipped out of his pew, his colleagues slipped into their coats and hats.

"I'll see you into a cab, Ms. Walker," the Reverend Brown said. Farnes smiled. That was Adam, ever the gentleman.

"Unnecessary, Reverend Brown," Ms. Walker said. "I'm just up Eighth Avenue and I have a very stout umbrella. The walk will do me good."

"Then, it's a walk," Brown answered. "But I'd be no man at all if I let a woman walk home alone on such dark and stormy night."

"I'd accompany you myself," Mr. Debbs cut in, "if I weren't going in the opposite direction."

"No need for apologies, Mr. Debbs," Ms. Walker said. "As always, you remain gracious, but contrary."

Farnes, having just reached the door to the back corridors beside the choir loft, smiled in spite of himself. He was glad that Adam and Ms. Walker were just as tired of Debbs's posturing and preening as he was. Debbs, for his part, either didn't get the joke, or refused to acknowledge it. His silence in answer to Ms. Walker's jibe was a great, black cloud in the sanctuary.

The Reverend Farnes turned and waved to them. "Safe travel, all," he said. "See you next Wednesday."

Adam gave the Reverend Farnes a friendly wave and smile as he escorted Ms. Walker down the aisle toward the narthex. Debbs was already marching ahead of them, not even a farewell offered. Farnes hated to admit ill will toward anyone, but he was starting to regret inviting the belligerent Mr. Debbs to join their committee.

XX

A steady rain fell on 137th Street, turning the gutters into roiling sluiceways and the normally bright streetlights into little more than tall and sickly kerosene lamps. Automobile traffic was thin, foot traffic almost non-existent.

The Reverend Adam Clayton Brown and Ms. Lucille Walker shared Ms. Walker's umbrella. Jebediah Debbs, still fuming, opened his own umbrella, grumbled a farewell to them, and trudged off into the April rain. Brown, for his part, was suddenly stung by a pang of regret.

Ms. Walker shook her head beside him. "He's so angry."

Reverend Brown shrugged. "We are all products of our environment, Ms. Walker. Far be it from me to second-guess the many trials and tribulations that have made the Jebediah Debbses of the world as they are." He looked into her brown eyes and shrugged. "Not a one of us is perfect, are we?"

Ms. Walker set them marching toward Eighth Avenue. "Hardly," she admitted. "Nonetheless, I have a hard time

3

summoning much sympathy for a man like that, all puffed up like an angry ape."

They fell in step, moving easily northwestward. The Reverend Brown knew that Ms. Walker could handle herself—she held a PhD, was a card-carrying communist party member, and often bolstered her husband in his union-building efforts when he grew disheartened. She could teach the lot of them a thing or two about courage and conviction, Brown supposed. Nonetheless, he felt it would have been a terrible impropriety if he'd let her walk the ten blocks home on such a night. He himself didn't care for the notion of walking alone in weather like this, and was glad of her company.

Idly, Brown wondered if that made him a coward.

"Maybe you were right," Ms. Walker said as they crossed Seventh Avenue. "Maybe this would be a night for a cab." The rain was so loud above and around them that they almost had to shout to be heard, even huddled so close together.

"We'll get you up to Eighth," Brown said. "Certainly we can flag you a cab there?"

Though the streets were almost deserted, there was movement in the windows and doorways of the brownstones, storefronts and homes they passed. Lamps glowed warmly behind milky curtains, attended by the moving shadows of their occupants. Brown stole glances at them all as they passed—cozy sitting rooms, welcoming cafes, warm parlors—and dreamed of his own little parsonage, his cozy kitchen, his warm bed, waiting.

"Do you know him well?" Ms. Walker asked.

"Who's that?" the Reverend Brown replied, drawn out of his reverie.

"Our Mr. Debbs."

Reverend Brown shrugged. "Not terribly well," he said. "So far as I know, he learned of our little committee via friends of the Reverend Farnes—much to the reverend's chagrin."

"He worked with Mr. Garvey?" Ms. Walker asked.

Brown nodded. "As I hear it, he was in Mr. Garvey's inner circle. When Mr. Garvey went to prison, that circle squabbled and tore itself apart. Mr. Debbs arose as cock of the walk."

"They don't seem to like each other," Ms. Walker said, a mischievous little smile on her lips. "The Reverend Farnes and Mr. Debbs."

"No, ma'am, they don't," Reverend Brown answered. "But, sometimes politics and activism make for strange bedfellows. If Mr. Debbs wants what we want, we're obliged to include him and see if we all can't contribute to the greater good, personal enmities aside. As annoyed as he may be, Barney understands that."

Ms. Walker looked a little shocked. "Barney?" she asked.

"The Reverend Farnes," Brown clarified. "We go way back—all the way to Seminary."

"Barney," Ms. Walker said. "I can't imagine the Reverend Barnabus Farnes letting anyone call him Barney…"

Brown shrugged. "Time and familiarity give me some privileges, I guess," he said, and felt a warm flush in his cheeks. He hoped Barney would make it home safe tonight as well…

They reached the intersection of 137th Street and Eighth Avenue then. Brown was about to search up and down the avenue for an approaching cab when a dark blue Packard careened around the corner from behind them. The sedan took the turn tightly and sent up a giant, shimmering sheet of gutter-wash as it did so.

Reverend Brown and Ms. Walker were both soaked, the water cold and shocking.

The Packard screeched to a halt in the street just before them.

"I never!" Ms. Walker said.

"See here!" the Reverend Brown cried.

The doors of the Packard opened.

Men with guns stepped out.

XX

While the Reverend Brown and Ms. Walker enjoyed their shared umbrella, Jebediah Debbs marched up Lenox Avenue, most dissatisfied with his experience among the Harlem Concerned Citizens' Brigade. The Reverend Farnes was haughty, the Reverend Brown so affable as to be laughable, and Ms. Walker a foolish, naïve bourgeois housewife playing leftist crusader once or twice a week between lavish parties at her posh Sugar Hill high rise. Debbs thought that perhaps, just perhaps, he might succeed in radicalizing these old guard Talented Tenth sorts, but he had been sorely mistaken. Their innate responses to the crises all around them were passivity, docility, assimilation, submission. Debbs would have none of it. Now that Mr. Garvey was doing time in a Georgia prison, the need for action was clearer than ever. Debbs was a revolutionary, and he would remain so, even if it meant trampling on smiling, agreeable house niggers like the Reverend Barnabus Farnes and company.

Besides, he thought, *they've never given me the proper respect. They condescend to me, sport at me to my face, behind my back. But they'll see… there's a war coming. When the guns roar and the billy clubs crack and the gutters run red, their sort will look to me and mine for protection… and we'll decry them for the cowards they are and throw them to the white wolves…*

A car horn blared at him, shocking him from his fuming. The car with the blaring horn—a Willys Overland with chrome trim—made a suicidal left turn to barrel west down 140th Street. The Overland swerved as it turned, tires squealing for traction on the rain-slicked roadway, and as it passed just before Debbs, it hit the gurgling rainwater in the gutter and splashed his trousers.

Debbs couldn't believe it. How dare that rascal leave him soaked and dripping there on the sidewalk! *This was a brand new suit!* And without even stopping to see if he was well before speeding on! The nerve! There and then, Jebediah Debbs was through being disrespected. Starting there and then—*at that very moment*—he would not countenance another insult, great or small.

They would pay. They would *all* pay…

But for now, there was no use stopping. The rain still fell and he still had several blocks to go before he reached his apartment house. Looking both ways, Debbs stepped off the sidewalk and crossed 140th Street. The rain beat down mercilessly on the cupola of his umbrella and raced in thick sheets over the deserted sidewalks. No one was out and about tonight—who would be, in such weather?—and he was glad of it. He wanted no company, no distractions. He just wanted to walk, and think, and work out his revenge for all the disrespectful, doubting fools that would be swallowed in the coming conflagration while he and his U.N.I.A. fellows stood tall and proud, strong and capable even in the midst of total, unbridled anarchy.

Because it was coming. Everyone had to know it was coming. Hundreds of lynchings every year… thousands over the course of the decades since the turn of the century… such bloodshed could not be allowed to pass without reciprocity. Blood cried out for blood. That was the point that Debbs had been trying to make to all these uptown gum-beaters, stormbuzzards and hanky-heads ever since he started drawing crowds on street corners, doing his damnedest to spread Mr. Garvey's words.

War was coming. They needed a plan of attack or a plan of escape. Anything less would result in their extinction. He heard the truth in Garvey's words even if others didn't. That's why he'd cleaned out the U.N.I.A. when Mr. Garvey was so unceremoniously railroaded by that kike judge and his bent jury. Anyone who didn't get the message needed to hit the road.

Debbs was approaching another intersection, and forced himself to look up and down all four streets as he approached, eager to avoid another close call with death this evening. What good could he do anyone if he were splattered all over Lenox Avenue, a broken rag doll in a tailored suit?

Turning to glance back over his shoulder, to see if any cars approached from behind, he noticed that he was being followed. He hadn't heard footsteps because the rain was far too loud.

Strange: his erstwhile shadow looked like a white man.

Debbs made the corner of 142nd Street and prepared to cross. He noticed someone else approaching from his left.

Another white man.

They did not carry umbrellas. They simply trudged along in the rain, hands in their pockets, collars high, hats sluicing rainwater off onto their coat mantles.

Immediately, Debbs felt a tingle of foreboding.

That's when the first drew a gun from his pocket.

XX

After his companions had departed, the Reverend Farnes took the stairs to the basement level, where many of the offices and meeting rooms of the church lay empty and silent. He shut off the lights, made sure the side door that led up to the street was locked, then climbed the stairs again. Above, he swept through his office and checked the back door that led to the little cluster of classrooms and the cloister that appended the rear of the sanctuary. Locked up tight. Time to go.

Farnes doubled back to the sanctuary and the choir loft. From the choir loft, he was able to turn off most of the lights in the sanctuary, save one circuit that left the big meeting hall dim and rife with shadows. Now that he was all alone, he could hear the sound of the persistent spring rain on the pitched slate roof of the sanctuary. He thought he had an umbrella near the front door—just beside the coat closet where his hat and overcoat awaited him. If not, he might have to venture all the way back to his office and call Fralene to come fetch him. At his age, it was the height of folly to walk home exposed to weather like this.

He rounded the choir loft, heading straight for the long aisle that bisected the sanctuary. At the head of the aisle, he stopped.

He wasn't alone.

"Who is that?" he asked, squinting in the uneven light of the shadowed sanctuary. It appeared to be two men, big and broad-shouldered, wearing dripping overcoats and soggy hats. They sat on opposing pews about halfway up the center aisle, sentinels guarding his last walk to freedom. In the mottled light, he couldn't see their faces, but he could tell they were white.

"C'mere, pops," one of them said, and slowly rose to his feet.

"Pops?" the Reverend Barnabus Farnes sneered. "Now, who are you to come into my church and talk to me that way?"

"Smart-ass nigger, in't he, Turk?" the man who'd called him pops offered.

The other stood. "Oh, he's a mouthy one, all right, Winch."

The reverend knew he should be scared—deep down, he was. But something else had hold of him—disbelief, an inconvenient rage that these two strangers could so casually march into his church—the Lord's house—and speak to him so. He considered trying to flee out the back door behind the choir loft, but that seemed somehow undignified. Pressing past them and escaping through the sanctuary was out of the question, too. He could only stand his ground.

They each stepped into the aisle and marched toward him.

XX

Reverend Brown could neither move nor speak. He'd been accosted by his share of white men on the street before—some of them wearing blue uniforms and carrying billy clubs, some just in their Sunday best. But now, standing here under a chilly

April shower with Ms. Lucille Walker trembling beside him under their umbrella, the two armed men approaching, Brown counted his lucky stars. He had always thought of himself as a brave man, but he wasn't sure how brave he could have been all these years if he had ever once stared down the barrel of gun, as he did now.

Perhaps that was the only place that his bravery came from? The fact that he had never *really* faced death? Never *truly* been tested?

The two armed men stepped onto the curb. A delivery truck rolled by up Eighth Avenue but didn't slow, let alone stop.

"What's the meaning of this?" Ms. Walker managed, trying to sound indignant but just sounding terrified.

Both men extended their weapons, leveled them in the reverend's and Ms. Walker's faces. Two thumbs cocked two hammers, almost in unison. Rain dribbled off the barrels of the guns, like drool off the snout of some hungry, rabid beast.

"You Brown?" one of the men said.

The reverend managed a nod. His voice had left him.

"You the Walker dame?" the other asked, cocking his head toward Lucille.

"Somebody!" Ms. Walker screamed.

The gunman right in front of Ms. Lucile Walker backhanded her with the fist that held his weapon. His iron-backed knuckles smacked hard against Ms. Walker's smooth jaw. Ms. Walker whirled out into the rain, tearing the umbrella from Brown's grasp as she stumbled. The wind caught the umbrella and blew it in pirouettes up the Eighth Avenue sidewalk.

Something overcame the Reverend Brown. He did not summon it and he could not name it. He simply lunged, laid hands on the man nearest to him, and shoved hard. The gunman gave a startled cry and stumbled backward. He hit the pavement on his back and his gun clattered away.

Then the reverend felt flesh, bone and blue steel slam like a hammer blow into his jaw.

He tasted blood. His vision was suddenly awhirl with stars.

Down he went. Ms. Walker screamed.

Before the reverend's vision cleared, he was struck again. It was a foot this time, the sharp shoe feeling like it was carved out of petrified wood. The reverend's breath fled like wind from a balloon.

"You don't wanna do that, teapot!" the gunman snarled as he kicked him, again and again. Ms. Walker was suddenly shoved down on top of him, still screaming. The rain beat down, a cold, sobering shower.

"The more you fight the worse you make it, see?" the gunman above him snarled. Then, to his companion: "Hank, you skinnin' your piece yet, or what?"

I thought I was brave once, the reverend thought, *but I was never tested… not like this…*

The other gunman was up now. Brown blinked again. He heard someone crying and realized it was him. Ms. Walker shook, curled against him there on the sidewalk.

The guns hovered above them, muzzles dripping.

"Why?" Brown managed, though he knew perfectly well.

"If you gotta ask," one of the gunmen said, "you'll never know."

Then, there was a sudden loud crash: crushed metal and shattering glass. For just a moment, the Reverend Brown thought the guns had fired and his world had ended.

Then he opened his eyes. He saw the gunmen turned away from them, staring at their Packard, its roof crushed under the weight of some fallen object.

A gargoyle in a top hat sat upon it.

XX

Jebediah Debbs faced his would-be assassins. He made no attempt to run, nor did he betray any fear. He'd seen their sort before and met them without fear. Usually they wore white sheets and hoods, rode snorting horses and loved to set things afire.

These two just happened to be wearing fedoras and raincoats.

"So, who is it?" Debbs asked.

"Who's what?" one of the gunmen asked in return.

"Who sent you?" Debbs said. "I think I've got a right to know."

The one on his right brought his weapon around in a flat arc, rapping him a good one on the back of his head. He knocked Debbs's hat clean off. The umbrella fell out of Debbs's hand and the wind carried it into 142nd Street.

"You ain't got a right to shit, sambo," the one who'd hit him growled. "Now shut those flappin' gums 'less you want a sound beatin' before we put you down!"

Debbs, though dazed and bent, managed a reply. "I'd like to see you try beating me like a man, instead of holding me at gunpoint like a coward."

The gunman right in front of him lowered his weapon a little, taken aback by Debbs's bravado. "You hear that, Charlie? Sambo here wants to go a round."

That was all Debbs needed. Still bent from the force of the blow, he hurled his weight forward and tackled the gunman with a guttural battle cry. After that, all he saw was a crimson mist and all he heard was the drumming of his pulse in his ears.

XX

"What do you want here?" the Reverend Barnabus Farnes asked the two intruders in his church. They were just a stone's throw from him now, still moving up the aisle and getting closer with every breath.

"That mouth of yours is gonna get you into trouble, old fella," the one called Winch muttered.

"Big trouble," the one called Turk added. "That's why we're here."

The reverend nodded. "Your masters can't think of nothing better than to send a couple a strapping young lads like yourselves uptown to bully an old preacher? Is that it?"

"Bully, hell," Winch said, just ten feet away. He reached into his coat and pulled out an automatic pistol. It was black and heavy and the reverend didn't care for the view down its yawning barrel, not one bit. "We're here to shut that smart mouth of yours."

Turk pulled a piece as well. "Permanently."

The reverend fought the urge to raise his arms, knowing they'd offer him no protection. What did one do when one stared down the barrel of a loaded gun? Just stand there, staring, and wait for the shots that would end you?

Their thumbs heaved back their gun-hammers almost in unison, the clicks of the mechanisms loud in the big, empty sanctuary.

Then, just as he expected those hammers to drop and a pair of bullets to roar out of those barrels and steal the breath he held in fearful anticipation, there was sudden thunder. It shook the floor, the walls, the ceiling. A rending crash followed as metal was torn into a thousand pieces and hurled in a thousand directions. A great flash of fiery light bled in through the narthex windows at the front of the building.

The hoods were both as startled by the explosion in the street as the reverend was. All three turned toward the far away narthex and stared.

"The car?" Turk asked.

"Go check it out," Winch answered. As Turk took off at a bounding lope down the aisle, Winch lunged toward the reverend and snatched him by his collar. "Come on, old man."

The reverend submitted, the hood's pistol hovering right in his face.

Turk hit the front doors just as Winch and the reverend entered the narthex. Once he'd opened those doors, they all had a good view. Rain sluiced out of the sky in fitful sheets. Directly across the street lay the ruins of an automobile—a flaming, riven hulk. Smoking debris littered the street.

"You gotta be fuckin' kidding," Winch breathed beside the reverend.

Turk was out on the stoop now, the rain pounding down on him. He slowly descended the steps, staring at the ruin of their automobile in disbelief. When he turned and looked back at Winch, his eyes were wide, his mouth working like a dying fish.

"The boss's car..." he managed.

Winch, now standing in the open doorway, peered out into the night, scanning the street. Silhouettes and puzzled faces were evident in windows and doorways up and down the street—everyday folks who'd heard the explosion, curious to see what the racket was all about. And here stood these two hoods, guns in hand.

It was almost as if someone had blown up the car on purpose. To draw them out...

Something shot out from behind the open door. At first, the reverend thought it might be a snake—odd as that seemed— because it moved so swiftly, with such intent. It whipped around the edge of the door—a fiery crimson lash—and wrapped itself around Winch's gun hand. With a yank, the gun swerved away from the Reverend Farnes, Winch's finger tightening on the trigger. There was a loud report as a shot went wild into the far railing of the front stoop. Then the crimson snake went taut and yanked Winch forward, away from the reverend, right to the edge of the church's front steps. Winch tumbled right down those steps, cursing all the way. It was a hard fall.

The master of that crimson snake stepped out from behind the church doors. The serpent was a long scarf, and it was wrapped around the throat of a terrifying apparition in a black overcoat and top hat. The reverend couldn't believe his eyes. This was the one that people had been talking about for months now—the vigilante sometimes called the Cemetery Man, sometimes Doc Voodoo or the Dread Baron.

The Reverend Barnabus Farnes retreated into the church narthex. He wanted God on his side at the moment. This hellion in whiteface might just have saved his life, but he was no ally the reverend would ever count as righteous or reliable.

Out in the street, Winch stumbled to his feet, face bashed and bloodied, coat torn, hat fallen free. Reverend Farnes realized what was about to happen and jogged sideward, out of the line of fire.

"Smoke that spook son of a bitch!" Turk shouted.

Both men raised their weapons.

The Cemetery Man's gloved hands dove into his coat and emerged laden with iron. The night exploded in a volley of gunfire as both parties loosed lead simultaneously. From his vantage just inside the narthex, the reverend clearly saw the hoods' shots hammer the Cemetery Man square in his chest.

His coat frayed, smoke rose from him, and he recoiled a little under the weight of the shots—but he didn't bleed. His feet stayed planted. His guns kept barking their bloody bolero.

The hoods in the street didn't have the same magic. The Hoodoo Man's shots tore through them like knives. In a moment, the raucous gun-music ended, leaving only the sound of the rain and a faint ringing in the reverend's ears. The Cemetery Man stood on the stoop of the church, back to the doorway. Turk and Winch lay in the street: smoking, bleeding, dead.

XX

Jebediah Debbs snatched the gun from the man he'd tackled and shot the other assassin. The gunman went sprawling in the gutter and didn't rise again, so Debbs assumed he'd hit his target. Once he knew he wouldn't be shot in the back, he attended to the man he had first overpowered.

He used the butt of the pistol on the bastard's face. He did not stop until all his teeth were bloody, shattered stumps and his gums swam in a sea of red. That task accomplished, Debbs rose and carried on with his heavy shoes and all the considerable weight of his body. The gunman, barely conscious, begged for mercy through his pain. Debbs offered none.

This was how they would all pay! Sometimes he imagined it was Brown beneath him, sometimes the Reverend Farnes. This is what they needed: corporal punishment; a good beating to put things in perspective.

When the man beneath him no longer moved, Debbs caught his breath and looked around. There was no one on the street. The rain still beat down mercilessly and there seemed to be no traffic up and down Lenox Avenue. He waited, almost willing someone to wander by so that he could show off his handiwork and proudly display his trophies.

Look at these dumb crackers I trounced! he'd say.

 But no one came.

A pity.

Giving the gunman's corpse a final kick, he lumbered away from the dead men on the street corner and strode right out into the rain-battered street. Halfway to his umbrella—still turning cartwheels all alone in the middle of Lenox—he realized that the blood-streaked gun was still in his hand. He put it in his coat pocket, a keepsake.

Then, Jebediah Debbs picked up his dancing umbrella, shook the excess water from it, lifted it above him, and carried on home. When he reached the opposite corner, he started whistling.

XX

Satisfied that his quarry was dead, the Cemetery Man holstered his guns.

There were onlookers choking 137th Street now, gawping at the fire-torn automobile, the dead goons, and the apparition of darkness on the church stoop. Reverend Farnes edged closer to his strange savior.

The scarf around the Cemetery Man's neck kept slithering and undulating as if alive. To the reverend's disbelieving eyes, it looked like the rain itself shunned him, drops pearling as though on oilcloth, then scurrying right off him, eager to leave him be.

"Thank you," the reverend managed.

The Cemetery Man turned his head a little, but didn't seem to want to look the reverend full in the face. "Dangerous business you're in, reverend."

"I could say the same," the reverend answered. "If punks like these don't get you, son, I promise the devil will."

The Cemetery Man turned his head, looking back over his shoulder. His eyes smoldered like banked coals and the old man thought he saw something like a laconic smirk beneath the cracked and fearsome war paint.

"You're welcome," the Cemetery Man said, then turned and leapt right off the stoop. Before all the wondering eyes of the onlookers, he bolted into a nearby alleyway and the shadows swallowed him. In the distance, a siren drew near.

XX

The policemen wore rain-slickers and moved with all the urgency of morgue attendants. The Reverend Adam Clayton Brown and Ms. Lucille Walker were curled up on the sidewalk, hunkered against the brownstone that loomed above them, trying to use its shallow stoop for cover. Ms. Walker's face was buried deep in the Reverend Brown's chest, sobs wracking her like tremens. Brown felt like every bone in his body were broken or cracked.

Bodies were strewn around them. The two gunmen lay in heaps on the sidewalk. The driver of the Packard—who had leapt from the car when his fellows were gunned down—sprawled in the street.

When the pair of policemen saw the carnage, and then saw the reverend and Ms. Lucille Walker hunkered there against the brownstone, they were at a loss for words. Brown saw it on their pale faces, in their staring eyes, in their gaping, soundless mouths.

"Who the hell did all this?" one of them asked.

Brown tried to speak around a mouthful of broken teeth, bleeding gums and a swollen, bleeding lip.

"Death," he said. "He wore a hat."

2

When Doc Voodoo was horsed, he was something like a spider on its web. All the threads of that web—converging on him—stretched out in myriad directions, anchored to the many souls in his vicinity. When danger neared any of those souls, it was like a bow being drawn across those strings, the note deeper or higher depending on how far away they might be, how soon the danger might be upon them. As he trotted the rooftops, vaulted above alleyway canyons and scanned the streets below, he could tune to those bowed web-strands, and hear everything that the souls attached to their opposite ends broadcast. He heard the dreams of sleeping children; the bitterness and anxieties of Pullman porters and longshoremen sozzled on hop or the demon rum; the fearful murmurings and inward prayers of beaten housewives, money-hungry molls, and little girls who didn't like the way their neighbors or their uncles or their own troubled fathers looked at them. He heard these things as well as the wind in his ears, the traffic in the streets, the chatter from speakeasy doorways and the syncopated thrum from cellar jukes and swank supper clubs. It was only his will—a concerted act of focus and concentration—that kept him from going mad.

He asked Ogou, the *lwa* that rode him, if there was anything he could do. Could he shut his ears, or dampen the strength of the signals?

This is being horsed, boy, Ogou answered gruffly. *If it's drivin' you crazy, how you think it strikes me? I hear it all, day in, day out, wherever I've got turf.*

Now, Dr. Dub Corveaux, in the guise of Doc Voodoo, fought to shut them out as he fled the scene of the takedown at the church. He'd arrived just in time—he was glad he did—but he'd taken an awful risk. His *maji* wasn't as strong on holy ground and Ogou could have been driven out of him. Saving the Reverend Brown and Ms. Walker on Eighth Avenue was one thing; standing fast on a church stoop was another. Luckily, it worked as always: he felt the force of the slugs—a dull and distant pain, pure kinetic force—but that was all.

But the reverend hadn't tried to drive him out. Presently, the *lwa's* presence was all that kept him alive. Once he was back in his peristyle, Ogou would draw the lead out, Erzulie would close his wounds, and by sunrise, he'd be able to stand in front of a mirror and not see a single blemish.

But his foolhardiness wasn't lost on Ogou. Not for a second.

Just what were you thinking, the war spirit growled, a voice in his head as clear as a spoken conversation, *putting yourself in jeopardy like that?*

"I couldn't leave him," Doc Voodoo answered aloud, jogging the length of a rooftop and leaping the thirty feet that separated this building from its neighbor. "Not after finding the Reverend Brown and Ms. Walker under the gun like that… knowing the Reverend Farnes might be next…"

Not my turf, not your problem, Ogou said.

"All due respect, Papa Ogou," Doc said, and leapt another alley, "any soul in need hereabouts is my problem. I see trouble on the way, I'm gonna make a stand."

You can't stand on holy ground, Ogou countered. *I got no power there. Just standing on that stoop, the reverend could've driven me right outta you if he tried!*

Doc's building and holy sanctum lay just ahead, an upper window yawning wide. He vaulted from the rooftop he'd just crossed, traversed empty space, then landed neat as a cat on the windowsill.

"I may be your horse," Doc said, "but I ain't your slave. If I gave you that impression, we can end this arrangement right now."

He stepped down from the windowsill onto the earth-covered floor of the attic in his brownstone, the secret vodou peristyle where all his power was concentrated.

Tough talk, Ogou snarled in his head. *How bad you think you're gonna be to these hoods and bootleggers when you ain't got my mojo at hand?*

"And how bad do you think you'll be without a horse to ride?" Doc countered. "I need you, you need me. Mutual benefit. The mutual goes out of that, you can find another horse to ride."

As he strode to the altar to strip his crime-fighting raiment, he sensed his other patrons—Legba and Erzulie—draw near in the holy space of the peristyle.

You shouldn't talk to Ogou that way, Legba chided. *He's the only reason those bullets ain't bleedin' you dry at present.*

"I saw someone in need, I came to his aid," Doc told them. Off came the hat; the dreadlocked wig; the bullet hole-riddled coat. "Isn't that what we're doing here? Helping? Defending? Reckoning?"

He clipped a pair of icemen gunnin' for the preacher man, Ogou said. *Stood fast right on the church steps.*

You know you can't do that, Legba countered. *You step foot in that church, Ogou's vulnerable! He could be yanked right out of you! With Ogou's power stripped, you're just a man in a funny suit!*

"Ogou's out of me, and Ogou's nothing but smoke," Doc answered. He tore off the crimson scarf; shrugged out of his shoulder holsters and waistcoat and yanked off his gloves. "We made a deal. You get a horse, I make a difference. I get protection, you get potency."

Here's your protection, Ogou said, and dismounted.

It hit Dub like a freight train. The bullets, still lodged in his chest, burned like molten steel drip-dropping from a crucible. He couldn't breathe, coughed up blood and spittle. More blood came streaming from his now-opened wounds as though someone had turned on a faucet.

Hurts like the devil, don't it, boy?

Hurt? Hell, Dub was dying…

Erzulie came to his aid. She horsed him herself—an alien, feminine presence in his body. She enfolded him and all the pain subsided. The bullets came burrowing up out of his tissues like blunt worms seeking the early morning sun and fell to the earthen floor with tiny, mute thuds. His breathing became regular again. He spat a wad of phlegm and blood from the back of his throat and wiped the rivulets of blood from his bare chest.

That wasn't funny, Ogou, Erzulie hissed.

Wasn't meant to be, Ogou answered. *This horse needs to learn his place.*

He's right, Legba said. *We're not just here to help the people that give us offerings and call our names, Ogou. We're here to show we've still got power…that we're still a force in the lives of these people. They've got to know that this world with all its electric lights and beating fans and motor cars ain't all there is…that something ancient, and righteous, and powerful can still watch over them.*

You should understand that, Erzulie added. *Ain't you the warrior, Ogou? Ain't you the champion of the weak against the strong?*

That preacher wanted to curse your name and cast you out, Ogou said to Dub Corveaux where he lay, still recovering from the sudden shock of his vulnerability sans Ogou's protection. *I heard the thoughts in his head, felt the fear and hatred in his heart. You saved his life and he still just saw you as demon from the pit.*

"We ain't doin' this for pleases and thank-yous," Dub Corveaux answered, struggling up onto his knees. "He needed helping and we helped him. You tell me I did the right thing, and I'll tell you I was disrespectful, and I'm sorry."

There was a long silence. He could not see them—unless they deigned to show themselves—but he could feel the three spirits moving in the space around him, like a trio of breezes. When they spoke, their voices seemed deep in his own psyche, almost indistinguishable from his own thoughts.

Peace, Erzulie said, and Dub Corveaux did not know if she spoke to he, or to Ogou, or to both of them.

This is a partnership, Legba added. *There's got to be respect and trust—both ways—or it ain't worth a damn.*

Dr. Dub Corveaux waited throughout a long, pregnant silence.

You did right, Ogou finally muttered. *But if you ain't careful, you're gonna get yourself killed. You end up in a corner I can't crawl into with you, there's no way I can keep you safe.*

"Fair enough," Dub said. "My apologies, Papa Ogou."

Another long silence fell. Through the still-open window at the far end of the room, the doctor saw pale, early morning light just starting to purple the black night. And just like that, Dub felt them depart—Ogou and Legba, at least. They went to whatever that place was that they went to when the sun was up, and they had no horse to ride. Only Erzulie lingered, still inside him, still drawing out the last of his aches and pains like soft lips drawing poison from a wound.

I know she's special to you, Erzulie said, *so that makes the old man special to you. But he's just one man, and he's got his own holy patron, besides. You can't risk yourself, and all the good you could do, by always putting that girl and her family first.*

"It wasn't like that," Dub said. "I came upon another pair—the Reverend Brown and that Ms. Walker from Sugar Hill—both under the gun. Once I'd taken out their gunmen I felt another threat nearby. It just happened to be the Reverend Farnes, and he just happened to be at the church. He needed me, and I did what I could to help him. Hell, I even shoved a flaming kerchief in their gas tank just to draw them outside, where I could take them."

You've got a good heart, Erzulie said, and he felt that she meant it. *But you've also got to use your head.*

Then she was gone as well, and it was time to climb down his secret stairs, shower, and once more play doctor.

3

Harry Flood knew that Dolph Storms didn't like early morning meetings—let alone the sort where he was required to present himself hat in hand and admit failure. Failure—weakness—was not in Storms's vocabulary. He'd been lucky enough to always be the strongest guy in the fight—or at the very least, the craziest, scariest, or sneakiest one. That string of success, from his days as a teenage street hustler until now, had spoiled him.

That, and the fact that he was a psychopath.

Flood tried to stay calm. He sat in his silk robe at the end of his big dining room table in the solar of his apartment just off Fifth Avenue, ministering to a generous portion of eggs and sausages and beans on the fine china before him. He ate placidly and sipped his coffee as Storms ranted. It was tiresome, but it was the only way to tire the asshole out. Let him talk, talk, talk… sooner or later he'd get dossed and shut his trap.

"Who the fuck is this guy?" Storms said for the eighteenth time. "This jig in the fright wig? Does this son of a bitch really think he can fuck with the likes of me? With the likes of you? Does he have any idea what sort of friends we've got? The serious ass-shredding we could give him if he pushes us too far?"

Flood refilled his coffee cup from a sterling silver pot nearby. He silently offered Storms the pot. Dolph paused his screed just long enough to push the empty cup beside him forward. Flood refilled the cup.

"You got somethin' I could put in this?" Storms asked. "Little hair of the dog?"

"It's eight o'clock in the morning," Flood said calmly. "Don't be such a goddamn rummy."

"You ain't had the night I've had," Storms growled. "I'm out seven guys. Seven!"

"No, I haven't," Flood said, returning to his breakfast plate. "Then again, I could've sworn you told me you had this. 'Don't worry, Harry,' you said—sitting right here at my goddamn table—'I got this.' Well, it looks to me like you haven't got shit. Shut up the crusaders—that's what you were supposed to do. Two old farts, a housewife and a goddamn tub from Jamaica!"

"Well, if it was so goddamn easy, why didn't you do it?" Dolph said, sipping his coffee. "Maybe the problem, Harry, is that you can't stand to get your hands dirty."

Flood pursed his lips. The prick. Impugning his rep like that. "Dolph, I was rolling swells with the Five Pointers when you were still a drop of pearl jam in your papa's schvatz. I got my hands so dirty in my day, I had to bleach 'em to get 'em clean again. These days, I keep your sort around to do the dirty work because I've had my fill of it."

Storms stared. Was that an insult, or a compliment?

Flood threw his linen napkin on the table. The light in the solar was grey and icy. Clouds still choked the morning sky and it looked like it'd be another rainy day—the third or fourth this week. God, Flood hated April.

"What do you want me to do?" Flood asked. "I've sat here listening to you bitch and moan—just like I've done the past six months. You want to run in Dark Town, you want to deal in Dark Town, you want to squeeze the jigs in Dark Town, but when that hoodoo spook shows himself, you hightail it and come sniveling back to me."

"Now look here—" Storms began. It was the word snivel. He hated that word. That's why Flood used it.

"No, you look here, Adolph," Flood said. "I paved the way for you uptown. Bankrolling another club for the Queen Bee settled her turf and opened yours. We ain't seen hide nor hair of that House bastard, and that's good news for you, because all his rackets needed supervision. You've done wonders for me and my partners, Dolph, and we appreciate it—same way we appreciate you keepin' the peace and staying out of the Queen Bee's honey."

"Despite what you think," Storms said, trying to sound erudite but still coming off like a bohunk from the Bronx, "I am capable of rational compromise."

"Well, I'm really fucking relieved to hear it, Adolph. Now, if you could just accommodate the price of doing business—"

"If it's my racket, ain't the price of business what I say it is?"

Flood leveled a finger. "It is with people like us—business men. But the hoodoo man ain't a business man. He's a goddamn vigilante, and he hates you as much as you hate him. Jesus Christ, he saved the Queen Bee's life, but he's been busting up our operations in Harlem just as bad as he's been busting up yours! He ain't exactly playin' favorites here."

"So why can't we whack him?"

Flood spread his hands. "I don't know—why can't you? I don't see his head here on my table. You slipping, Dolph? I gave you one goddamn errand to run—"

"Technically," Storms said, "it was four errands."

"Regardless, you blew it," Flood countered.

"Those were my best guys," Storms growled. "That's how seriously I took that job, Harry. They were my best, and now they're all wearin' iceboxes at the city morgue." Storms grimaced. Once again, he didn't like having his manhood impugned. "If I'm gonna bring him down, I need free reign."

"Well, that ain't gonna happen," Flood said with finality. "My partners don't want uptown turned into a bloodbath. We make a lotta money off those supper clubs and gin mills because, if you haven't noticed, booze ain't legal, and downtown swells got a taste for that uptown jig hopscotch. But if you start batting the beehives and getting those downtown swells stung—I promise you, the boys in blue aren't gonna be in our pockets anymore, they're gonna be on us like flies on shit."

"Well, what do you suggest?" Storms asked, draining his coffee. "I did it your way. Your marks are still breathin' and I'm out men."

"Goddamn it, Dolph! Didja ever think the problem was how your boys did the job? Pulling their guns out on the goddamn street? They were supposed to do these crusaders nice and quiet like! Not a trace, I said! They just need to disappear, I said! It'd be like they just ran away! Now you got a baker's half-dozen of dead triggermen courtesy of that goddamn hoodoo man! But I also got partners, Dolph! Men in high places, who expect me to manage messes like this. How many more chances do you think I get after the job got so botched?"

"Give me a second shot," Storms offered. "Only, my way."

"This was your way—"

"Not the way I wanted. I was tryin' to keep it sweet and lowdown, in deference to you and your, uh, partners."

"You're not gonna do shit!" Flood roared. "Making them disappear was one thing. Now the whole goddamn city knows somebody's gunnin' for those four boat-rockin' jigs. Any one of 'em turns up dead, it's not gonna scare anybody! It's gonna make 'em mad, and we're back to the boys in blue, and flies on shit. Remember that? Didn't I just cover that with you?"

Storms shook his head. "Why should a couple nigger preachers with big mouths get everybody's panties in such a twist?"

Flood rolled his eyes. "They're goddamn crusaders! People love crusaders—white or black. They mouth off one too many times about cleaning out the dirty cops in their precinct or running the rackets out of Harlem, white folks downtown start thinking the same way. 'Golly-gee, those teapots uptown cleaned up with some speeches and parades! Maybe we could do the same on the Bowery? Or in Yorkville? Or in the Tenderloin? Or in Hell's Kitchen?' One good apple can spoil the whole rotten barrel."

Storms leaned forward. "Then give me free reign."

"No!" Flood shouted. "You ignorant son of a bitch! You rub 'em out now, you're just gonna make 'em martyrs! And right now, even if they just disappeared, you'd do the same! So long as you're workin' for me, you need to use your head, you dumb kike!"

Storms glared at him. He didn't like being talked to that way. What did Flood care? He didn't like having to explain the nuances of their business to a gorilla like Storms. How the man had gotten to be as powerful as he had with so few brains, Flood would never know. If Storms wasn't such a good earner, or such a useful bulldog, he'd probably just have him aired out.

But right now, they needed a solution to their problems. The preacher had a big mouth, and the hoodoo man had a long reach. What to do? What to do…?

Then it hit Flood. There might be an answer, and the hoodoo man gave it to him.

Flood leapt up from the table and pointed toward the foyer. "Out. I'm onto something."

"What?" Storms asked.

"Don't worry about it," Flood answered. "You just get back to the Bronx and take care of the day's business. I gotta make some calls. When I need your help, I'll let you know."

Storms rose from the chair where he slumped. He was big, standing upright—a full head taller than the five-foot, five-inch Harry Flood. Nonetheless, Flood wasn't scared of him. Dogs just needed to be taught who was boss. As long as they knew that, they'd never bite you.

"That hoodoo man crosses me again," Storms said, "I'm gonna have his head."

"He crosses you, you're welcome to it," Flood answered. "Just don't go stirring up Harlem to roust him out, you hear me? Remember what I said: you stir up the bees—"

"Yeah, yeah, we get the flies. Fine."

Flood gave him a pat on the shoulder. "Get the hell outta here. I got work to do."

4

Dr. Dub Corveaux put on his best mask of concern before knocking on the Farnes's door. This wouldn't be easy—acting like he'd just heard of the Reverend Farnes's run-in with gun-toting hoods this morning when he was the one who gunned down those hoods the night before. But duplicity was starting to come easily to him. He didn't like lying to Fralene, but the alternative was telling her flat out that he let a vodou deity ride him like a horse most nights and used dark, unearthly powers to fight crime. At best, she'd believe him and slam the door in his face—she was a good Christian girl, after all—no traffic with the elder powers for her, thank you very much. At worst, she might think he was crazy and call the police, or the fellows with the straitjackets.

So he lied, as he'd been lying for the past few months. It wasn't so impossible. He just pretended that when he was 'in character' and roaming the streets, it wasn't him at all. It was some other man out there striking terror into the hearts of Harlem's evil-doers, while he, Dub Corveaux—physician, intellectual, man of reason—remained at home in bed, merely dreaming of the adventures of the nighted avenger that some called the Cemetery Man, others Doc Voodoo.

Sometimes, he almost believed it.

The door opened. Fralene looked like she hadn't slept all night, and for perhaps the first time in the six or eight months they'd known one another, she didn't look put together and squared away. She looked weary and scared.

He started his act before she even got a word out. "What's this I hear?" he asked. "Is your uncle all right?"

Fralene's mouth snapped shut, all the words she'd been ready to offer evaporating. Instead, she simply waved him in and closed the door behind him. She led him down the short hallway to the kitchen in the back.

Fralene's teenage brother, Beau, sat at the little kitchen table, eating eggs and toast. "Morning, Doctor Dub," he said.

"Top of the morning, Beau," Corveaux answered. The boy didn't look upset about anything. Dub wondered if he'd even been told.

"Coffee?" Fralene asked.

"Please," Dub answered, and she moved to the percolator to pour him a cup.

"You're late, Beau," she said.

"I got time," he answered.

"You need to go, Beau," she said with more force.

He didn't argue. He just scooped up the last of his eggs with the final wedge of toast, popped the toast down the hatch, and rose from the table. As he squeezed past Dub, he gave the doctor a familiar look. The I-can't-wait-until-my-sister's-no-longer-my-guardian look. Dub just gave the boy an understanding smile and a clap on the shoulder as he left them.

Fralene handed over a cup of coffee—black, just the way he liked it. Her own cup was pale with cream and probably sweet as candy. They heard the front door slam as Beau headed out for school.

"Are you all right?" Dub asked, studying her. "You look like you haven't slept a wink."

"I haven't," she said. "Who told you?"

"I was over at Dexter's for breakfast. I didn't even get around to ordering. I heard someone talking about it and I came here, straight away. How is he?"

Fralene shrugged and shot a wary glance down the side hall that led to the reverend's cramped little study. The old man liked to withdraw there when something laid heavily upon him. It was his prayer sanctum and his thinking place, all rolled into one. "He keeps saying it was nothing. Just threats. The Reverend Brown's in far worse shape—"

"Brown, too?" Dub asked. He was good. Maybe he needed to hit the stage?

Fralene nodded. "Apparently, Reverend Brown and Ms. Walker were walking together. Gunmen stopped them. Brown tried to resist and they beat him silly before..."

She trailed off.

"Before what?" Dub asked. "Did someone come to their aid?"

Fralene seemed to think long and hard about her answer, then nodded, never raising her eyes.

"Well?" Dub insisted.

Fralene's eyes met his. She looked like she almost couldn't summon the words. She clicked her teeth. Rolled her eyes. Sipped her coffee. "Would you believe, the Cemetery Man?"

Dub widened his eyes. He couldn't help smiling a little. That was okay. It would read like incredulity. "You're joking."

"That's what Ms. Walker told me!" she hissed, as though afraid her uncle would hear her. "And that's just what Uncle Barnabus said, as well! He said that those two hoods showed up, talking tough and waving guns in his face. The next thing he knew, the Cemetery Man had come to his aid. Some of the people I talked to—people who saw the whole thing—said the same. He's no joke, Dub! He's real!"

Dub sniffed. "I'll believe it when I see it. What about the other fellow on the committee? Debbs?"

She leaned closer. "That's the strangest part! The police say they found two more dead men up Lenox—one stomped to death, the other shot. But when Ms. Walker called Mr. Debbs to ask if he knew anything, if he was alright, she said he acted as if he didn't know what she was talking about. 'I had a lovely walk home,' he said to her. 'No trouble at all but the rain. Yourselves?'"

Dub considered. That did sound strange. Two dead gunmen on a Lenox street corner, right on Debbs's path home… but Debbs acted as though he hadn't seen a thing? Dub knew for a fact he hadn't gotten that far the night before, so if Doc Voodoo didn't air those two out, who did?

"Go talk to him," Fralene said, cocking her head toward her uncle's study. "He likes you. Respects you. You can tell me if you think anything's wrong. Out of the ordinary or worth worrying about, anyway."

He nodded and headed for the side hall, coffee still in hand. "You've got one thing to worry about," he said as he moved past her. "You're uncle's making powerful enemies. If they're sending gunmen to threaten him, they're playing for keeps. And now that these two are dead as Julius Caesar…well, I wouldn't be surprised if the bad guys try again. They're not going to let a slight like that go unanswered."

"Just talk to him," she said. "Please."

He stared at her. He hoped she could see the concern in his eyes. It was absolutely genuine.

He knocked on the door of the reverend's office, announced himself, then opened the door and slipped inside. The Reverend Barnabus Farnes sat in his wooden secretary's chair beside his writing desk, one hand in his lap, the other on the desk. His fingers drummed out a troubled tattoo, and he stared off into space, distant and contemplative.

"Reverend?" Dub asked. "You all right?"

The reverend waved one hand dismissively. "There's no need for you to trouble yourself over this, doctor. No need at all."

"I beg to differ," Dub said. "Somebody threatens one of my most treasured friends, he might as well threaten me. You want to talk about it?"

"Nothing to talk about," Farnes said with a shrug.

Dub sat in the little wooden chair that lived beside the door. He waited in patient silence, sipped his coffee, let the old man grow used to his presence.

"He gunned them down, right before my eyes. Right on the steps of my church."

Dub blinked. "Who did?"

The reverend turned and stared at him. "That Cemetery Man. I saw him with my own two eyes. I've heard the talk…but who could believe such talk?"

"What was he like?" Dub asked.

The reverend shook his head, shrugged again. "Terrible. Haunted. Just seeing him put a fear in me. Even though he saved my life, he put a fear in me."

"What sort of fear?"

The reverend sighed. "Is that what we've come to? Emancipation, education, equality, success—we've striven to rise above our roots—the primitive savagery we were torn from, and the primitive savagery we were delivered to in slavery, and the chaos and abuse and disrespect since our emancipation— but this is how we do battle with our enemies? Possessed by dark forces, dedicated to the left hand path."

Dub shifted uncomfortably in his chair. "Now, reverend, this fellow came to your aid—"

"And I thank him," he said. "But damned if I'm not still haunted by the look of him. The smell of him. The shadow that he cast, even in the middle of a dark and stormy night. What makes him any better than those men that came to kill me, eh? What makes him any better than the people who would oppress us, and discount us, and exploit us for their own gains? Because what else are these devilish powers he serves but gangsters offering patronage? Power for subservience! Agency for the sacrifice of one's soul."

Dub sat forward. He really didn't like the direction this conversation was going in. "Did you ever consider," he offered, "that this fellow's not in league with any devilish powers at all? Maybe he just wanted to strike fear into the hearts of the corrupt in this town, so he chose this Halloween costume—war paint, a fright wig. Hell, those guns of his alone are pretty scary—or so I've heard."

"You weren't there," the reverend said soberly. "I know you've been to war, but I been walkin' the earth a lot longer than you, doctor, and I've seen more strange than a book-learned youngster like you will ever conceive of—"

I sincerely doubt that, Dub thought, but bit his tongue.

"—and I'm telling you, that man carried a wild and terrible power with him! Hell follows with him, just like the Good Book says! And while I'm grateful as can be for his intercession, I'm still haunted by what I sensed in him."

Dub raised an eyebrow. "And what is that?"

The reverend searched for the right words. "He carries a great weight on his shoulders," the reverend said. "The sort of weight that'll crush a man if he doesn't get out from under it."

Dub sipped his coffee again and lowered his eyes.

XX

When he finally emerged from the study, he found Fralene more or less where he'd left her—in the kitchen, sitting at the table, staring into her coffee cup. He took a seat adjacent to her and met her thousand-yard stare, but didn't touch her. Her gaze shifted a little, settling on him.

"Well?" she asked.

"Your grandfather's not a man prone to tall tales," Dub said. "So I can only assume he saw what he says he saw."

"So there really is some crazy man running around Harlem in skull-face popping gangsters and putting the fear of God in sneak-thieves?"

Dub sipped his coffee. There was only one swallow left. It had finally gone cold. "We've heard the stories. I know we've had our giggles over them. But here's a reliable witness that we both know. Why fight it?"

"What did he do to deserve this?" Fralene asked. "Why on earth would a couple of armed hoods need to threaten that man? What did he ever do to them? Or the others, for that matter?"

"Do you really have to ask?" Dub said.

Fralene stared, waiting for elaboration.

"The Harlem Concerned Citizens Brigade? They may not have a lot of money or muscle, but they've been making an awful lot of noise. And with people like your uncle and the Reverend Brown and that demagogue Debbs involved… well, those are some high-profile, well-known noisemakers. If they're decrying corruption at the street and municipal level, then they're basically calling attention to how the mobs have their fingers in every pie around here. The mobs don't like to be called on the mat like that."

"Well, what are they supposed to do?" Fralene asked. "Stand by and watch as the cops ignore real crooks to shakedown store owners for protection money? Stay quiet when white swells from downtown come up this way to watch cabarets and jazz bands and swill bootleg liquor in clubs that black folk aren't allowed to patronize? Put up with innocent business owners being terrorized and muscled by gangsters like that Queen Bee woman, forced to buy into her illicit gambling and liquor businesses?"

Dub shook his head. "Nobody buys into bolito or bathtub gin at the point of a gun, Fralene. Anybody who buys in is just as guilty as the people they're buying from."

That made her hot. "So now you're an expert, Mr. I-don't-want-to-get-involved?"

He knew where this was going. He didn't like it. The worst fights they'd had in the months past always started when his strict policy of neutrality in social matters arose. "Fralene, I don't see what one's got to do with the other…"

"It's got everything to do with it," she shot back. "Maybe if a few more smart, successful, strong young men like yourself stood up for this community, then frail old men like my uncle wouldn't have to—and they wouldn't end up as targets for the kind of men that came to kill him last night."

"So you'd rather I was a target?" Dub asked. Oh, how he'd love to share with her what it felt like when Ogou dismounted and he felt those bullet wounds start to bleed…

"I'm saying that if more men like you made noise, you wouldn't be targets, because you wouldn't be perceived as weak, or frail, or vulnerable."

Dub stood. It was time to go. "Fralene, I know your uncle's advanced in years, but I think you're selling him short. There's nothing weak or vulnerable about him. Maybe that's part of the problem. Maybe if he can't handle the consequences of his crusades, he should find different associates and keep his mouth shut."

She looked at him with a terrible coldness in her big, brown eyes. He sensed something ugly coming, but it still hurt when she said it. "Now you're talking like a god-damned coward, doctor. I never figured you for a coward."

He had a number of retorts in mind, but none of them would do him any good at present. He snatched his hat up off the kitchen counter and placed it on his head. "Sorry to disappoint you," was the only reply he could muster. He made for the front door.

She didn't follow him.

5

Rachel Gooden—known to most in her neighborhood as Mambo Rae Rae—opened the doors of her botanica every morning at ten o'clock. Customers didn't usually show until much later, sometimes not at all. Business had been slow, of late. She blamed it on the times: there was too much hope, too much prosperity. When people were happy, content, and employed, they didn't come seeking hexes, charms or packets to improve their situations. They just spent their money on food and drink and gambling and carousing. Good times were hard on her business.

Still, after making some offerings to Filomez for success, she opened those doors every day, read the latest gossip rag, and waited.

But this morning was different. When she moved to the front of the shop and drew up the shade on the door before unlocking it, there were people waiting outside for her: Madame Maybelle —known to most in her neighborhood as the Queen Bee— na pair of her bodyguards, and some white men in expensive suits and overcoats. Rae Rae didn't like the look of them. She thought long and hard before finally throwing back the deadbolt and opening the door. The little bell above the door tinkled ominously as she greeted them.

"Miss Merriwether," Rae Rae said.

"Good morning, Miss Rae," the Queen Bee said as she strode in, her associates trailing behind her. It was a small shop, and crowded. Once all six were all inside, there was barely room to move. Rae Rae squeezed past them, seeking the protection of her rightful place behind the counter. The white men in the Queen Bee's company were unfamiliar—the boss of the group short and stocky but imperious, the other two tall, muscled Irishman with doughy faces. Rae Rae had a vague notion of who they might be. She'd heard Madame Maybelle was doing business with Harry Flood these days, and that's precisely who the pugnacious little dandy in the fine gray coat and homburg probably was.

As Rae Rae slid behind the counter, one of the Queen Bee's associates locked the front door and drew the shade down again.

Oh, dear. Not good.

"I'm open for business," the mambo said.

"Not yet, you're not," the Queen Bee answered.

Rae Rae tried to maintain her composure. "I can't waste the day with my doors shut."

"Honestly, Rae, what difference does it make?" the Queen Bee asked. "We both know you're underwater."

Rae felt a cold knot in her belly. She'd have to move Filomez to a smaller shrine. Clearly his ministrations weren't profiting her for shit.

Still, she tried to play it cool. "I ain't under nothing," she lied. "It's a business, like any other. It's got good days and bad days."

"You're into Little Al for fifteen large," the Queen Bee countered. "He's a free lender, but that generosity's got a price. How many points did you agree on, above the principle?"

"What business is it of yours?" Rae Rae asked.

"Don't argue, Rae Rae. Little Al's one of mine, and you know it. If you're in to him, you're in to me. What's the vig?"

Rae Rae hated the Queen Bee right now—absolutely hated her. How dare she march into Rae's own store and humiliate her like this—in front of strangers, no less! So what if she'd had a few bad months? Wasn't everyone entitled? And Al wasn't exactly rushing the payback, either. Matter of fact, he'd been more than willing to defer payments a few times in exchange for more immediate modes of exchange. Rae Rae might be forty, but she was still a good looking woman. She could still be sweet, even to a fat, self-important loan shark like Little Al.

"What's the vig?" the Queen Bee demanded.

"Fifteen points!" Rae Rae shouted. "Not that it's any of your business!"

Goddamn the Queen Bee, she kept her cool. "My shark, my money, my business."

The little bulldog in the expensive duds piped in. "Nice place you've got here, Miss, uh, Gooden, was it?"

"Who are you?" Rae Rae asked, not bothering to feign courtesy.

The little man stepped forward, smoothly drawing off one of his gloves and offering his hand. "Harry Flood, miss. I really appreciate you agreeing to see us so early in the day."

She shook his hand, wondering when, precisely, she'd been given the opportunity to agree or disagree. "What's this about?" she asked, to no one in particular. "Honestly, I've got to open those doors."

Flood drew out a money roll, peeled off a fifty-dollar bill, and laid it down on the counter. "This is for your time," he said. "You're a businesswoman, after all, and your time is precious."

Rae Rae stared at the fifty where it lay. She was almost afraid to touch it. She looked to the Queen Bee—smirking and silent—then back to Flood. "I don't understand," she said.

"We just need a few minutes of your time. Maybe even some coffee or tea if you could provide it."

Rae Rae studied the odd little band again. What the hell was she about to get herself into?

She snapped up the fifty and shoved it into the cash register drawer. "All right, then. Step into my parlor."

They followed her into the little passageway that led upstairs. Once they were all gathered in Rae Rae's cramped parlor and sipping chicory coffee from old, chipped cups, the Queen Bee laid out the problem. Once she'd finished, Flood took over.

"So, you see our conundrum," he said. "This Reverend Farnes is being rather vociferous in his protests to our uptown investments. As you can imagine, this is rather awkward for us. Any action we take to quiet down such a seemingly frail, innocent old bird will obviously make us look like common thieves and street thugs—an impression we feel there is no need to make."

Rae Rae listened, thoroughly amazed that they were doing this song and dance for her. The bottom line was, they didn't like the Harlem Concerned Citizens Brigade, and they especially didn't like the Reverend Barnabus Farnes. But how could they shut up one obstreperous preacher without killing him outright, for doing so made the man a martyr and made the lot of them—whom suspicion would fall on immediately—look like the bloody murderers they were.

So, they needed the reverend to discredit himself. And for that, they needed him hexed.

Which was where Rae Rae came in.

"In a weird way," Flood said, smiling and sipping his coffee, "this Hoodoo Man I hear so much about gave me the notion. I mean, if he can use these unseen powers for his own ends, why can't we just as easily use them for ours?"

"You know about the Hoodoo Man?" Rae Rae asked.

Flood got very serious all of a sudden. He stared down into his chicory coffee—full of milk, but without sugar—and took a deep breath. Finally, he raised his eyes to hers. His expression was grave.

"I saw him," he said, "with my own two eyes. If anyone had told me about him, I wouldn't have believed them. But that night that everything went hinky at Aces and Eights, I saw that man do things no man should be capable of. He took bullets square in the chest with little more than a shrug, and he jackrabbited right up into a second-story window from street easy as a guard dog hops a low fence. I don't know what he's into—superstition's never been my area of expertise—but I'd lay good money on the fact that he's the real deal, not just some quack in Halloween make-up."

Rae Rae stared into her own coffee, which she had not touched since pouring it. "So you think I can summon something that powerful for you? And control if for you?"

"I don't think we need something as powerful as him," Flood countered. "All we need is something to make the general populace fear for the good reverend's sanity. A temporary madness, maybe. A sort of hysteria."

"It's not that simple," Rae Rae said. "If I do what you ask, there's only one way to guarantee the efficacy of the powers I invoke. We've got to plant something bad—real bad—right in the reverend's body, and let it grow their like weeds in a garden. If it takes, most likely it won't kill him…but it could get bad. Very bad. Like locked in a padded room in a hog-tied dinner jacket bad."

Flood gave only the most curt and casual of shrugs. "So long as the man's not physically harmed. He's old and frail, after all. We're not animals."

Rae Rae had to think long and hard about this proposal. All she had to do was to prep the reverend by some subterfuge, give a demon access to his weakened body, then let the demon take over. She'd seen such hexes worked before—though she'd never attempted such a thing herself. It was like watching someone slowly go crazy. Little by little, the rider wore its horse's resistance down, until finally there was nothing of the horse left at all, just a shell that the demon could puppet however it liked. And the worst of them—oh, they loved to puppet a horse! Once they were firmly planted in the saddle, there was no dislodging them.

It could work.

Best of all, they'd offered to square her with Little Al. They'd clear her debts and slide her a few hundred besides. Being flush again, with money in her pocket—that could take her a long way. Hell, she might even leave Harlem behind. She'd been thinking lately that the cold winters had just about done her in. She was ready for something new. Maybe California, with its warm Santa Ana winds and golden sunshine. Lots of folks were going west these days…

But what they asked of her… hexing a man of God. A thing like that had terrible consequences. Flood and the Queen Bee only wanted to avoid killing the man to avoid turning the general populace against them—but what about the Powers That Be? Laying black hoodoo on a good man like the Reverend Farnes was almost as bad—maybe even worse—than just killing him.

If she did the laying, wouldn't that come back to haunt her?

But squaring up with the shark and putting some bills in her pocket could help her start again. If she started again, she could make everything right, couldn't she? Eventually? Wasn't that what new starts were for?

"We need your answer," the Queen Bee pressed.

Rae Rae squared her shoulders and looked the Merriwether woman in the eye. "I'm considering it," she said.

"Don't consider too long," Flood said. "This is a delicate matter, and it needs seeing to."

"I'm taking a lot of risk upon myself if I do this," Rae Rae said. In truth, she was already imagining how far the money might go. And hadn't she been snubbed on more than one occasion by the good Reverend Farnes? Hadn't he deigned not to greet her with more than a grunt and a nod on the street? Hadn't he held out his hands and said a prayer more than once when he passed her botanica, as though her store was somehow accursed? Who was he to judge the efficacy of the powers that she held traffic with? To deem her—a hard-working, conscientious businesswoman—some sort of blight on the community?

"We all take risks," Flood countered, finishing his coffee. "If we're men—or women—of substance, then risk is our meat and mead, right? This is a simple proposition. We need a simple answer."

Rae Rae started to smart off again, to tell Flood that he could not possibly understand what the price of so cruelly employing supernatural forces could be. But then, she noticed something.

The Queen Bee's bodyguards, silent and seemingly disengaged throughout the entire conversation, were staring right at her. Their hands were planted firmly in their coat pockets. She wasn't imagining things when she thought she saw something hard and heavy stirring in one of those pockets.

Likewise, Flood's men hovered right behind her. They'd taken stations by the window, presumably to watch the street.

But from where they stood, they could easily flank her and hold her still.

And the Queen Bee's bodyguards would then have an immobilized target. Pop-pop! Two slugs, right between the eyes, or right between her breasts, and she'd be done.

She did owe the Queen Bee's shark an awful lot of money. If she turned them down, would they want her possibly telling anyone else about the offer they'd made? The terrible plan they were intent upon?

Your choice is already made, she thought. *And even if you hadn't made up your own mind—which you have—they wouldn't leave you any options.*

Their minds were made up when they walked in the door.

She finally sipped her coffee. It was cold now. Her hands were shaking.

"I want the money up front," Rae Rae said.

The Queen Bee reached into her own pocketbook and drew out a roll of bills—twenty tens, crisp and clean. She offered the roll in her elegant, gloved hands. "A retainer," she said.

6

The Reverend Adam Clayton Brown, Jr., convalesced in a room with three other patients at Harlem Hospital. According to the nurses, his roommates included an appendectomy, a rummy with pneumonia, and a fellow plastered in half a dozen places who had been struck by a freight truck. Beside these sorry fellows, Brown himself felt he'd gotten off easy: missing a few teeth, face bloodied, bruised and swollen, a couple ribs cracked, his right forearm in a cast. The doctors had assured him that he was lucky that he hadn't bled internally. Just a few inches one way or another, and that gunman's Florsheims might have sent him to the morgue instead of the sick ward.

Brown contemplated this as an overcast light crept in through the open windows. He thought of how close he'd come to death, and how he had a man in a Halloween costume to thank for every breath he now took. He thought of how he'd gone digging down in the muck of his own spirit for courage, to meet his end like a man, but seemed to find none at all. What he did to protect Ms. Walker had largely been done in fear, by simple reflex. The rest of the time, he was rooted, staring down the gaping barrels of those two pistols, terrified of what the next moment might bring. He did not remember ever making a conscious choice to do this or do that because it was the *brave* thing to do—the *right* thing to do—he only remembered being angry and scared.

Where was my faith, then? he wondered. *Where was my determination to meet my Maker with some dignity? Why should I have been so scared, if I believe that Jesus will receive me when my days are done?*

The answer frightened him so much, he could barely allow himself to give words to the thought.

It was in the midst of his struggle not to admit his own mortal terror and faithlessness that a tall, thin figure appeared in the white-framed doorway of the large hospital room: the Reverend Barnabus Farnes. Brown saw his old friend's face fall in despair, then realized what a fright he must look. Brown tried to force a smile, but it hurt.

Farnes removed his hat and strode toward Brown's frame bed. Across the room, the pneumoniac coughed violently, shuddering with the weight of all the fluid choking his lungs. To Brown's right, the fellow who'd lost his appendix muttered in his sleep.

Farnes slid an old wooden chair up beside Brown's bed and sat in it. He drew a breath. "My God, Adam… what'd they—"

"I'm sure it looks worse than if feels," Brown said, and this time he forced himself to smile, pain or no. "Really, I don't even know why I'm here—"

"Because a couple of gun-jacks beat you within an inch of your life," Farnes said. "All for having the temerity to resist them."

"I didn't resist much," Brown said quietly.

Farnes laid one long, weathered hand over Brown's on the shaggy wool blanket where it lay. "Nor I," Farnes said, but Brown knew that probably wasn't true. "I've never stared down the barrel of a gun before. Not an experience I hope to repeat anytime soon."

Brown nodded. A shudder ran through him—involuntary, unstoppable—in answer to the image of those gaping gun-barrels. That view of the void would haunt his memory, he was sure of it.

"Are you all right?" Farnes asked. They'd been friends a long time—forty years, almost. In all that time, they had come to know one another's secret signals and wordless bluffs all too well. Sometimes, Brown thought that the two of them remained such close friends because each kept the other honest, grounded.

But that wasn't entirely true, was it? The simple fact was that Brown had always looked up to Farnes, even though they were just a hair over five years apart in age. Farnes, who was always upright, always righteous, always fair, if a little stern; Farnes, who never quailed, never held his tongue, and never backed away from a fight, verbal or otherwise. Brown had done his damnedest in his life and ministry to be as brave as he believed Barnabus Farnes to be, and often convinced himself that he succeeded.

Last night, he failed. Miserably.

"What's gotten into you?" Farnes asked. "Are those tears?"

Brown realized that his vision was tear-blurred now, even though he wore his glasses (spares, brought from home by his housekeeper; his everyday pair were now fragments of wire and glass in a gutter on Eighth Avenue). He almost hadn't noticed. "Maybe I'm just tired," he said. "The doctors tell me rest is all that'll heal me."

"Prayer might not hurt, either," Farnes said, smiling a little. If he smiled at all, it was usually only a little. For Brown, that was enough.

"Is that why you came?" Brown asked. "To pray with me?"

"I'll be happy to do so, if that's what you want," Farnes answered. "But I actually came to speak with you."

Brown stared, waiting for Farnes to continue. Farnes didn't. He simply sat there, waiting in grave silence for Brown to give him verbal leave to continue. "Go on," Brown said, curious.

Farnes inhaled. Exhaled slowly. "Did you see him?" he asked.

Brown thought of the top hat. The skull face. The barking pistols. "I did," he said. "I owe him my life."

"As do I," Farnes said, sighing. He rubbed his furrowed old brow. "I suppose we all do."

"All of us?" Brown asked. "Debbs—"

"Debbs swears he didn't have any trouble," Farnes said, "but the police told me there were two more dead gunmen up on Lenox and 140th Street. That's right on his path home."

Brown stared. "Do you really think he could have—"

"I don't know," Farnes said.

"But he's alive?" Brown asked. "He's safe?"

Farnes nodded. "Ms. Walker called him late last night." He reached into his black topcoat and drew out a small, folded card. "He sent this this morning, via runner—one of those youngsters hangs around Liberty Hall."

Brown took the card, opened it. Written in simple, ropy cursive were the words, *Safe and sound. Thank you for your inquiry.*

"You sent for word of him?" Brown asked.

"No," Farnes said. "I didn't. That's what shames me. After those men came for me, and I found out they'd come for you… well, Mr. Debbs just wasn't on my mind. But he should have been. Debbs knew it, too, else he wouldn't have ended his missive that way. *Thanks for your inquiry.* I must admit, Adam, I'm more than a little disappointed in myself."

But you were just thoughtless, Brown reflected. *Not cowardly, like me.*

"I can only assume the Cemetery Man did all four of us a kindness, coming to our aid. Maybe he just got to those men before they ever caught up with our Mr. Debbs."

"Who is he?" Brown asked. "This Cemetery Man?"

"I can't say," Farnes answered. "But he frightened me. "

Brown nodded. He owed the Cemetery Man a great deal as well. Was that a good thing or bad? Being in hock to a devil of that sort?

"As for my other question," Farnes added, "perhaps it's too soon to ask, but I'd be remiss if I didn't."

Brown waited. Farnes seemed to take a long time to ask it.

"Should we continue?" Farnes asked simply.

Now it was Brown's turn to be silent. All his mixed emotions—his fear, his shame, his guilt, his indignation—roiled within him. His reflex was to say, no, absolutely *not.* Their near-death experiences proved that they were taking a great chance, speaking out against corruption in their community without more solid backing from the community itself, or the authorities.

But could he say such a thing to his old friend? Could he be so cowardly, here and now, after he had replayed the previous night's events in his head over and over and cursed himself for a yellow-bellied fool over and over again?

"It's done, then," Farnes said. "You need say no more, Adam."

"No!" Brown suddenly hissed. "It's *not* over! We can't just… *shrink* like that! Not now!"

"Do you mean that?" Farnes asked.

Brown smiled weakly. He managed to nod, but the movement was barely perceptible. "Of course," he said. "It's the right thing to do."

But, oh God, *how I wish I didn't have to do it.*

Barnabus rose from his seat, now towing over Brown where he lay on his lumpy hospital bed. "This was a bad idea," Farnes said. "I shouldn't have come to you so early. You need to rest. Forgive me, Adam—"

"No," Brown said, and without thinking about it, reached up and took the Reverend Farnes's hand. "It gave me pleasure, Barney. Really, it did."

Farnes looked down on him, a smile on his lips but a terrible sorrow and pity in his eyes. Brown could not tell if that look suggested that Farnes thought he, Brown, was pitiful and contemptible—a thing to be felt sorry for—or if it bore some terrible guilt and shame—as if Farnes somehow held himself personally responsible for Brown's present state.

Brown withdrew his hand. He managed a smile of his own, but knew that his eyes probably betrayed him. "Don't trouble yourself, old friend," he said. "We'll talk later, when I'm a little further recovered."

Farnes nodded. "That we will."

Then Barney smiled again—small, but clear—put on his hat and went on his way.

7

Jebediah Debbs sat in the parlor of his cramped little apartment in a glowering three-floor walk-up north of 147th Street. He was rocking in his favorite chair, a cup of cooling chicory coffee beside him on the scuffed old end-table. This was his thinking place—this cramped, cozy room filled floor to ceiling with books and second-hand furniture, the scuffed old wooden floors padded by a fading, threadbare mock-Turkish rug. He felt cocooned when in this room, his parlor window looking down onto a filthy alleyway and the backside of the building behind his own. Here, away from the noise of the world, and the blank, expecting stares of his followers and the judgment of his so-called *peers*, Debbs could order the storm of suppositions that skirled through the dark corridors of his mind. He could ponder. He could decide.

Having finished his eggs and toast, his ham and sausages, and having sent Calvin, his house-boy, away with his breakfast dishes, Debbs had decided a few things.

First: he didn't need to waste his time in the Harlem Concerned Citizens Brigade any longer. Those gunmen last night proved it: the heebs and the wops from downtown didn't cotton to niggers shooting off their mouths, knew all niggers could be cowed with fear and intimidation. Observing the likes of Brown, or Farnes, or prissy Ms. Walker, what else could they think? But no more would Debbs go the peaceable route prescribed by Farnes and company. No, Debbs would take the fight to the enemy, right out into the streets if need be.

Thus, his next decision: he would not be merely *concerned* for Harlem's welfare—he would *fight* for it. He would form his own committee, and it would be a vigilance committee. They would walk the streets in ordered squads, like soldiers, and they would defend the poor, cowed sheep of this Negro Babylon against the wolves that encircled and slaughtered them: the errant downtown gangsters; the soiled and compromised Irish policemen; the Uncle Tom politicos who gave black money to white extortionists for 'protection'—anyone who stood in the way of progress. Debbs and his followers would die like men before they would live any longer like domesticated animals.

And finally, his most important decision: if they were going to defend Harlem, they needed arms. After all, a well-armed citizenry was essential to the security of a free state, was it not? Some of his followers no doubt had weapons of their own— old squirrel poppers and breakaway shotguns inherited from relatives out west or down south; cheap pistols bought in the heat of passion or acquired in Saturday night dice games; knives; blackjacks.

But that wouldn't do—those were the weapons of cheap hoods and criminals. No, if Debbs and his followers would stand against the forces that conspired to keep Harlem in chains, they would have to be outfitted accordingly. They would need firepower—*heavy* firepower—elsewise they would be no better than a country fire watch. Debbs knew of only one person who could possibly provide him with the contraband he required, at reasonable cost, and without threat or interference.

He had often heard that the Queen Bee was a reasonable woman. Surely, she could understand the need for a troupe of proud black Ajaxes to defend themselves against the white rabble. Debbs could even frame his request as one with advantages for the Queen herself: provided that she did not threaten the street folk or interfere, Debbs could promise to defend her interests as well.

He had no intention of keeping that promise, of course. But making it might get him what he wanted.

He was proud of himself. How he had ever managed to rise so far above the fools and the sheep and the scoundrels around him, he would never know—but somehow, he'd done it. He had outsmarted them all, and now it was time to show them just who had their best interests at heart. If they would not stand up for themselves, he'd be their master, and he'd force-feed them every bitter pill necessary to flush the slave mentality out of them.

These were his decisions. He was quite proud of them. He felt, in fact, like the only brave and thinking man in Harlem.

Because I killed them, he thought. *Farnes and Brown and Ms. Walker—they needed that haint in the hoodoo garb to save their quivering necks! But not me! I needed only my courage and my strength and my bare hands!*

If they couldn't do what was necessary themselves, he would happily do it for them.

8

It took Mambo Rae Rae the better part of the week to prepare. The sort of *wango* she was about to unleash was sensitive, frightening stuff. Missteps had to be avoided, because they could prove disastrous—even fatal. She consulted her reference books (largely useless except for some particulars regarding circles of protection) as well as her personal diaries. In those diaries, she kept records of all the rituals she had ever witnessed, so that she could later recall the details, the mishaps, and those actions that proved most efficacious. It was the little things, often, that got one in trouble—omitting a crucial phrase, offering the summoned *lwa* inadequate or offensive gifts. Rae Rae had to do everything right, or the only person who ended up hexed might be her.

Following her initial study, a trip to Bellevue was in order. There, she called in a favor from a regular petitioner and initiate—a laundress with access to a number of corridors and stairwells. The young lady guided Mambo Rae Rae through the Bellevue labyrinth and into an unused basement chamber beneath the lunatics' wing. There, Rae Rae took a measure of soil from the earthen floor, knowing that the grief and madness poisoning it would have powerful *namh*, for both the summoning and the hex packet she'd have to use on the reverend.

Once the earth had been secured, Mambo Rae Rae spent several hours over the next two days observing the Reverend Barnabus Farnes himself. He usually rose early, spending the first hours of his day in Biblical study and contemplation. He took a simple breakfast, then spent the rest of his morning and afternoon attending to church business, sometimes visiting needy members of his congregation. Usually, he didn't return to his home again until well after dark. Then, after supper with his niece and nephew, he'd retreat again into his study for more reading, and perhaps some writing before he finally took to bed around ten o' clock. Rae Rae assumed the evening sessions were probably when he prepared his Sunday sermon. What else could he be doing, bent over his writing desk, scribbling away with a fountain pen as the Good Book and other tomes lay open around him? She saw him at work in this way through the side window of his house, two nights in a row, and the sight made her both sad and angry.

So serious, she thought. *So studious. Does the man derive any joy at all from his own faith? Or is it all just an academic exercise to him?*

Well, she would just have to remind the Reverend Barnabus Farnes that all the unseen powers—from the god he served to the *lwa* she held commerce with—were more than abstract ideas in dusty old books, more than Sunday sermons and rules inscribed on stone tablets or reproduced in cross-stitch for parlor walls. Those powers were *alive*, and they were about to lay their dread gazes upon the Reverend Farnes in a most direct and unpleasant fashion.

Around nine o'clock on a Thursday evening, Rae Rae set out to accomplish the first phase of her plan. She borrowed a broken-in Holmes sedan from a hotel maitre'd who often paid her for love charms and Tarot readings, then lit out for Queens. Although clouds cloaked the stars and there was no moon to speak of, no rain was forecast for the evening. She would enact her ritual under the open sky, in the most remote location that she could think of which also met the ritual requirements.

Her destination was a wasteland of soot and ash known colloquially as Mount Corona, but officially, it was the Corona Ash Dump, in Flushing. The only mountains in Mount Corona were mountains of ashes hauled from furnaces and butt-cans all over the city, deposited out on Flushing's edge like the ghosts of hills flattened by the city of skyscrapers and high-rises she left behind. She needed a crossroads and she needed privacy. On a moonless midnight, she guessed the ash fields would offer both.

She arrived at the intersection of Corona Avenue and an unmarked country road with only an hour to spare before midnight. She parked her borrowed car off the road, its headlamps pointed into the intersection. With no moon or stars, no street lights or civilization near, her only light were those two glaring orbs at the nose of the car and a small lantern that she'd packed in an old, picnic basket with her other ritual implements.

Rae Rae left her picnic basket on the road's verge, withdrew a fat shard of chalk from her coat pocket, and went to work. She sincerely hoped no one would drive past as she saw to her business. Aside from the fact that she might look silly— or if it was a cop, get arrested—there was the very real risk of compromise or infestation; of the forces she dealt with slipping through the protective barriers she would establish and fleeing into the world via any unprotected passers-by. It would behoove her to move fast.

She worked by the garish light of the car's headlamps—a light that spread in a shallow arc across the intersection, throwing every stone and ripple into sharp relief and making of her own shadow a slanting, elongate giant. In the intersection, she drew a large circle, and around the circumference of that circle she drew protective *veves* and inscribed words of power. Satisfied with her handiwork, she fetched a corked bottle of good, imported rum infused with gunpowder and placed it in the very center of the circle. If all went according to plan, the *lwa* she intended to summon would manifest inside that circle, and the words of power and *veves* she had inscribed around it would keep it well bound.

Next, she drew another circle—this one much smaller—just outside the larger circle, on the south side of the crossroads. This would be Rae Rae's second line of defense: an extra, added layer of security between she and the powers she hoped to invoke. With any luck, two circles of protection and proper liturgy would keep her safe.

At least, she hoped they would.

Kalfou was not to be trifled with.

Mambo Rae Rae had only seen Kalfou summoned twice in the whole of her forty-three years of life. Both manifestations were memorable in the worst ways, and still sometimes terrified her when she dredged up their memories and dwelt on them too long. One of the mounted horses had squatted by a bed of smoldering coals, scooped up an enormous handful, then opened his mouth and shoveled them down his gullet. She remembered the smell of burning flesh as he held the coals... the choked, inhuman laughter he'd offered as he chewed and swallowed them. The laughter had been Kalfou's. The screams that followed when Kalfou dismounted and departed were the horse's.

The other manifestation had been a young woman—a beautiful girl whom everyone agreed was the prettiest maiden in the village. When Kalfou mounted the girl, she'd astonished the onlookers with an absolutely gut churning sexual display, dancing and exposing herself so lewdly that even Rae Rae—no Puritan, and no angel—had been shocked. When her dance was done, the girl had shattered a number of rum bottles left on the Petro altar and eaten the broken glass as though it were rock candy. She wasn't so pretty after that.

Kalfou. The Lurker at the Threshold. The Haunter of the Crossroads. Chaos Incarnate. He was Papa Legba's vile twin, eager to throw the doors between the two realms wide at the slightest provocation and set terrible powers loose in the mortal world.

Rae Rae took an awful risk, calling Kalfou alone like this while simultaneously trying to bind him, denying him a horse to ride. He could take that as a sign of her mistrust, her fear, or her ignorance and burst his bonds just to prove he could. She might end the night burrowing into one of those ash mounds nearby under his control, then suffocating once he'd departed. Of course, it was possible that, having no horse to ride—no mouthpiece—he would not be able to make his presence known. She would have to simply make her petition and depart, hoping that he left the *pwen* she asked for in the rum bottle after he'd finished it all. That was sometimes the way of things with the *lwa*: results were not immediate, but left pending some behind-the-curtain manipulation.

Part of her hoped that would be the case. She didn't relish facing Kalfou alone on this ash-littered crossroad in the middle of the night.

Rae Rae emptied the rest of her implements from the picnic basket: a knife; a *kwa-kwa* rattle, to provide some rhythm for her Petro song; a small, red velvet bag filled with six silver dollars and some of the lunatic earth from the Bellevue cellars; and finally, an old flour sack, tied shut, moving the slightest as she lifted it out of the basket. There was a black tomcat in the flour sack, caught that very afternoon after she'd enticed it with a dish of laudanum-laced milk.

The mambo took the flour sack and her ritual knife out to the center of the big circle. There, she laid the bag down beside the bottle of gunpowder-laced rum, gently probed the cat's shrouded shape with her fingers, and plunged her knife into the kitty's throat. It squalled a little when pierced, then mewled sedately as its lifeblood flowed out of it. Rae Rae left the dying feline in the blood-stained sack and moved hastily into her own circle.

She turned her back to the big circle and knelt in her own. Wiser *boukour* than she recommended keeping one's back to Kalfou in such situations, lest you engender his fury or worse—invite him to mount you. The car was still parked on the opposite side of the big circle, headlamps pouring their harsh light over the crossroads and throwing her shadow out before her, a long, lean, darksome marionette that scarcely seemed human, even as it matched her movements. She considered doubling back to the car to turn off the lamps, but the offering was already bleeding its last inside the summoning circle. She had to get started.

The mambo stitched a rhythm with her *kwa-kwa* rattle, and began her song. She was astonished by how quiet and deserted the world around her felt, out here in the middle of nowhere, on a night blacker than a coal vein and twice as cold. Tendrils of ash skirled off their scudding mounds as winds whispered through the wasted grounds, making shadows of their own as they danced between she and the car lamps at her back.

She closed her eyes. Beat time with the rattle. Sang. So alone, in the center of those roads to nowhere, she started to hear sounds in the world around her that could not be real. Small scuttlings magnified. Sarabandes made of phantom breezes. A chanting voice in the rattle that shook in her hands, stitching the terrible, unyielding tripartite beat.

The blood was spilt to draw him. If she wanted to petition Kalfou, she would now have to offer him payment.

Still keeping time with her rattle, still singing her song, Rae Rae lifted the little red velvet bag, heavy with silver and poisoned earth. She sang the last verse—the verse about a suitable offering and gratitude eternal—then pitched the bag backward over her shoulder. It landed seconds later with a musical tinkling, somewhere behind her.

Then, Mambo Rae Rae waited. Her song was over. To finally open the door and bring Kalfou through, only one action remained.

She bent forward, kissed the paving three times while saying Kalfou's name in between, then finally made fists and rapped them in rapid succession on the same patch of asphalt.

She kept her eyes shut. She listened. She hoped.

If he manifested, there would be some indication: words on the wind… a new tremulousness to the air… the sudden arrival of a flock of crows or a bevy of dump rats, acting as Kalfou's envoys. Anything was possible. She need only listen for it.

Because she *would not* open her eyes. She could not. If she opened them and saw something—a new shadow cast alongside her own by those glaring headlights—dear God, Mambo Rae Rae might go mad!

She waited. The temptation to open her eyes—to crack them just the slightest, like a child playing possum for a parent trying to drag them out of bed—was almost unbearable. But she fought the urge. If she opened her eyes, even the slightest, and saw something moving in the light of the headlamps, she might be further tempted. She might want to open her eyes all the way… to look over her shoulder.

But she knew that someone—some*thing*—might be standing in that circle if she turned and looked over her shoulder. And she would not want to meet that someone's gaze. Not now. Not ever.

A new breeze mowed through the ash lands that surrounded her. Somewhere she heard the flap of small, leathery wings. Insects seemed to be swarming over her bent knees, but she knew that was just aching muscles and an active imagination.

She waited.

Waited.

Shit.

Did she do something incorrectly? Were the circles of protection a misguided addition? Had her song not been loud enough, or long enough? Perhaps the tomcat wasn't a suitable offering? Kalfou, being famously hostile and recalcitrant, might not appear for anything so base as a stray tom. If it had been *her* tomcat and not a stray—an animal she owned and felt some care and affection for—that might have made a difference…

She counted to twenty, slowly. Still, she heard nothing. Felt nothing. There was only the susurrating nocturne of the night breezes through the ash lands; the great, high lonesome of a Queens wasteland at midnight. Mambo Rae Rae sighed. She would have to approach this differently… get the help she needed in some other way.

She opened her eyes.

There was a long dark shadow in the light of the headlamps that as not her own.

A cold hand fell on her neck and caressed her, so cold it burned like red-hot iron.

Mambo Rae Rae shot to her feet. Reflex had almost forced her to bolt from the circle—to run, as far and as fast as her feet could carry her. But she resisted the urge. Her feet stayed planted. She kept her back to the great summoning circle, but her eyes lay on the broad pool of light that stretched before her… that separate, alien shadow that swayed behind her own.

He was here now. *Kalfou.* She knew it. It had been his cold-hot hand on the back of her neck.

A series of terrible sounds rose behind her: canvas, tearing slowly under strong, sure hands; small, wet twigs cracking and breaking; a viscous sucking mingled with the gnashing of teeth on cold flesh.

Kalfou was eating the tomcat. It took every ounce of Mambo Rae Rae's experience and self control to keep her feet planted inside her protective circle. She forced her eyes to rise from the shadow that rocked and gamboled around her own. She focused on the slope of an ash-pile a hundred yards beyond her protective circle. After a few moments of enduring those terrible sounds— Kalfou, eagerly tearing away at his offering—something flew into her peripheral vision on a low, flat arc, hit the verge of the highway, and tumbled off into the patchy, dead grass beside it.

The feline's remains. Broken. Bloodied. Mangled by strong hands and teeth.

Mambo Rae Rae drew a deep breath, her chest suddenly feeling like it was bound in a corset. The light from the car headlamps made it possible for her to see her breath bloom in the near-darkness. Had it grown colder out here since Kalfou's arrival?

Of course it had.

I should never have done this, she thought. *Never, never, never, ever.*

Kalfou spoke, his voice in the very center of her brain, moaning like an autumn wind through the eaves of a drafty old house.

You dare call me out for a bloody black stray and a bag of coin?

She wanted to scream but fought the urge. She had business to transact. She had to see to it, or all of this—the moral hazard she'd undertaken, the terror of occupying this circle while Kalfou manifested just a stone's throw behind her—would all be for nothing.

"I called you for business, dread Kalfou," she said, her voice sounding strange and distant in her own ears, like someone else's voice, speaking someone else's words. "Hear me and help me if you would, then be on your way if what I offer isn't pleasing to you."

There was a long silence. Dear God, could she feel him standing right behind her? At the very edge of his circle and hers? Banked coal eyes boring into her, cold hands ready to reach out and caress the back of her neck again? She wanted to turn around—needed to turn around, to assure herself that he wasn't there, that his terrible hands weren't about to fall on her.

No. Not one look. Not a single glance, however oblique. Dealing with him was dangerous enough. Looking upon him could be the end.

Instead, she made her request. "I need an in-dwelling," she said.

You want me to horse someone? he said, disdain and contempt dripping from his voice like spittle from a lunatic's lips. As he carried on, the sound of his voice grew to an elemental roar in her mind and even in her ears—the sound of a cyclone tearing *across a prairie, hungry for your shotgun shack and its pitiful earthen foundations...*

Me? he continued. *Dread Kalfou? The Haunter of the Crossroads? The Lurker at the Threshold? You want my might and power and sublime corruption poured into the stinking, leaking, rutting vessel of some sad, sorry mortal—*

"Not you," Mambo Rae Rae corrected. "Someone in your employ will do just fine."

Who's your victim? he demanded.

"A holy man," she said. "An uppity, meddling old Christian. I have punishment to be meted, Kalfou, and one of your *eskó* spirits could do me a great favor by breaking this horse who's earned my enmity. Use the rum bottle if you like, once you've drunk your fill. This is no demand, only a petition. I gave offerings in good faith. I beg your aid now."

Mmmmmm, Kalfou purred. *Been a looooong time since I had me a Christian holy man...*

That elemental voice made of wind and ruin gave something like a long and pensive sigh. Rae Rae saw the shadow that attended her own flicker in the garish light, as though its form were mutable, its substance, variable. Then, she heard the tiny sound of her bottle being lifted from the paving.

Kalfou drank all the rum and gunpowder in a single, long draught.

It's done, Kalfou said. *Take your vessel and be on your way.*

Mambo Rae Rae almost turned on her heels, ready to hold out her hands and accept the proffered bottle. Luckily, she stopped herself before turning around—before stealing that glance she so desperately wanted to steal.

Why should it be so hard? Why should looking into the face of ruin seem like such a treat, and not the terror it was? Why do I have to fight the urge...?

"No, thank you, Kalfou," Rae Rae said as politely as she could. "Just leave it where you found it—corked, if you please. I'll take it into my keeping once you're on your way."

The Lurker seemed to laugh. It was the sound of a half-rotted corpse twirling in a squeaky gibbet.

Clever girl.

"I could never look on one so terrible," Mambo Rae Rae offered demurely. "One so beautiful."

It's true, he said, thoroughly smug. *You could not.*

She waited. How would she know when he'd gone? Really, truly gone?

I expect more for this than flesh and coin, Kalfou said, his voice sounding distant now, as though receding down a long passage.

Rae Rae almost responded with a question of her own. But then, she realized what the only appropriate response could be... and what that would mean for her. Could she quail now, when she'd come so far? This was yet another test, and she had to pass it if she wanted to leave this place alive.

"A favor is owed, then," she said, her voice catching in her throat. "I'm your humble servant."

Once more, the wind laughed. Then, all at once, the night seemed warmer and more welcoming, the darkness not half so dark. Rae Rae counted to one hundred, slowly. It seemed to take an eternity. When she was finished, she felt reasonably sure that Kalfou was gone. The only shadow on the roadway now was hers.

Rae Rae turned and stared into the large circle behind her. It was empty, save for the rum bottle, once again corked. She knew she had left the bottle in the very center of the circle, at least twenty feet away from her. It now stood at the circle's very edge. If she knelt again and stayed within her own circle, she could reach out and grasp it.

That was where Kalfou had stood… just an arm's breadth away from her, separated only by arcane symbols and an unbroken chalk line.

Rae Rae snatched up the bottle. It twitched in her hands as though alive, the spirit within sloshing the last of the remaining rum, bathing in it.

Rae Rae held the bottle tightly to keep it safe and hurried back to her borrowed car.

9

"Maybe you should slow down," Fralene Farnes said to her Uncle Barnabus. She couldn't bear to look at him. She felt like a coward for even suggesting such a thing. There were few hard and fast rules in the Farnes family, but among those few was, *Never back down from a fight.*

They were in Dexter's, one of their favorite breakfast spots. Her Uncle Barnabus sat across the table from her, nursing a cup of black coffee. It had been Fralene's intent to ease into her argument for Uncle Barnabus adopting a lower profile, but as silence expanded in the absence following the departure of their waitress the words seemed to come bubbling out of Fralene like a spring from rocky soil, completely unbidden.

"Slow down?" Uncle Barnabus asked.

Fralene stared into her own coffee, pale with milk and very sweet. Was this a failure on her part? A capitulation?

No. She just didn't want her uncle to end up dead—or worse—simply *vanished.* She had imagined it once or twice: how one night, he simply wouldn't come home from the church; and although they would beg aid from the police and the community, and the city would be scoured, high and low, he would never be found. Nonetheless, Fralene would know what became of him. Everyone would know.

And his vanishing would increase their collective fear, and assure their silence.

"There's nothing more to prove," Fralene said. "These gangsters… they've already tried to kill you once. Why provoke them again?"

"You're afraid," Uncle Barnabus said, and it sounded like an accusation.

She finally managed to look him in the eye. "So what if I am?" she asked. "Fear tells us what's important, what's worth fighting for or fleeing from. I don't want to lose you, Uncle Barnabus. Not like this."

"Fair enough," he said, his aspect softening. "I suppose this isn't my choice alone. You and Beau have a stake in it, too, seeing as I'm the one takes care of you two."

She could tell he was struggling. Whenever he wrestled with something—a hard choice, a difficult dilemma—his tone and demeanor softened. It was as if all his energies—normally so intent, so vital—were suddenly turned inward toward finding a solution to a problem. Thus, the exterior he so carefully cultivated—the thick, righteous skin; the schoolmaster's judging gaze; the unsmiling, stone-set mouth—fell away, the energies necessary for the sustenance of his mask otherwise engaged, the soft and compassionate man beneath revealed.

"I don't like asking," she said. "I hate it, in fact."

"You needn't worry," Uncle Barnabus said. "We're meeting tonight, but… well, let's just say I think it might be little more than a motion to dissolve." He looked at her, and Fralene could see the sadness and defeat in his eyes.

"I feel like I'm hamstringing a lion," Fralene said. "Leashing a big, brave bear."

He smiled a little. "Me? A bear?"

Fralene studied him and smiled as well. "Maybe neither. You're more like a stubborn old horse." They both laughed. "You understand my point, though?"

"Perfectly," he said, sipping his coffee. He took in their surroundings. Dexter's was slow this morning, only a handful of other patrons spread out among its counter stools and little tables. "Maybe I should look before I leap for once. Think before I speak. It's not cowardice, Fralene, it's just… just…"

She took his hand. "You live for the fight," she said.

He stared at her, as though the words both surprised and satisfied him. "Yes, ma'am. Yes, I think that's it. But that isn't good enough when people you care about get hurt. When I saw Adam in that hospital bed, all bruised and broken…"

He went silent. Fralene laid a hand over his on the table.

"I understand," she said. "But this time, let's both admit that there are other things worth fighting for. Other things worth living for."

He nodded a little. Fingered his coffee cup. "Sure there are."

A long silence fell between them. Each sipped their coffee, studied the other patrons, laughed quietly to themselves as the owner, Dexter, told one of the counter customers a rather blue joke about a priest, a rabbi, and a spokeswoman for the Temperance movement. Fralene's eyes grew wide when she heard the punch line.

"Oh my," she said.

"Come off it," Uncle Barnabus said joshingly. "You're no babe in the woods, young lady."

"But I *am* a proper lady," she assured him.

"No doubt," he said. "It's just not good to be shocked too often. We can opt out of certain things in this life… try to rise above certain human foibles… but feigning shock when there's no reason for it… or feigning offense just because of who's watching you… those are bad habits to get into. They breed hypocrisy… self-righteousness."

Fralene studied her uncle. She liked him when he was like this. Less serious, less flinty. "Uncle Barnabus, are you telling me I should laugh at Dexter's naughty joke?"

He shrugged a little and never raised his eyes from his coffee cup. "If it's funny."

"You *are* going soft," she said.

He shook his head, raised his eyes and studied her slyly. "Just remembering what's really important. And laughter's important."

She nodded. "Duly noted."

"What about the doctor?" her uncle asked. "Does he laugh good and often? Does he make *you* laugh?"

Fralene stiffened. She didn't really care to discuss her relationship with Dr. Dub Corveaux with her uncle… especially when they were on the outs at present. She sipped her coffee and wouldn't meet his gaze. "He laughs. Sometimes I think he could fiddle while Rome burned around him."

"That's my fault," her uncle said.

"What is?"

He sighed. "That serious streak in you. You're not terribly forgiving, Fralene."

"It's not a matter of forgiveness," she said. "It's a matter of responsibility. He lives here, works here, makes money off of these people… but he won't do anything for the community save stitch a few scars and set a few broken bones."

"That isn't enough?" her uncle asked.

"In *this* place? At *this* time? No sir, it is not."

He smiled. Chuckled. He was thoroughly amused by her seriousness.

"What are you laughing at?" she asked. "Are you taking his side?"

"Do you forget where your good doctor's been and what he's seen, young lady?"

"Forget what?"

"He was in France," her uncle said. "In the trenches. Your doctor's seen things you and I can't even imagine. Blood, death, sorrow, fear. And hasn't he talked about some bad business with his parents, down in Haiti? Wasn't his father killed by men with cane knives?"

"What does all that prove?"

"Baby girl," her Uncle Barnabus began, a smile on his lips but his eyes dead serious, "you've never seen blood, or death, or even real pain. Sorry to put too fine a point on it, but there it is."

"Now, wait a minute—"

"Let me finish," he said. The schoolmaster was back. "I can understand that you've got passions and beliefs. We all do. What I'm asking you to suppose is that your good doctor may not be as willing to 'get involved', as you call it, not because he's a coward or a fiddling cricket, but because he's had his *share* of getting involved. He's seen things—maybe even *done* things— that you and I can scarce imagine the weight of. I think you can cut the man a little slack."

"This is an important time," she said, back still ram-rod stiff. She knew she couldn't win this argument, but she persisted anyway. "We could all have something real here—true and honest and real—that we never could have had before. If we fail to do what's right in the face of an indifferent city administration, corrupt policemen, and predatory criminal enterprises… well, my God, what are we? What *good* are we, to ourselves or anyone?"

He reached across the table and laid one rough hand on hers, with all the gentleness of a surgeon. "Then maybe it's something else."

"What else?" Fralene asked. She had no idea what he was suggesting.

Her uncle smiled at her—a smile that said she was an ignorant child, but he loved her anyway.

"Didn't you just tell me that fear teaches us what's important? That sometimes, we should listen to that fear and respond to it? Fralene, maybe he *is* afraid of something."

"But—"

"Stop arguing," he said gently. "You know I'm right."

She didn't have a response.

"He's a good man, your doctor," the reverend said. "You keep expecting him to keep pace with you in the course of your social crusades and such, you're like to drive him away."

The bell above the café door tinkled as someone stepped in. Fralene's back was to it, so she couldn't see who had just arrived. Her uncle, however, focused on the newcomer, frowned, and took a long, slow sip of his coffee. Fralene heard a voice from the counter—a woman.

"Cup of coffee and a sour cream donut, Dex."

Fralene raised an eyebrow, as if to ask her uncle who it was that had just arrived and soured him with their very presence.

"That hoodoo lady," he whispered.

"Miss Gooden?"

He nodded. "She's eyeballing me, too. Tryin' to be sneaky about it, but I see."

Fralene leaned closer, smiling in spite of herself. "Maybe she likes you, uncle. Aren't you in the market for a new missus Farnes to keep the parsonage clean and host your tea parties?"

"There never has been a missus," the Reverend Farnes said, "and there never will be. Now… enough out of you, young lady. Respect your elders."

Fralene smiled. She enjoyed these quiet times with her uncle. They seemed to have so few of them lately.

Their waitress arrived with their breakfasts. The two dug in.

"She's still lookin' at me," her uncle muttered, raising a spoonful of fried mush to his frowning mouth. When he swallowed it, he made a strange face.

"Something wrong?" Fralene asked, pouring syrup on her hotcakes.

"I think this is yesterday's mush," he said, but lifted another spoonful and kept eating.

10

It was storming outside. Dub could barely hear the wango drums or the mambo's song as the recorded summoning skirled out of his Victrola's horn. Down came the deluge, making thunder on the roof of his brownstone and filling his peristyle with a maddening clatter.

Still, Dub held his concentration and repeated the familiar rituals. He poured offerings of his good family rum, lit cigars for Ogou and Legba and set them upright in an old trepanned skull, then burned dried sage and set some cones of frankincense smoldering. Offerings settled, he danced in a circle—stomping, clapping, chanting—until he felt the doors between the worlds ready to burst on their etheric hinges. When he fell to his knees, kissed the earth, and knocked upon it three times, the Guinee door swung wide and the *lwa* stepped through.

Dub addressed Erzulie directly. "I suppose there's no appeasing Danto? No end to this blasted rain?"

'Fraid not, Erzulie answered. *Sister Danto and me, we ain't on speaking terms.*

Goin' soft, Ogou snarled. *A brave man likes the feel of nature on his face.*

"And a wise man knows when to come in out of the rain," Dub countered. He slipped on his *veve* pendants, his dead man's socks, his grave-digger's boots. Then came the purple-and-black striped waistcoat gifted him by an *houngan* in Haiti, his long, coal-black trenchcoat. Finally, he loaded and holstered his pistols, then pocketed some govi grenades.

The boy ain't wrong, Legba said. *This storm's more than just the wind and rain. It's portent and prologue. It carries something with it. Can't you feel it?*

"I feel it," Dub said, donning his dreadlock wig and top hat.

I feel it, too, Erzulie agreed. *Like it ain't gonna wash things away… it's just gonna set them loose.*

Dub dipped one gloved hand into the bone powder that made his face into the fearsome mask that all evil-doers in Harlem had come to dread.

Well, if the storm's set something loose, Ogou broke in, *best to get to business, neh?*

Dub cracked his neck, stood ready. "Let's get horsed."

Ogou mounted.

Doc Voodoo, the Dread Baron opened his black eyes.

XX

Neither rain nor sleet nor snow now hail could keep the almost-dissolved Harlem Concerned Citizens' Brigade from meeting. Fralene tried to talk her uncle out of it, but he wouldn't hear of it. The meeting was scheduled and he would follow through, hell or high water. Fralene might not have been so worried if he didn't seem so out of sorts. But, she'd noticed something working on him all afternoon and evening—a malaise, an irritability that was not his normal prickliness. What if he was coming down with something?

But, no, her uncle had insisted. If it might be their last official meeting, they should damn well *have it*, and not call it off on account of rain like a baseball game. Fralene supposed she could accept that, but insisted upon accompanying Uncle Barnabus. She would make sure he took a cab and didn't try to just walk under the inadequate cover of his umbrella. All their family needed after all they'd been through recently was her uncle contracting a fever or pneumonia. And wouldn't that just be the choicest irony? Barnabus Farnes: survived gun-toting assassin, done in by spring rains.

So here they were, at Mother Zion African Methodist Church, sitting among the pews, four individuals dwarfed in the sanctuary's big and empty interior. The Reverend Brown walked with a cane and still sported a cast on his arm, but his face looked far better, not half so swollen, bruised, or lacerated as it had been. Still, Fralene thought he looked rather deflated, his natural, almost childish spryness and vigor beaten out of him, his spirit cowed and broken. Fralene hoped the reverend's

70

spirit would mend, and made a mental note to check on him in a week or so, perhaps by bringing him a pot of beans or a pie from a neighborhood bakery.

Ms. Walker had escaped the encounter with no physical signs of distress, but Fralene thought she recognized in the normally poised, elegant, middle-aged matron a strange sort of shuttered silence more common to wallflowers and shrinking violets; as if she were a once-spirited filly, broken by a harsh, cruel trainer. There was still a faint bruise on her cheek, as well. Fralene tried to make chit-chat with Ms. Walker as they waited for the arrival of Mr. Jebediah Debbs—both to put her at ease and to try and probe the depths of her distress—but Ms. Walker was not forthcoming regarding her feelings. She simply matched Fralene's idle chit-chat but failed to illuminate further how her struggles with fear or anxiety might still be affecting her.

Uncle Barnabus checked his pocket watch. "Twenty minutes," he grumbled. "Where in Sam Hill is that man…"

His face was twisted and creased in ways that she'd never seen before. Uncle Barnabus seemed more deeply troubled—more resentful, more angry—than Fralene had ever seen him to be. He checked his watch again and again, groused continually, and in between seemed to struggle for breath, sometimes mopping his brow with his handkerchief.

He doesn't look good, Fralene thought. *I just might have to fetch a doctor for him this evening.*

And Dub's the nearest doctor.

No. She wouldn't. She couldn't. She hadn't spoken to Dr. Dub Corveaux in almost a week, and she would not approach him now. If he wanted to smooth things over and apologize for being so stubborn, let him; she would not be the first to back down just because she needed his professional services. There were other physicians in Harlem, after all…

Besides, she had nothing to apologize for.

Did she?

"Perhaps we should begin?" the Reverend Brown offered. "After all, this isn't a formal gathering, is it? If Mr. Debbs arrive, we simply—"

"Have you got somewhere to be?" Uncle Barnabus asked him.

There was a momentary silence. The bristly tone of the question, aimed at one of Uncle Barnabus's oldest friends, caught them all off guard. It wasn't right.

"No, Barney," the Reverend Brown said. Fralene hoped that would settle her uncle a bit. Brown was the only man who ever called her uncle Barney.

That was when the doors of the sanctuary thumped and opened wide. Mr. Jebediah Debbs strode in, barrel chest puffed out before him, looking almost infernal in a rusty orange suit and waistcoat, a matching Homburg on his melon head, and a long raincoat trailing behind him like a royal mantle. Two men accompanied him—young men with wide shoulders, heavy expressions and grim, determined mouths. Fralene wondered just what Debbs was aiming at, arriving with such a clatter and trailing these two hangers-on. From the looks of the three other committee members surrounding her—her uncle included—they were all equally puzzled.

"I apologize," Debbs said in his booming basso voice as he marched down the aisle toward them. "I had urgent matters to attend to before arriving, and they could not wait."

"Knows how to make an entrance, don't he?" Uncle Barnabus muttered.

Fralene stared. The venom in his voice; the slightest hint of country ham and corn pone. Her uncle was born in the South, but he hadn't been there since he was a child, and he was downright fussy when it came to how he spoke and what impression he made on anyone who heard him.

That tears it, she thought. *He must be feverish.*

Debbs arrived at their pews. He did not take a seat himself. He simply stood in the aisle, officiously planting his thick fingers in the watch-pockets of his waistcoat, then let his two companions take up positions on either side of him. They crossed their hands before them.

"Down to business, then," Debbs said with a haughty lift of his chin. "Have we considered my proposal of a rally to support our cause?"

"I didn't know that such a motion was on the table," the Reverend Brown said.

"It most certainly was not," Ms. Walker added.

"It most certainly *was*," Debbs said. "Check those minutes from our last meeting, Ms. Walker, and you'll see that I broached just such a subject—"

"In any case," the Reverend Brown countered, trying to bring the rising tension in the sanctuary down, "this isn't a formal meeting. We're here to discuss how we feel in light of our… experiences last week. To put it plainly: do we carry on, or do we retire?"

He looked to the others, seeking even unspoken support from them. Ms. Walker nodded. Uncle Barnabus just looked to Debbs.

Fralene studied the big agitator. A twisted smile bloomed on Debbs's dark lips—a smirk of self-satisfaction.

"Just as I thought," he said. "The enemy threatens you, and you're all ready to fold. I thought I was in the company of lions, but apparently, there are only lambs hereabouts."

"We haven't decided anything yet," the Reverend Brown said.

"Of course you have," Debbs countered. "You've made your decisions. Well, I'm here to tell you, I've made mine. You can see my decision standing right here on either side of me."

They all studied the two young men at his elbows, not sure what he meant.

"Gentlemen," Mr. Debbs said to his companions, "show my colleagues the level of our resolve."

Each opened his raincoat. Each had a pump-action shotgun hanging by his side from a leather strap over his shoulder.

Brown seemed terribly affected by the sight. "How dare you," he whispered, "bring armed thugs into a house of God!"

"These are not armed thugs, reverend," Debbs said. "These are members of the newly-formed Harlem Vigilance Committee. If our protectors are corrupt and our enemies armed, we have no choice but to protect ourselves. If you lot are determined to dissolve the Concerned Citizens Brigade, I'm here to offer you membership—or sponsorship opportunities—for the Vigilance Committee."

"You're mad," Reverend Brown said. "You're just going to make things worse."

"Violence isn't the answer, Mr. Debbs.," Ms. Walker added.

"You are a strutting peacock, aren't you, Debbs?"

Everyone fell silent. Those words had come croaking out of the Reverend Barnabus Farnes. Fralene couldn't believe her ears. Nor, apparently, could anyone else.

Uncle Barnabus sat in his pew, hands clasped imperiously before him, eyes down. He said nothing. There was only the sound of his breathing.

"Uncle Barnabus…" Fralene began.

"What did you say to me?" Debbs demanded.

"I said you're a strutting peacock with a mouth as wide at the Brooklyn Bridge," the Reverend Farnes answered. "Didn't you hear me the first time, or are you deaf, as well?"

The thorniness in his voice was unmistakable. Fralene had heard her uncle adopt a stern attitude when dressing down someone for a failure of character before—lies, deceit, self-pity—but she'd never heard him simply insult someone because he did not like them, or thought them overly proud. The Reverend Brown and Ms. Walker stared at the Reverend Farnes with a mixture of incredulousness and pride. However shocked they were at his words, they clearly, secretly, agreed with the spirit of them. Ms. Walker even had to raise her hanky and hide the smile that bloomed on her normally-dignified face.

"Now, see here—" Debbs began.

"Ain't nothin' to see but a fat, blustering carpet-bagger, trumpeting Africa for the Africans, offering salvation with one hand and stuffing his pockets with the other."

Fralene leaned closer. "Uncle Barnabus, is this really—"

Uncle Barnabus shot to his feet. "I didn't say a word to you, missy!" he roared, and Fralene felt herself thrust back into her seat simply by the power of his voice. "You ain't part of these proceedings, so just keep yourself close by and quiet, you hear?"

The Reverend Brown's face grew dark and heavy with concern. "Barney, this isn't necessary—"

"And what would you know about it, whitey?" Farnes growled.

Fralene couldn't believe her ears. Her breath caught in her throat. The Reverend Brown's mouth fell open. He didn't just look shocked... he looked *wounded*.

"That's right," her uncle continued. "You heard me, Brown. Look at you. If everybody didn't already know your name and know you were a preacher man up here in nigger heaven, you could probably waltz right into a West Egg country club, couldn't you?"

Fralene rose and laid hands on him, trying to urge him to sit. "That's enough," she said. She'd never seen him like this, and it scared her.

Uncle Barnabus yanked loose from her, snarling in her face. "Take your hands off of me, you mealy-mouthed little brat! Ain't it enough I fed and clothed you when your parents departed this sickly planet? Now you've gotta tell me my mind when I'm freely speakin' it?"

"Reverend," Ms. Walker interrupted. "This is most irregular."

"That it is," he answered. "But it oughta be the norm, you ask me. I've had just about enough of all your preening and whining and bickering—the lot of ya. If any one of you had sand, you'd have been drumming up supporters one by one— but no. Strength in numbers, right? So you come crawling to me, begging me for help, as though I've got nothing better to do than baby-sit the lot of you."

"I expect an apology," Mr. Debbs said. "And I'll have it."

"It's in the post," her uncle said dismissively. "Keep an eye out for it, why don't you?"

The Reverend Brown was on his feet now, stepping up to her uncle's left elbow. He wore a mask of grave concern. He'd known her uncle for a long time—longer than Fralene herself had been alive. He knew this was an unheard-of mode of speech for him.

"Barney," he said, "come on now—"

"Get your hands off of me you high yalla house nigger!" the reverend roared.

Ms. Walker shot to her feet. "I don't think we're ready for this discussion," she said, trying to maintain her composure. "Maybe we should adjourn for the night."

"I'm not leaving here without an apology," Debbs said.

"Mr. Debbs," Fralene offered, "I'm sorry. My uncle's a little under the weather—"

"What do you know about it?" her uncle growled. "What do you know about anything, you spoiled, frigid little minx? When's the last time you did an honest day's work, eh?"

Fralene felt the sting of tears. *What was happening?* This wasn't like him.

"Take him home," Brown said. "Call him a doctor. This isn't right—"

"*Call the doctor,*" her uncle tittered. "She'll call the doctor, all right. He'll come running, too, like a stray dog sniffing a bitch in heat..."

Fralene actually felt a fist close on her beating heart. Her breath caught in her throat and she could not inhale or exhale. Those words—so bitter, so hurtful. Where had those words even come from? She'd never heard anything so terrible from her uncle's mouth, not in her life.

Ms. Walker didn't even spare a word. She turned to leave her pew, but Debbs and his bodyguards blocked her path. They were not trying to keep her there—they simply didn't bother to move aside. Debbs was still intent on Uncle Barnabus, his honor challenged. He shook one fat finger at the old man.

"Everyone will hear of this," Debbs growled. "Everyone will know what a cruel and ungracious man you are, Reverend Farnes!"

"Coming from a thief and a rabble-rouser like you, Debbs, I couldn't imagine a finer compliment."

Debbs lunged toward him, his pointed finger becoming a fist. "Now, see here, old man!"

Fralene's uncle surprised her by pushing right past her and swinging out of the pew into the aisle. He stood toe to toe with Debbs.

Then he shoved him.

Debbs stared, gape-mouthed. His bodyguards were shocked as well. What should they do when their employer was threatened by a septuagenarian man of the cloth?

"Get out!" her uncle roared.

"You can't," Debbs sputtered.

Her uncle strode forward, shoving him again. Debbs stumbled backward. His bodyguards retreated without making any move to help him.

"I said get the hell out of my church, you preening pig!" Uncle Barnabus snarled. He drove Debbs and his bodyguards right down the aisle toward the narthex and the front doors. "Get out and take your field hands with you! You ain't nothin' but a fat bag of wind and I don't suppose I'll take any more sass from you!"

Fralene looked to the Reverend Brown, to Ms. Walker. They were all equally terrified and perplexed. They hurried out of their pews and followed.

Debbs's bodyguards reached the doors before he did. Each took one and opened it, providing their employer with a wide escape hatch out into the wet, drizzly evening beyond. Fralene was halfway up the aisle when those doors opened. She saw Debbs stumble out; saw his bodyguards follow; saw her uncle reach the threshold and throw his arms wide to keep the doors from closing.

When Fralene, the Revered Brown, and Ms. Walker reached the narthex, they saw what waited in the street outside.

Mr. Jebediah Debbs had brought an armed mob.

There had to be two or three dozen of them—men of all ages, shapes and sizes, carrying pump shotguns and automatic pistols and revolvers. Debbs stumbled down the church steps and was caught in the welcoming net of his little merry band. He recovered, straightened his hat on his head, then turned to face Uncle Barnabus where he still stood in the door.

"Come on, then!" Debbs challenged. "Come bully me here and now, with my Vigilance Committee at my side!"

"*Your* Vigilance Committee," Uncle Barnabus sneered. Fralene and the others hung back, in the center of the narthex, fearful that something terrible might happen next.

It just takes one itchy trigger finger, Fralene thought. *Just one, and all hell breaks loose…*

"You can take your Vigilance Committee," her uncle growled, "and march 'em back up to your tenements on your block, and you can all chew on my bony black ass, for all I care! If these dumb Negroes think you're a man worth following, Debbs, then they deserve whatever they got comin'!"

"A reckoning's coming!" Debbs answered, shaking that thick, prophetic finger of his again. "The wheat will be winnowed from the chaff, Reverend Farnes! The faithful from the weak!"

"Reckon your ass outta here!" Farnes roared. "Every goddamned one of ya!"

Then he tugged the doors shut, and they met at the threshold with a thunderous crash that seemed to shake the very walls of the church. A terrible silence followed.

Uncle Barnabus turned and faced his fellows—Fralene, the Reverend Brown, Ms. Lucille Walker. He studied them like they were the lowest forms of life he'd ever encountered.

"Best close your mouths," the Reverend Farnes said, "'fore you draw flies."

Then, the Reverend Brown stepped forward and struck him.

Fralene gasped in spite of herself.

It was open-handed, and probably not as hard as it could have been, but the sound of flesh on flesh was terribly loud in the wide narthex. Fralene saw something change in her uncle's eyes when he was struck—as though he'd awakened from a sound sleep, or been interrupted in the throes of a nightmare. He blinked, staring into the Reverend Brown's round, blushing face.

"Adam?" the Reverend Farnes said, sounding bewildered.

The Reverend Brown saw the change, just as Fralene did—and somehow, that sudden change, even more so than the venom that had been pouring out of him, scared the holy man even more. He looked to Fralene.

"Get him home," Reverend Brown said.

Her uncle turned and stared at her, still blinking. His eyes were watery and perplexed. She could see the desperation in them, the fright.

"Mr. Debbs?"

"Don't worry about him," Ms. Walker said. "There's more than a little provocation in that man…"

Fralene laid hands on her uncle's right arm. "Come on, Uncle Barnabus. Let's go home. You just need some sleep."

"I'm not myself this evening," he said weakly. "Those words…"

XX

She found his coat and hat. They waited for the armed vigilantes out front to disperse, then Fralene walked her uncle home, the two of them huddled beneath an umbrella. He was dazed and silent most of the way. It occurred to Fralene to talk about his outburst as they walked—to settle him, to try and get to the bottom of things—but every time she stole a glance at him, she was so stunned by his stricken stare and downturned mouth that she could not bring herself to speak. She just kept walking, and held his arm a little tighter.

It was only when they were home, their coats and hats hung on their familiar hooks by the door, that she could bring herself to ask him what was wrong.

"I can't explain it," he said. "I just sort of went away…a daze of some sort. I heard those words, but they sounded like someone else's. Far off. Then, when Adam struck me—"

"I'm sure he didn't mean it," Fralene offered.

"It was right and proper," her uncle said, shuffling where he stood, seemingly lost as to where he should go next. "I wasn't myself, and that slap was all that brought me out of it."

"Would you like some tea, maybe?" she asked.

He glanced toward the kitchen, then shook his head. "No. No, you go on to bed."

Then he turned and shuffled off toward his den. Fralene watched him for a few moments, then stepped after him.

"I could cut you a slice of pie, if you want," she said. "Or some warm milk?"

He stopped. Straightened. He spoke without turning around to look at her. "What part of 'no' did you not understand, you nagging bitch?"

It was *that voice* again. The one he'd spoken in at the meeting. The most disconcerting thing about it was how unlike him it sounded. Not just the words, but the very tone and timbre. It was like someone else's voice, imitating her uncle's, dripping with venom and malice, the subterfuge not entirely complete.

"Uncle," she said. It was all she could manage. Her voice caught in her throat.

He slowly turned. His eyes bore into her, dark and contemptuous. "There go the tears," he said, sneering. "Hear the little bitch whine."

"You can't talk to me like that," she said.

"I can talk to you any goddamn way I please," he said. "You think this is *your* house? You think *your* sweat and tears and hard work went into these walls and these floors? You're a guest here, little girl—a guest of my good graces!"

She wanted to run away from him, but she refused to. Something was very wrong—more wrong than she'd ever imagined a thing in her life could be. She'd heard of old men and women going senile, getting confused, sometimes getting hostile or obstreperous because they didn't know where they were, what they were doing, or who they were doing it with. But this was different. He seemed to be speaking in another voice, acting like another person.

"Well?" he asked. "What do you got to say for yourself, you freeloadin' ninny?"

She stepped forward, determined not to abandon him. "I don't know what's wrong with you, uncle. Maybe you're sick—"

"Sick," he sneered. "I never felt better, girl."

"—or maybe you're just tired or confused. Either way, I'm not walking away from you. Why don't you let me help you up to bed? If you could just rest awhile—"

He lunged suddenly, a movement so quick, so threatening, that Fralene actually cried out as he did so. His arms stretched out, his palms slammed against the wall, and before she knew it, Fralene was trapped between them where she stood. Her uncle's glowering face hovered inches from her own. "I've slept long enough, missy. Longer than you can imagine. I don't think I'll be warming any covers this night—"

Fralene struck him, just as the Reverend Brown had—open-handed, right across the face. "Wake up!" she screamed.

He was stunned for only a moment. The venom never left him. "Wide awake, little girl," he said.

She had no choice. She threw herself forward and shoved him as hard as she could.

Her uncle went stumbling backward, collided with a little table beside the sofa, and caught himself just before he went sprawling. He stared at her in surprise… then surprise turned to fury.

"You little bitch," he snarled, and lunged.

Fralene dove sideward and plunged back into the foyer. Perhaps if she could get upstairs, to her room, lock the door—

Her uncle barreled after her, growling as he came. Fralene leapt onto the stairs and tried to climb, taking two and at time—

But she was too slow, too clumsy. She tripped and fell forward, nearly eating the stair runner and slamming her head hard on the stair above her. One knee had also collided with the leading edge of a stair and it blazed with pain, unlike anything she'd ever felt.

Then her uncle was upon her. He snagged a handful of her hair, lifted her head, and forced her to look into his leering, wrinkled old face. His eyes were mad and frightful, his tongue running over his lips.

"Don't you ever run away from me, you—"

And then, Fralene heard something else: heavy footfalls thumping down the staircase from above. She rolled her eyes and jerked her head sideward just in time to see Beau—her little brother Beau—rushing down toward the two of them, a look of confusion and worry on his face.

"Fralene, where the hell's—"

Her uncle looked up at the boy, sneered, then growled as an animal might, teeth clenched, the sound rising out of his chest and gullet.

Beau didn't hesitate—perhaps he couldn't, because momentum was carrying him downward. He slammed right into the two of them, seemed to roll over Fralene where she lay prone on the stairs, then collided with their uncle. In that confused instant, Fralene saw a tangle of limbs, her uncle's hands torn from her blouse and hair, Beau's hands falling on the old man, heard curses and a shout of fright from her younger brother.

Then they went rolling down the last few stairs, a heap of shoulders, elbows, feet and knees. When they hit the foyer floor, Beau was on top. Their uncle wasn't moving.

Fralene forced herself to her feet, using the bannister for support. She descended the last few stairs to the foyer floor and stood above them. Beau was just regaining his senses. He had a bad knot rising on his forehead and some blood trickling from his bitten lip. Under him, Uncle Barnabus stirred a little, but didn't seem capable of waking up.

Beau looked terrified. He stared at their uncle as he struggled to his feet. "I didn't mean to," he said. "I just heard you two yelling. I came to see what was wrong and he had his hands on you and… and… I didn't mean it! You've got to believe me!"

Fralene held Beau's face in her hands. He was seventeen years old, but at that moment, he looked like the scared and frightened child she still thought him to be. "It's alright," she said quietly, trying to control the sound of her voice, to project confidence, control. She was failing miserably. Her own hands were shaking.

"What's wrong with him?" Beau asked.

One of Uncle Barnabus's arms suddenly flopped out, his hand grasping emptily at the air. He muttered something incoherent. Fralene and Beau fell into one another's arms, terrified by the sudden spasm.

But he didn't wake, and he didn't rise. He lay there, still unconscious, breathing shallowly.

"I'll explain while we work," Fralene rasped. "Just help me, Beau. We're going to fix him."

"Get you girl…" Uncle Barnabus muttered, voice slurred and far away.

The danger hadn't passed. He was knocked silly, but he wasn't himself again. Fralene and Beau had to put him away somewhere—lock him up where he could do no harm until she could bring someone who could help him.

"What the hell's wrong with him?"Beau asked.

Fralene disentangled herself from Beau, grabbed one of her uncle's bony legs, then looked to her brother. "Help me," she said.

"Help you do what?" he demanded.

She cocked her head down the hall beside the stairway. "We're taking him to the basement."

11

The ice truck wasn't cool any more. The air was warm and moist, and the rain beating down on the roof reverberated within like the roar of Niagara Falls. It had been Willie's idea to climb in here. All his deliveries for the day were done and the boss—his father—didn't mind if Willie sometimes took the truck for a spin once there was no more block ice. You'll like it, Willie had told Esther. It's dark and cool. Private.

But Esther didn't like it—not one bit. With the two of them squeezed into the dark little refrigeration space, the outer door barely cracked, the air had turned swampy fast. Esther's head was pounding. The darkness and the noise drove her batty, and Willie's not-so-gentle insistence on reaching up under her skirt to yank down her drawers was starting to scare her.

"No," she said again. "We can pet, all right? But you ain't getting' into my knickers, Willie Bunyon."

"Come on," he groaned, and tried to slide his hand up there again, ragged nails raking her bare legs. He got one hand on her drawers and yanked again. Esther tried to wriggle away from his hand, but he only yanked harder. She heard something tear and tried to pedal out from under him, legs scrambling for purchase.

"That ain't right, Willie," she said. "That ain't right at all—"

"Baby, you know it's right," he murmured in her ear. He then licked her lobe, nibbled it. His probing fingers brushed her privates. The sensation was terrible and exciting all at once— mostly terrible. It all seemed so wrong all of the sudden—laying down here in the back of a damp, empty ice truck with Willie Bunyon rutting and grab-assing atop her.

"You better stop," Esther said.

"Ain't stoppin'," Willie assured her. His hand dove for her privates again.

She locked her legs shut, laid both hands on his chest, and shoved.

Willie was a big, thick fellow. It wasn't easy raising him up. He stared down at her, small, dark eyes narrowed in the darkness.

"Woman, what are you on about?"

"I ain't havin' you manhandle me in this ice truck," Esther said. "I said pettin' and that's all."

"Pet, hell, baby," he said, and there went his hand again, searching under her skirt for the place that he'd uncovered when he tore her panties away. "All we been doin' is pettin'."

She squirmed. Kicked. She wanted to lock her legs again, but she couldn't kick and close all at once.

Her protests seemed to excite him. He set himself atop her, all his weight pinning her, then he reached down with one hand to open his fly. Esther tried to wriggle out from under him, but he really had her now. He dropped one leg between her knees and prized them apart.

"Willie, quit it," she said. She sounded like a child to herself, quavering and fearful.

"Just a little," Willie said, and worked her skirt up with a sweep of his engorged cock. "Just a little bit of sugar, baby—"

The little door to the icebox suddenly swung open. Second-hand street light dulled by falling rain spilled inside. Esther screamed, she was so surprised, and Willie raised his eyes.

"Push on, nigger!" Willie said, not sure who was bursting in on them, but rebuking them with authority just the same.

Esther couldn't see the man in the doorway clearly. The ambient light was too dim and it came from behind him, making him little more than a wall of darkness punched out of the shimmering curtain of rain. The only thing she could see clearly puzzled her.

He wore a top hat.

Then one gloved fist reached into the icebox, snagging Willie by the collar. Willie was dragged bodily off of Esther, kicking and screaming as he went.

Esther scrambled up off her back and onto her knees. She couldn't find her panties in the dark. She did her best to make sure her skirt was down and her blouse buttoned, then dove for the icebox door. It was still swinging on its hinges.

When Esther opened the door and stuck her head through, she saw Willie on his knees in the street, mouth agape, eyes rolling in his brown face like two big stones. The stranger in the top hat loomed over him, Willie's collar in one hand, a big black gun in the other. The gun's muzzle lay firmly against Willie's temple.

Strange as it seemed—even to her—Esther screamed. "Don't hurt him!" she cried, and did her damnedest to scurry out of the icebox. It was tough, negotiating that little portal. When she tried to plant one foot on the rear bumper, she slipped and dinged her other shin hard on the lip of the door. Instead of trying to right herself, she just threw her body forward and landed face-first in the rain-swollen gutter.

The gunman loomed over her. His face was dead white, painted like a skull, and he had a head full of weird braids that flared out from under the top hat like a lion's mane. He glared at her with dark eyes.

"Don't hurt him!" she sobbed, crying as much from the pain of her awkward landing as for Willie's well-being. "He didn't do nothing!"

"That's right!" Willie chimed. "I didn't do nothing!"

The muzzle of the gun pressed hard against his forehead. "I didn't ask you any questions," the gunman snarled.

Esther threw herself at the gunman's feet. "Please! Please! I'll be good from here on, mister! Just don't hurt him! He don't deserve it, he don't!"

"Yes, he does," the gunman said.

"Please," Esther pleaded.

"Run home, Esther," the gunman said, and Esther thought hearing her name from his lips was the most terrifying sensation she'd ever known.

"What?" she asked.

"Don't you leave me!" Willie said.

"I said, run home," the gunman repeated. "Your mama's waiting. Tell her Willie here got fresh, and you don't think you're gonna see him anymore."

"What?" Willie asked

The gunman turned his dark gaze on Willie. "I wasn't talking to you."

Esther was on her feet, her legs loose beneath her like a couple of licorice whips.

"Please, sir… please."

"Go," he said.

She went, leaving one of her shoes where it lay in the roiling gutter.

XX

Ace Fincher emerged from the basement into a dim, rain-beaten alley. He supposed he should be worried about the lousy weather—maybe even button his overcoat—but neither the chill, the rain nor his health were concerns at the moment. He had pretty big knot of mazuma in hand—over a grand if he counted right—so his first order of business wasn't buttoning up or taking shelter from the rain: it was getting the hell out of Harlem, before somebody dry-gulched him and took it on the lam with his scratch.

Ace came uptown because he knew two or three of the seats at Rondo's game would be occupied by high-rollers prone to crash-and-burn gambling binges. One of them, Fitzwilliam Jones, a.k.a. Fitzy, was a small-time con man and some-time pimp who'd been downtown just the night before. Fitzy had lifted a bundle off a drunk Mick in Danny Doll's gang. Word had it Fitzy had started shooting his mouth off before he even made it back uptown, gum-flapping to a back room croupier, a speak-tender, and a nigger hack about how he'd taken one of those Hells Kitchen 'tater-eaters to town and now he'd have a hefty poke to buy into Rondo's Wednesday night basement game. Ace—being unaffiliated with any particular crew and moving in many nefarious circles—had overheard talk of Fitzy's braggadocio and knew that he'd be wise to find out who Rondo was and where his game was happening, before somebody else got wise. The Micks might come gunning for Fitzy if word got back to them. Worse, Fitzy could come up this way and just blow the whole poke in the game, pissing all that cash away on a couple of able card-sharks who were probably conning the con-man from the moment he sat down at the table.

So it was Fitzy's hijinks that led Ace uptown. He was even more delighted when he saw the other two players.

Blue Lou Bundy was the dealer, the ranking sharp at the table. Everybody called him Blue Lou because he never smiled, but Ace figured it could just as easily be for how dark he was—like, made-of-African-tar dark— so black he really *was* almost blue. Ace knew Blue Lou by reputation, and he knew that his sour puss and doped demeanor hid a canny mind, a wad of dough, and a savage temper.

Sitting on Blue Lou's right had been Brown Tom. Word had it his name was really Tom Brown, but somewhere along the way, somebody'd called him Brown Tom and it stuck. He was a grass dealer and petty thief who sometimes made ends meet playing slap bass in speakeasies and at rent parties. When Ace arrived, Brown Tom was grinning ear to ear telling Rondo—the host of the game, but not sitting in—all about how he'd found his girlfriend, Debbie, going down on some high yalla bohunk rail porter—walked right in on them. He'd been packing at the time, so he drew his piece, smacked Debbie head-wise, then leveled his popper in the bohunk's face. Poor sap was scared so bad he pissed in Debbie's face. Brown Tom told that pissin' John to empty his pockets, and Brown Tom hit the mother lode. The poor sap pulled a five hundred dollar stash (apparently, he'd had a good night in Atlantic city just before he made it to the Apple). Brown Tom took the whole five C's and shook down Debbie too—who he actually had no special attachment to— and got another fifty. Off he went, leaving the bohunk shaking, Debbie with piss on her face, and himself with a fat wad of lettuce.

Ace knew when he heard Brown Tom's story that he'd come to the right place. When Fitzy arrived, it was clinched: Ace would take all three of these teapots for a ride and he'd leave this basement with all their money or not at all. The jigs didn't want to let him sit in at first, but Rondo knew Ace's name and reputation and said it was okay—providing the rest of them knew not to give Ace an inch of wiggle room. Ace even demonstrated his honesty by stripping his jacket and rolling up his sleeves.

Funny part was, in the end, he barely used any of his tricks: he was on, and his card mates were decidedly off. After three hours, Ace had the whole pot. He didn't even have to break a sweat or load his hand to do it.

But they were pissed.

Man, were they.

Oh, they stayed cool. They didn't whine. Didn't make threats. Didn't even beg for another chance. They were soundly whipped, and they knew it—but their chilly silence and smoldering acceptance of their losses convinced Ace he needed to air out, fast.

So he tipped his hat, made gracious obsequies, and fled the basement, with Rondo laughing behind him, dressing down the three big losers for being so stupid as to let Ace take them to the cleaners.

Fuck 'em. They were all grifters. This was the game. Every hand was played fair and square.

But that didn't really make Ace feel any better as he marched through the dark and rainy alley toward Fifth Avenue just up ahead. Crying fair and square really wouldn't take you far if your card mates were poor losers. Fair and square didn't put your teeth back in your head or work out the kinks in your broken fingers.

So Ace ankled it. He'd scurry to the train station and head back to his end of the Apple. If he was smart, he'd sock a chunk of this cabbage for a rainy day and only take a small portion of it to Moshe's casino on Saturday night.

If he was smart.

The problem was—though he hated to admit it—sometimes, he *wasn't* smart.

And sometimes, he was *too smart* by half.

He wondered which it was that undid him this time—not smart, or too smart—when a big, broad shadow suddenly stepped into his path, blocking the mouth of the alleyway and his Fifth Avenue escape.

It was Blue Lou. Nobody else had a head so much like a melon or shoulders that wide.

Ace froze in his tracks. Rainwater spilled off the drooping lip of his hat and ran riot down the shoulders of his rain coat. He quickly stuffed the wad of cash into an inside coat pocket.

"That you, Lou?" he asked.

Blue Lou didn't say anything.

"Did I leave something?" Ace asked, hoping the answer was, *Yeah, you dumb heeb—you forgot your cigarette lighter. Damn fine one, too. Shame to lose it.*

But no. That wasn't the response he got.

"You're *gonna* leave something," somebody said behind him. Ace turned a little, just to get a look.

Brown Tom and Fitzy stood about twenty feet behind him, blocking a retreat.

Eyes forward again. Ace saw Blue Lou take a single long step forward, then heard the thunder crack of the knuckles on both his big, black hands.

"Come on!" Ace said, his voice wavering and whiny. He turned sideways, so that they were to his right and left instead of in front and behind. "I won those hands fair and square, fellas! If you don't want to lose, you shouldn't oughta play."

"You stiffed us," Fitzy said. He and Brown Tom were close in now. Although it was pretty dark in the alleyway, Ace saw that Brown Tom had a pistol in his hand—probably the same pistol he'd used on the high yalla bohunk. Fitzy had something long and shiny: a stiletto. An ugly one, too.

"Jesus Christ, what a bunch of little girls," Ace snorted, shaking his head. It was all bravado. He was scared shitless. "You can't stand losin' so you gang up on the guy who beat you, fair and square."

"Fair and square is my foot in your ass," Fitzy said.

"Fair and square's our money," Blue Lou said, and Ace didn't care for the depth and darkness of the man's voice—not one bit. "Right now."

Ace went into his pocket and produced the wad. He started stripping bills off.

"Fine," he said, "I'll take back my buy-in, and you chiselin' jigs can take the rest. But I'm gonna tell everybody about this! Queens to the ferry, nobody's gonna sit for a game at Rondo's anymore, and you three can just sit there all by your lonesome and have a circle jerk!"

"Buy-in, hell," Brown Tom said, and raised his pistol. It was small and short, but goddamned if looking down that barrel didn't make it look like a howitzer. "You just drop that green and run, Abe."

Ace couldn't help himself. A terrible indignance overtook him. He heard himself raging before he could even employ his better judgment and keep his mouth shut. "You gotta be fuckin' kidding me! Is this really how you Uncle Toms play cards?"

Fitzy had him then. He slammed Ace up against the bricks at his back. Ace saw stars. The money fell from his hands. He felt something sharp at his throat.

"This look like I'm fuckin' kiddin', asshole?"

Blue Lou grabbed his coat in one ham fist.

Brown Tom leveled the gun at his head.

Then somebody jacked the pump on a scattergun and everyone froze.

Scattergun? Ace didn't remember any of these guys packing heat that large. But he sure as shit knew what the *ka-chak* of a shotgun pump sounded like.

He opened his eyes. His three assailants were all frozen in position, crowded around him like dogs about to tear into crippled prey. All eyes stared at the mouth of the alley that spilled onto Fifth Avenue.

There were a bunch of niggers with guns there, standing shoulder-to-shoulder, two or three deep.

A fat man with skin the color of a Hershey bar stood in the center of the armed posse.

"What's all this about?" the fat man boomed.

"None of your goddamned business!" Brown Tom snapped. "Push on, all of ya!"

More guns rose, muzzles trained on the tight little band of erstwhile poker buddies. They were packing serious hardware: shotguns, Tommies, a bunch of shiny blue six shooters that looked brand new.

"Explain yourselves or face the consequences!" the fat man demanded.

"Fine," Fitzy said, lowering his knife and stepping toward the vigilantes. Ace couldn't believe his eyes. He'd never seen so many armed jigs in one place before. This was a nightmare! He was never coming up to Harlem again! *Never!*

"This sumbitch cleaned us out!" Fitzy said, pointing at Ace. "Sneaky fuckin' Heeb thinks he can slink uptown and roll hard cash off a coupla hard-workin' niggers, he's in for a nasty lesson."

Ace still couldn't countenance being called a cheat when he hadn't actually cheated. Hell, he could barely tolerate it when he *did* cheat. "I didn't cheat!" he cried. "Honest to God, these guys let me into their game Dand I beat 'em, fair and square! Is this justice? Buncha sore losers rolling me in an alley cause they didn't like losing to a Lower East Side Jew?"

The fat man and his posse stared for a long time, studying the four of them. The rain beat down. Ace wondered what might have happened to the money he dropped. For all he knew, it could've been washed into the gutter by now.

"Hand him over," the fat man said. He meant Ace.

"The hell," Blue Lou growled.

Bolts were drawn and shells pumped into chambers.

The fat man drew a deep breath. "Hand. Him. Over."

Ace was thrown to the pavement. He landed facedown in a stream of water gurgling toward a storm drain. When he looked up again, the posse was right on top of him. They'd marched into the alley and closed their circle. Every one of them stared down at him like he was the lowest piece of garbage on the planet. The muzzles of their shotguns and Thompsons yawned, deep and black.

The fat man leveled a finger at him. Ace thought it might be the finger of God, pointing down from on high.

"Teach this Son of Abraham that if he wants to play games of chance for money, he can do it downtown, among his own kind."

"Goddamn right," Fitzy said.

Then the fat man raised his finger and pointed at Fitzy, Blue Lou and Brown Tom. "And teach these degenerate field niggers what hard-working, law-abiding Harlem citizens think of gamblers and thieves."

Brown Tom raised his pistol. It was a ridiculous moment of bravado, staring down all the firepower that the vigilantes carried.

Somebody's shotgun roared.

Hell broke loose.

In the confusion, Ace tried to crawl away.

He didn't make it.

XX

Doc Voodoo never pulled the trigger on Willie Bunyon. He just wanted to scare the bejeezus out of the kid, and yanking him out of the ice truck then putting a gun to his head seemed to do the trick. Erzulie had given him this tip, based on prayers from a Creole widow worrying herself sick over her daughter's escapades with Willie the Iceman. Willie's intent was probably more youthful exuberance than deep-seated viciousness or criminality, but once he had a taste for forced couplings in the back of his ice truck, there was no telling where his appetites would go.

So Doc intervened—none too soon, by the look of things.

The rain fell all night. Apart from keeping Willie out of Miss Esther, the Dread Baron had already foiled two armed robberies, scared a would-be arsonist straight, and beaten a dirty cop to a bloody pulp after the cop had forced a hard-working mother of three to give him a blowjob. He hadn't fired his guns all night, and no blood had been spilt—at least, not fatally. It was just a riot of rottenness, vice and predation, seemingly stirred up by the rain like a colony of roaches scurrying out of a leaking wall.

The vibes on the web drew him further uptown, toward the Harlem river and the Bronx bridges. All the while, he found his mind and heart wandering back to Harlem center; back to the Mother Zion African Methodist Church; back to the Reverend Barnabus Farnes.

Maybe the reverend had his own divine protection—but that still didn't quiet Dub's heart. He wanted to keep the man safe. If anything happened to him…

Stop it, Ogou said.

"Stop what?" Doc asked. He stood at the intersection of three dark alleys, in the shadows of a troupe of brick walk-ups.

You're mind ain't in the moment. You keep drifting.

"Well, I'm just a horse. What else should I do when you're riding me?"

Ogou seemed to growl—a low, throaty sound in the center of Dub's consciousness, like the low and hungry snarl of a lion contemplating a meal.

You've got a whole territory to protect here, Ogou said. *You can't go putting the needs of one old man or one woman—however fine she might be—above the work we've got for you.*

"You've got to admit," Doc answered. "It's been small time, all the way."

Maybe, Ogou said. *But that's what you're here for.*

Somewhere off to the east, Doc caught a signal: the frightened screams of a child as a shadowy beast lumbered out of the dark toward her, snarling and shouting, battering anything in its path with its fists. She prayed for rescue without knowing who or what she was praying to.

That'll be her father, Ogou said. *She can't see his face when he gets like this. She just sees a monster.*

"So do I," Doc said, and checked his pockets for govi grenades.

Some perditious flames would cut the kiddie-beater down to size.

XX

Fralene took an awful risk, leaving Beau alone with their uncle locked in the basement. Generally, that lock was sturdy, and she'd removed the key, but he seemed different in his present state: stronger, more agile. Just to be safe, she and Beau had shoved an old sideboard in front of the basement door. If the lock didn't hold him, the sideboard probably would.

Probably.

She'd heard of lunatics being granted greater-than-normal strength like that. She prayed to God he wasn't going crazy. She couldn't handle that. Illness or a brain fever or some such—that was fine, that could be treated. But the idea of watching the kind and gentle man who'd raised her and Beau slowly go murderously bonkers filled her with a terrible dread.

Her umbrella did her little good. The rain slashed down on an oblique, soaking everything below her shoulders. She had tried calling Dr. Corveaux, but he didn't answer his phone. Either he was out for the evening, or he was so soundly asleep that he couldn't hear it ringing. It didn't matter. She needed him. All personal entanglements and stresses aside, she needed a man—a strong man who wouldn't be afraid to face her uncle in his present state—and she needed someone who could diagnose him, possibly even sedate him. There were other doctors in Harlem, but Dub was the closest. And she knew he could keep a secret.

Her shoes were soaked through and her feet and stockings squelching when she reached Dub's brownstone. She let herself in on the first floor, where the offices were, then took the stairs as quickly as she could up to the second. At Dub's door, she pounded hard with her fist.

There was no answer. No sound of footsteps. Nothing.

Fralene rapped again. "Dub!" she shouted, knowing that he was the only person living in the brownstone, thus, the only person who she could disturb. "Dub, wake up, I need you!"

Again, she waited. No answer.

She pounded again. Tears stung her eyes. She was losing her grip. She didn't like to lose her grip. If he answered this door and saw her crying like this, disheveled like this, frightened like this—what would he think? He'd think she was a weak, hysterical woman, just like so many others she knew. She hated that thought; loathed it, in fact. A part of her felt that if he saw her in this state—he might never want to see her again.

He couldn't ever know how frightened she was capable of being; how helpless she often seemed. He'd lord that over her, she knew it. They all did. Men. Goddamn all their composure and cheap machismo and condescension.

She pounded again. "Dub, please!" she screamed, but she knew he would not answer. He wasn't home.

And where could he be at such an hour? Out carousing in some gin joint? Charming some prettier, livelier, more promiscuous woman? Smiling the way he smiled? Laughing and joshing the way he so often did, his masculine seriousness disguising a rakish—sometimes even childish—sense of humor?

Fralene's knees failed her. She didn't fall, precisely. She simply slid down the immovable barrier of Dub's door and folded herself into the doorway. The only sound in the second floor hall was the rain beating the street-front window, and her desperate sobbing.

XX

Doc Voodoo was passing by when he felt it: a terrible malignancy; a rotten soul infecting a human host, laughing inwardly at the opportunities that lay ahead for mischief and destruction. He slid to a halt, mid-way across a rain-battered rooftop, and waited, trying to locate the source of the signal— the other end of the web-strand now vibrating.

What are you doing? Ogou asked.

"Listening," Doc said. "Do you mind?"

Move it, Ogou insisted. *There's more work to be done.*

Doc had it now: the evil entity was just a block or two northwest… a creature not of this plane, locked inside a physical form… and locked somewhere else, as well.

An attic?

No. *A basement.*

When that little bitch gets home, it kept thinking. *Oh, when that little bitch comes home, she's gonna have a big surprise coming to her…*

Doc moved toward the thought-signal, drawn like a lodestone to an iron bar. There was another signal coming through—interference, behind that primary voice. Someone in need. Someone calling for help. But though he knew that both phantom transmissions came from the same source—the same body—the one in need sounded weaker and farther away than its more obnoxious, ill-intentioned companion voice.

That's not a human spirit, Ogou said, sounding more than a little worried.

Where am I? the needy one cried, again and again. *What's become of me? Is this the other side? Is this death? Where's my Lord to greet me? Where's the golden light of my salvation?*

Locked down here, the other growled inwardly. *Sneaky, tricky, scheming little slut. Just you wait, sis. Just you wait til you come home. You'll find me right where you left me, playin' possum, and oh, what a surprise I'll have in store for you!*

You best move on, horse, Ogou snarled.

"That ain't natural and you know it, Papa Ogou," Doc answered. "That's something from the other side… something that's crossed over and taken up residence."

Like I've crossed over and taken up residence in you, Ogou snarled. *Now, let's move!*

"You're in me by invitation," Doc said in answer. "You know that what we're hearing isn't a spirit anybody invited in… it's something that forced its way in and took over! You can hear the host, like two radio stations fighting over the same frequency."

Your night's done.

"Pardon me if I say the hell with that," Doc said, and backed himself up to get a running start.

You want me to dismount, boy? Ogou said. *You want to see how this leap goes without me on your back?*

Truth be told, Doc didn't know if Ogou would or could do such a thing. He'd acted of his own accord the other night, hadn't he? When he'd come to the reverend's aid at the church? Ogou blustered and roared then, too—but he didn't stop him.

Maybe he *couldn't* stop him.

"Back me up or stand aside," Doc said, then broke into a run and launched himself from the rooftop. He sprang skyward, travelling in a long, shallow arc before landing at last on a rooftop across the broad, deep span of the street that he'd traversed. When he hit the tarpaper, he broke into a run again, making straight for the source of the diabolical signal.

As he neared his next launching point, he tried to orient himself… and suddenly realized where he was headed.

"No," he said, feet pounding away as he neared another ledge, another long drop. "No way this is gonna be—"

Maybe you don't want to get involved in this one, boy, Ogou said.

Too late. Doc leapt off the rooftop, this time not aiming for an adjacent roof, but for the street below.

He dropped five stories from the top of the brick walk-up he'd just jumped from and splashed down in the center of the street, knees bending to absorb the magically-blunted force of the landing. When he straightened up, he realized he was right where he feared he'd be.

The home of the Reverend Barnabus Farnes.

Fralene's home.

12

The house didn't carry the same charge as the church, even being the home of a holy man. Doc Voodoo felt a reticence in the walls and foundations to accept him—a weak but insistent force, like a strong wind blowing in his face as he marched into it—but it didn't stop him from opening the door and stepping inside. He was still safe. Still horsed. Still Doc Voodoo.

Then he felt the full force of that malignancy emanating from the basement: a soul full of poison and rot, rife with nightmare impulses. He closed the door behind him and moved through the foyer toward the hastily-barricaded door to the basement, beneath the main staircase. The evil that he sensed down there—waiting in the dark, delighting in its own twisted fantasies of terror and fear—put him on guard. He wanted to draw his guns, but knew he could not; would have felt safer if he loosed the *Machette d'Ogou*, but dared not.

He couldn't spill the host's blood, after all. It was the Reverend Barnabus Farnes—Fralene's own upright and kindly uncle—possessed by something terrible and unknown.

How was that even possible?

Who is that? the thing in the basement asked itself. It sensed him now. *Who is that tromping through my front door?*

"Ogou?" Doc asked.

I told you not to come here, Ogou said.

Doc heard quick, heavy footsteps thumping up the basement stairs, then the basement door buckled in its frame.

"I know you're out there!" the thing in the basement croaked, still throwing all its weight on the door, again and again. The door buckled. The sideboard scooted, forced away from the buckling door just an inch. "I know you're out there and I know you ain't like the rest! I can smell that red-iron sumbitch ridin' you, friend! I can tell you ain't yourself, same as this here holy man!"

Then, Doc heard a sudden, in-drawn breath off to his left. He spun, hands falling toward his holsters and the pistols they held. He stopped short of drawing them when he saw who had made that tiny sound.

It was Beau Farnes, Fralene's younger brother. He stood in the doorway that led from the front hall to the kitchen—seventeen years old but looking like a wide-eyed, scared kid.

And why shouldn't he be scared? He had his possessed uncle locked in the basement, and here stood the Cemetery Man, in his very own front hall.

Doc slowly removed his hands from his coat. He showed his empty hands to the frightened boy. "Stay calm," Doc said, his voice still sounding like iron scraped ominously along iron. "I'm not gonna hurt you."

Beau stared. Swallowed. "Jesus," he breathed.

"Who's out there?" the thing in the basement growled. "Who you talkin' to?"

Doc pointed to the basement door. "That's your uncle down there, isn't it?"

Beau, dumbfounded, just nodded his head. His eyes looked like they were ready to pop right out of his head and he couldn't seem to close his mouth.

"Calm down," Doc said.

Beau nodded again. Swallowed again. He didn't look any calmer.

Doc decided to get back to business. He turned back to the basement door and studied it. He whispered to himself, a question just for the spirit that currently rode him. "Who is he, Ogou?"

Ogou was silent for a time, studying the etheric signature of the spirit on the other side of the door. *He ain't one of mine*, he said. *I got no jurisdiction on this one.*

"Legba? Erzulie?"

Them neither, Ogou answered. *Somebody else is runnin' this one, and it ain't anybody we hold favor with.*

"Lemme out!" the basement thing shouted, its body still hammering against the locked and barricaded door. "It's been a coon's age since I been loose! Time's a wastin', friend, and I ain't aimin' to waste it!"

Doc marched forward, planted one boot on the sideboard, and shoved it back against the buckling door again. "Not on my watch, you son of a bitch!"

He threw a glance back at Beau. The boy stood against the door frame, clutching it fearfully.

There was a pause. The thing stood just on the other side of that locked door, and Doc almost fancied he could hear its infernal mental wheels turning—smell the smoke rising from the stripped and rusted clockwork of its diseased mind.

"Who are you?" the thing asked. "What do you care what mess I make of these mundanes?"

"Forget who I am," Doc said. "Who are you?"

"You don't know, I ain't tellin' you," it said.

"Who sent you?"

"Go spit," it said.

Doc huffed. He spoke to himself again. "Ogou, tell me something—"

Nothin' I can tell you, Ogou answered. *It ain't Rada, and it ain't Petro. Maybe Ghede, but that's just a guess.*

Ghede. The dead, the ancestors… and the infernals. If that was the way of things, Ogou was right: neither he, nor Legba, nor Erzulie could help Doc with a Ghede run amok. He'd have to figure out which Ghede Baron held sway over this punk, then try to get it recalled.

And getting a Ghede Baron to call back a spirit already loosed—probably by someone's command—meant he'd have to do that Baron some favor as well, or give him something in return.

This was getting worse all the time.

The door shuddered on its hinges as the thing in the basement threw its frail old host body against it. "Awfully quiet out there, buck! What you thinkin' about got you so quiet all of a sudden?"

Doc had a new idea. He turned to Beau and motioned for him to stay back. The boy nodded and cowered against the door frame. Then, Doc grasped one end of the blood red scarf that hung round his throat—the *Serpent d'Ogou*—and yanked it loose. The scarf coiled and undulated in his hands like a silk snake, restless and alive. He heard Beau gasp at the sight.

"Oh, somebody's makin' plans," the thing whispered. "What you thinkin' about, buck?"

Doc raised the serpentine scarf to his face, cradling it in both hands. He spoke to it. "Hold him," he said.

The scarf quivered in his hands, affirming his mandate.

Then Doc pivoted sideward, laid one boot on the sideboard again, and shoved. His superhuman strength sent the big, bulky buffet scooting lengthwise down the hallway. The basement door was suddenly free and clear.

The thing in the basement threw all its weight on the door and it burst open on its hinges. The door bolt tearing right through the old wood of the jamb and littering the hall with splinters. There before Doc Voodoo stood the Reverend Barnabus Farnes, hands grasping and eager, dark eyes bulging lunatic-wild and teeth gnashed in a feral snarl. Carried by his momentum, he collided with the wall opposite the basement door then turned his brimstone gaze on the Dread Baron. That was good. Doc wanted the demon's attention on himself, not on the scared kid in the kitchen doorway.

Doc studied the reverend, fighting to stay in character and not reveal the horror he felt. Here was the same man he knew from countless hours spent in his parlor, his study, his kitchen, his church. It was the same Reverend Barnabus Farnes in shape, but not in aspect: it was the holy man's hellish twin, a diabolical doppelganger. This old coot looked nasty enough and determined enough to tear a man limb from limb with his bare hands and his snarling teeth.

The demon in the guise of a man studied Doc and sneered. "What you dressed for, buck?"

Doc threw the scarf and the great length of crimson cloth came to life as it flew, it's light, silky material acquiring an inexplicable weight and heft. The demon tried to snatch the slithering scarf from the air, but it fell on him like a striking snake and coiled around his arms, his torso, his upper legs. He stumbled forward and tried to struggle as the scarf constricted, then he lost his balance and pitched forward, landing hard on his face and writhing in the grip of the fiery red rag.

"The hell you say!" he spat and hissed. "The hell says I, this rag can't hold me!"

"It can and it will," Doc said, kneeling beside him and yanking the writhing demon over on its back.

Beau suddenly shot forward. "Don't hurt him!" he cried, his concern finally overcoming his fear.

Doc looked up at him. "Don't worry. I won't."

The thing in the reverend spat up at him. "You and your fright wig and your skull face! You don't scare me, buck! Nothin' scares me now that I got me some real estate on this plane!"

"You're just a squatter," Doc snarled. "Who called you?"

"Ain't tellin' you nothin'!" the demon spat.

Doc snatched a handful of the scarf and hefted the reverend off the floor. He held him high in one hand, as though he were only a child, and shook him hard. *Who called you?*

Beau shot forward again. He was right at Doc's elbow now, grabbing his arms, tearing at his coat. "Don't hurt him!" Beau shouted. "Come on, you leave him be!"

Doc didn't have time to explain to the kid that the roughhouse routine was part of an act to try and persuade the demon that he would really start causing him some distress if he didn't talk. Of course he didn't want to permanently hurt the Reverend Farnes—but he couldn't exactly stop his act and explain that to the kid.

So he shoved Beau away. The kid went sprawling.

"Jesus, Mary, Joseph and Herod called me!" the demon sang. "Or maybe Mammy Laveau!"

"Wrong answer," Doc growled, and slammed the bound reverend against the wall.

"No!" Beau shouted from where he lay.

Doc threw a glare at the kid. "Stay out of this and stay quiet!" he snarled.

The demon-haunted feet kicked and bucked against the wall, seeking solid ground and finding none. He didn't want to damage the reverend, but intimidation was in order to get the demon talking—to learn its name. Only with its name could he hope to have any power over it.

"You've got nothin' on me!" the demon hissed. "I'm here and I ain't leavin', so you might as well let me go!"

Doc was just about to tell him that wasn't going to happen when the front door lock tripped and the door swung wide and someone stepped in from the rainy night. Reflex ruled. Doc's one free hand dove into his coat, snatched one of his pistols from its holster, and leveled the weapon at the open door and the figure framed there.

It was Fralene Farnes. He didn't know if the fear in her eyes came from staring down the barrel of his gun, or seeing him—

the Cemetery Man himself—standing in her own foyer holding her demon-possessed uncle aloft like a lunatic in a strait jacket. Her eyes bulged in her rain-soaked face like two white stones and her mouth fell open, seeking a scream and not finding it. Something fell from her hands and thumped as it hit the welcome mat beneath her.

Doc studied what she'd dropped: a black doctor's bag.

Dub Corveaux's doctoring bag.

His bag.

"Where did you get that?" he snarled, feeling a fury rise in him that he hadn't summoned or expected.

She found her scream then and let it loose. It filled the foyer, the house, the stoop behind her, the street outside.

The demon in his grasp laughed like a loon, trembled like a giggle-addled child.

Something heavy suddenly slammed into Doc from his right side. It was Beau Farnes. The kid took him in a flying tackle, and down they all went—demon-possessed reverend, *lwa*-ridden crimefighter and gangly teenager, all in a big knot.

Doc moved fast when they hit the floor. He dropped the demon, threw off Beau, then shot to his feet again.

He made the doorway in three long strides, yanked Fralene inside, and slammed the door behind her. She tried to break and run, but he took her by one thin wrist and drew her right back into his embrace. One arm locked her in and his gloved hand fell on her open, screaming mouth. The other planted the muzzle of his weapon against her forehead.

Oh, dear, Ogou chuckled.

Doc didn't listen. He had to quiet her. If he could do so faster with fear than reason, so be it. He thumbed back the hammer of the pistol and growled in her ear.

"Quiet," he said.

Her gagged scream became a fearful whine.

"That girl's got a mouth on her," the demon said from where it lay on the floor, still held fast by the crimson scarf.

"You, too!" Doc snarled. He looked to Beau. The kid was cowering on the hallway floor, completely out of his depth. Doc held him with a steely glare for just a moment—long enough to silently urge the young man to stay the hell out of the way and keep his mouth shut. Then, Doc spoke again to Fralene, his voice softer now. "I ain't here to hurt you, or your uncle over there. I'm here to help. I need you to keep your mouth shut and listen to me, sane and sensible-like. You think you can do that?"

She nodded, but he could feel her shuddering against him, her body trembling in the throes of fight-or-flight, heart hammering inside her like a pile-driver.

He counted to five, saying nothing while he did so. Finally, he spoke to her again. "I'm gonna let you go. I want you to go over there to the foot of the stairs. Sit down if you have to. We're gonna have us a little palaver. You up for that?"

She nodded. Doc took his hand off her mouth and gently thrust her away from him. Fralene spun to face him. He held up the pistol, let her watch as he slowly lowered the hammer, then he stowed it in his shoulder-holster once again. He showed she and her brother his empty hands.

Fralene backed into the stairs and nearly fell onto them. She caught herself on the bannister, though, and gently lowered herself down, sitting as he'd commanded. She couldn't take her big, brown eyes off of him. He tried to read her. He saw fear, wonder, disbelief, even disgust—but she seemed more in control of herself now, her initial shock passed.

Beau, meanwhile, was frozen in place. It appeared that tackling Doc when Doc had pulled a gun on Fralene was all the juice the kid had in him. That was fairly impressive, given the circumstances.

Still, there was business to be attended to. Doc glanced down at the doctor's bag and nudged it with the toe of one grave-digger's boot. "Where'd you get this?"

"The doctor's," Fralene said, voice catching in her throat. "Doctor Corveaux's."

"He gave you this?" he asked.

She shook her head, looking a little ashamed. "He wasn't there. I picked the lock with a hairpin. Let myself in. Found that and took it."

"You can pick locks?" Beau said, as though it was the most shocking thing he'd heard or seen all night.

Doc stared at Fralene. *Picked the lock?* He had no idea she was so endowed. He resisted the urge to smile a little. "And what did you plan to do with it?"

"There's morphine in there, and a needle," she nodded toward the bound reverend on the floor. "I was going to try and sedate him."

"Sedate me?" the demon said. "Girl, all you'd do is get my blood up—not to mention my—"

"Quiet!" Doc roared. Fralene and Beau both jumped, even though he was speaking to the demon. He turned to her again. "You know how to give a shot like that? How much of that dope is safe to give?"

She shook her head, eyes welling up with tears. "I didn't know what else to do. Doctor Dub wasn't home. I needed him—I needed his help—and he wasn't there! I had to do something!"

"There are other doctors," the Baron suggested.

"Nobody can see him like this!" she wailed, suggesting her trussed-up uncle, tears pouring forth. "He's a good man! A kind man! This isn't him!"

"This *is* me," the demon sang.

Doc leveled a finger at him. "If I have to tell you again—"

"You'll what?" the demon challenged. "Hurt me, buck? *Kill me?* You ain't gonna do shit so long as you give a good goddamn how the good reverend comes out at the back end. Don't you threaten me!"

Fralene was up off the stairs, backing into the little dining room to the right of the foyer, suddenly eager to be away from her uncle. Doc took a step toward her.

"Don't run," he said.

"What's wrong with him?" she asked.

"Nothin'," the demon said. "Right as rain, li'l miss!"

"He's got something inside him," Doc said. "Something not human."

Fralene stared, trying to make sense of his words. He narrowed his eyes. "You're a church-going woman. I shouldn't have to spell this out for you."

She shook her head, mouth working but no words readily available. "I don't—I can't—how could that be?"

"Look at him," Doc said. "Hell, miss—look at me. What do you think you're in the middle of here?"

"Even so," she said, "why him? Why now?"

"I haven't got any answers," Doc said. "But I can find them. We've just got to keep him under wraps a bit."

"Wrapped up good and tight," the demon said, straining against the *Serpent d'Ogou.*

Fralene shook her head. It was too much for her to take all at once. She stared at the Doc, trying to make sense of the

Halloween sight of him. "Who are you? How'd you even get in here?"

"I'm a friend," Doc said, then nodded toward Beau. "Just ask your brother. We've met."

She looked to Beau. Beau, seemingly ashamed, gave her a nod. Fralene clung to the wall, staring at Doc, stealing glances at her bound uncle, trying to reason out what she'd stumbled into. Finally, he thought he saw the fear and confusion subsiding in her. "What can I do?" she asked. It wasn't a plea or a lament—it was just a simple question in search of a direct answer.

He gently kicked the doctor's bag over to her. It scooted to a halt at her feet. "Go on and pull the morphine and hypo out of there. You're gonna give him a shot."

"You ain't givin' me nothin'!" the demon snarled, struggling again but making no headway. "That won't do a goddamn thing to me!"

Doc leveled his burning gaze at the bound man. "Then what are you so worried about?"

The demon didn't have an answer for that.

13

Dr. Dub Corveaux was awakened from a sound sleep by someone frantically pounding on his apartment door. Being one floor up from the front door, he could barely hear it—but it was unmistakable and undeniable nonetheless: hard, fast, insistent. He drug himself out of bed, slipped into a silk house robe, and trudged downstairs to answer it.

He knew it would be Fralene—in his guise as Doc Voodoo, he'd given her specific instructions to seek out Dr. Dub Corveaux as soon as the sun was up. He'd only managed a couple hours of sleep, but that didn't matter. Part of being horsed and doing his work on the streets at night was a special sleep dispensation from his *lwa* patrons. Ogou, Erzulie, and Legba made sure that his body felt strong and rested, and that he dreamed and stayed sane, no matter how little actual sleep he managed to snatch. As he approached the door, he prepared himself to seem groggy, confused, even a little annoyed when he found out that Fralene had broken in last night and stolen his doctor's bag.

He opened the door. There she stood, looking sleepless, beautiful, haggard and terrified, his doctor's bag clutched in her hands. Dub stared. Blinked. Raised his eyebrows. It was a fine performance.

"Fralene?" he asked, as though his eyes deceived him.

She offered the bag. "I was here last night, when you were out," she said. "I broke in and I stole this."

He stared at the bag as though he barely understood what she offered him. Then he looked to her again, incredulous. "You what?" he managed. He really deserved an award for such a performance. Maybe he belonged on stage?

"Let me in," Fralene commanded. "Make me some coffee and I'll explain everything."

He did as she asked. She waited in silence while the chicory coffee percolated. When he set a cup in front of her—heavy on cream and sugar, the way she liked it—she took a single, long gulp, then began her tale without preamble. He had to admit, her forthrightness surprised him.

She told him of her grandfather's strange behavior; of walking him home; of his sudden attacks before she finally managed to drag his unconscious body to the basement and lock him in. Then she told him how she'd come here late last night, looking for him, desperate for his aid.

"Where were you?" she demanded, a tad too acidly for his taste. "I needed you, Dub, and you weren't here!"

He raised his hands. "We had no plans, Fralene. Last time we talked, you didn't seem to need me for much of anything. I was just letting you enjoy a few evenings without me."

Her gaze was harsh and demanding, but she held her tongue. He sensed the doubt and division in her—she wanted to grill him, but she was afraid of what she'd learn. Moreover, even if she learned something terrible—horror of horrors, that he'd been out with another woman, balling the night away at a rent party—she knew she had no ground to stand on, no right to dress him down for such a decision. Hadn't they argued? Weren't they, in some small sense, on the outs? Hell, had they even made their association official or public somehow? Held themselves out as steadies?

No, she found no words, she just glared at him, as though his perfect right to an evening without her—and without explanation—infuriated her.

He held his ground. "Did I misunderstand?" he asked. "Were our last words of a kind and loving nature that I misinterpreted?"

"Forget about it," she said tiredly. "Just let me finish."

He resisted the urge to smile. That was his girl: clearly in the wrong, but loath to admit it. Hard-headed and troublesome as she could be, he admired her spirit…

"So, I came here," she continued, "I pounded. I called. I waited. When you didn't show up and used a hairpin to pick your lock."

"Where did you learn how to pick locks?" he asked.

"A woman's got to have some secrets, Dr. Corveaux. If I gave them all away I'd be a might less compelling, wouldn't I?"

Yes, indeed, you would, Miss Farnes, he thought.

"Anyway, I let myself in"—she said it as though it were a natural right, like breathing or liberty or suffrage—"and when I saw no sign of you but stumbled upon your bag, I decided to take it. I guess I was thinking I could put my uncle out. Make him a little more manageable until I could see you again and get your professional opinion."

"My professional opinion," he began, "is that you don't need to be administering hard narcotics to anyone if you don't know how they work or what the right doses are."

"Well, I wasn't alone," she said. "When I got back to the house, someone was waiting for me."

He stared, waiting. The reticence in her eyes suggested that even now, after holding court with Doc Voodoo in her own foyer and watching him drag her drugged uncle down into the basement and lock him there, she could barely believe it—nor did she want to admit it. Finally, she took another sip of coffee, drew a deep breath, and spat it out.

"It was the Cemetery Man," she said. "The one everyone's talking about. He was in my home, Dub!"

He hoped he could maintain his poker face. He even considered joshing her—suggesting that she was crazy or that he didn't believe her—but he knew that that might drive her over the edge. She was emotionally ragged at the moment— vulnerable. To misuse her at such a time…

He simply frowned and raised one brow higher. "In your home?"

"I saw him!" she said, eyes wide in disbelief and desperation. "Beau wasn't telling tales. He's real, Dub! When I got back, there he was in the foyer, wrestling with Uncle Barnabus! He had him all trussed up with a big red scarf! And he drew his gun on me when I walked in!"

Dub shrugged. "I'm sure it was just a reflex. Fella like him…he tangles with some rough sorts. He didn't hurt you, did he?"

"He scared the hell out of me," she said with some finality. "But no, he didn't hurt me. Once he'd gotten me over my shock and quiet, he even struck me as…I don't know. Gentle, somehow. Concerned…"

He hoped to God and all his angels she never told anyone that. That would be disaster for Doc Voodoo's reputation. The scourge of Harlem, gentle and concerned when alone with a lady in her parlor.

"He suggested the dosage," she said. "He seemed to know what he was doing."

"Makes sense, I guess," Dub conceded. "He probably has to see to his own wounds, after all."

"Uncle Barnabus bucked and squirmed and said the most awful things…but the drugs worked. He was out soon enough, and that Hoodoo Man carried him down into the basement and helped me better barricade the door. He told me to come see you as soon as the sun was up, and to bring back your bag."

"Glad to know he's looking out for me," Dub said with a slight smile. "I never knew you had it in you, Miss Farnes."

"What?"

"Petty larceny."

"Maybe if you'd been here—"

He held up his hands. "Enough. I understand. Charges won't be pressed. And for the record, I'm very sorry I wasn't here. Sounds like you had a hell of a night. You needed someone. At least the Hoodoo Man was there for you, right?"

She nodded, then leaned forward over her coffee and shook her head absently. "God, those eyes of his. Black and deep, like a couple of open manhole covers. And that voice…"

"Can I fry you up some eggs?" Dub asked. "Make you some toast?"

She nodded absently, off in her own world. He set to work on their breakfast. When he'd eaten and she still picked, he excused himself to get dressed before venturing back to her house with her. When he emerged, Fralene sat blank-faced over her breakfast plate, food half-eaten. She looked like she wanted to collapse, but wouldn't allow herself the luxury.

"Are you sure you're up for this?" he asked. "You could stay here for a bit if you liked. Let me handle—"

"No," she said with finality. "I can't sleep until I know he's safe. Let's be on our way."

So, off they went, he with his medical bag in hand. When they reached the Farnes house, it was just past seven in the morning. Beau was in the parlor, sleeping on the sofa. He stirred when the two of them entered, but Fralene urged him back to sleep, assuring him she'd wake him in time for school. The exhausted young man obliged.

The place had a drear, funereal pall upon it, as though someone had just died. Dub noted with some surprise how clear and unmistakable the feeling of wrongness was in the air—even when he was not horsed, not sensitive to such things. Anyone with even passing sensitivity would notice it, he assumed. One glance at Fralene told him he was right. She looked like she was standing in the foyer of a haunted mansion in the Jersey pine barrens—ancient, gloomy, frightening—instead of the entryway of her own house. She wrapped her arms around herself, shuddered the slightest.

"Do you feel it?" she asked.

He nodded. No need to lie. "Yes, I do. Where is he?"

"The basement," she said, indicating the door beneath the stairs, barricaded with the familiar sideboard. Dub set down his doctor's bag, laid his shoulders against the sideboard, and with a few, grunting shoves, managed to slide it out of the way. Then he took up his bag and looked to Fralene.

"Is there light down there?" he asked.

"There's a light bulb—but who knows whether he's broken it or not. Here—" she hurried out of the room and when she returned, offered him a little stub of candle in an old-fashioned candlestick. She struck a match on the sideboard and lit the candle. "This should do, at least until you orient yourself."

Dub took the candle and studied her one last time. She was exhausted and terrified. He leaned close and kissed her forehead. "Stay here," he said, then slipped into the basement and closed the door behind him.

14

It was a morning like any other: Dolph Storms taking breakfast at Mischki's Delicatessen while the boys—Toby, Spengler, and Monk—watched and waited. When they showed up for duty every morning, they should've already eaten (Dolph had told them this more than once), so that Dolph could nosh in peace while he read the morning papers, went over the racing forms, and drank copious amounts of black coffee spiked with schnapps (courtesy of the flask in his coat pocket). The boys could slurp a little coffee if they wanted, but that was all. No noshing on the big man's clock. Those were the rules.

Monk Lasky was glad of it this morning. If he had tried to eat with Dolph in the midst of the *plotz* now unfolding, Monk thought he probably couldn't digest. They were usually guaranteed at least one shit-fit every week during breakfast— Dolph wasn't a morning guy, and he sometimes took bad news— even the sort in the newspaper—personally. But *this?* This was bad. Monk wouldn't be surprised if some unlucky schlub who crossed Dolph's path today suffered a completely unwarranted beat-down because of it.

It all started when Dolph saw the thing about the darkie vigilantes on page eight. It was a tiny article—just a column, maybe four or five paragraphs—but somehow, Dolph had glommed onto it. He was hot before he even finished it.

"Goddamn nigger meshuggeners jumping Moses on a pogo stick!" he roared. There had been half a dozen other patrons in Mischki's then. By the time Dolph's tirade was done, most of them were dropping change on tables and making for the doors.

Monk shared worried looks with Toby and Spengler. *Not good.* What could get the boss so bent this early in the morning?

The boss yelled for Mr. Mischki to bring him a phone. Mr. Mischki took up his Ameche and trailed it, long cord and all, over to the boss's table. Dolph barked at the operator for his connection and waited. He was calling Mr. Flood.

Monk shuffled his feet and stared at the boss's unfinished breakfast—bagles, lox and cream cheese. The boss had only finished half of it. The smell of those lox made Monk want to yark.

"Yeah, Harry," the boss said when Mr. Flood picked up, "you see this happy horse-shit on page eight? Yeah, yeah! What the fuck is that jungle bunny cunt up in Darktown doing, anyway? Yeah, I know they're not a gang—I can fuckin' read, you condescending prick! But, seriously, *what's goin' on up there?* Didn't it occur to anybody that arming niggers who ain't on our payroll is bad for business? Next thing you know, they're gonna think they got the law behind 'em!"

Monk and the boys waited. On the other end of the phone line, Mr. Flood said his piece. Whatever he said, the boss didn't buy into it. His face got red and his mouth twisted into a snarl.

"Look, Harry, you can handle this garbage any way you like, but I do business up in Harlem, and I'll be goddamned if I'm gonna let some fly-by-night vigilance committee tell me when and where that business transacts! I'm telling you here and now, any of those scattergun spooks cross my path or interfere with my business, I'm gonna give 'em what for, and how!"

Mr. Flood countered with his own tirade. The boss seemed to take that a little calmer. He was past the point of arguing now. His mind was made up. Monk and the boys knew that once the boss's mind was made up, things would quiet down. It was the making up of his mind that caused trouble. Making up his mind—especially when someone else tried to make it up for him—always put the boss out of sorts.

"You told me to wait, Harry! You told me you had a plan for those preachers trying to rain on our parade! It's been a week now, and what's happened, huh? Just where the fuck are we compared to last week? I waited for you to try it your way, and now we got niggers with guns out in the streets—and they ain't even *our* niggers!"

Flood interrupted. The boss was getting hot, but he fought to control it. Monk was proud of him. The boss had come a long way keeping a lid on his rage. It'd been nearly a month since he'd killed anybody, and at least a week since he knee-capped that mouthy shyster up in Queens.

"I'm done," the boss said finally. "Far as I'm concerned, the best defense is a good offense! I think it's time we showed these sons of whores that they ain't the only vigilance committee packin' heat. *Nah.* Discussion's done. Finish your fuckin' bangers and mash you poncey Mick."

The boss hung up the phone then. There was a long silence as he drew out his flask, topped up his half-full cup of coffee with schnapps, then drank the whole brew down in a single gulp. He then picked up his uneaten lox—leaving the bagels and the trimmings behind—and ate the cold pink fish with relish.

"What's the deal, boss?" Toby asked. Toby always asked when they were all wondering. He could get away with it.

"Deal is, we're goin' on safari," Dolph answered. "I've had it up to my eyeballs with uppity niggers. All Flood sees is dollar signs. He don't understand that keeping the natives in line is part of runnin' a business uptown."

"So we gotta keep our eyes peeled," Toby asked, "in case these jigs with the guns come around?"

"Eyes peeled, hell," the boss said, a crooked smile bending his livery lips. "We're takin' the fight to them, Tobes. We're gonna light those porch monkeys up like the Fourth of July."

"Nice," Toby said.

"Fuckin' A," Spengler added.

Monk figured he better chime in, too. "Open season," he said, but he didn't really know what that meant.

The boss stood up, yanking crumpled bills from his pocket and tossing them on the table. "First things first, boys. Those preachy niggers need to be put down for some dirt naps. Hoodoo Man or no Hoodoo Man."

15

The only relief from the greasy darkness in the basement were three tiny slivers of murky light filtering in through a trio of cloudy little windows at street level. In that wan and sickly light, the brick walls were bleached of color and character, while the huddled shapes of old furniture, shelves of jarred jam and canned vegetables, and drawers and boxes full of tools and memories glowered in the tombish air, made nebulous and sinister by their swaddling of shadows. Dr. Dub Corveaux stopped at the foot of the basement stairs and blinked, trying to allow his vision to adjust to the darkness.

It was no use. He might as well have been stumbling through a black and white flicker-show, a world of deep blacks and pale grays, with little substance or gradient between them.

"Who's that?" someone said.

Dub knew that it was the reverend—though the voice was tinged with a venomous razor-edge that he'd never heard before.

"Reverend Farnes?" the doctor asked.

"You know better than that, buck," the demon said with the reverend's lips.

Dub stepped closer. Would it recognize him? Would the guise of Doc Voodoo still be apparent to the thing in the preacher, even if Dub no longer wore it?

"I'm sure I don't know what you're talking about," he said in his most reasonable voice. "It's Doctor Dub, reverend. Fralene asked me to come take a look at you—"

"Where's your *met tet*, horse?" the thing in the reverend said.

Dub stopped where he stood. This was going to prove more difficult than he thought. If Fralene came down here and heard this thing calling him out…

"I'm still all trussed up and waiting for you, buck," the thing said. "This scarf of yours—it's got me wound up tight. Where'd you ever get such a thing?"

All right, then. He had to sedate the reverend again, fast. He crouched at the foot of the stairs, opened his doctor's bag, and went rooting inside. There was a small flashlight in the bag. When his hands fell on it, he drew it out, activated it, and allowed its weak little beam to stab into the dark in search of his adversary.

There. The reverend lay where Doc Voodoo had left him, over in the very center of the cellar. He smiled devilishly under the probing flashlight beam. Dub felt a chill run down his spine when the old holy man's eyes flashed like the eyes of some wild beast in a forest. The look in those eyes… the malign grin… that might be the reverend's body, but it wasn't the reverend's soul animating it. The *Serpent d'Ogou* scarf still held him, tight as a hungry boa constrictor.

"Go on, buck," the demon said. "Let me out of this thing and we'll talk."

Dub shook his head. "I don't think so." He lowered his eyes and the flashlight beam to his open doctor's bag. He had more morphine and a hypo needle ready to go, loaded before he and Fralene had even left his apartment.

XX

Fralene stood near the basement door for some time after Dub had gone down into the darkness. She watched it as though something might suddenly happen. The door might buckle. Her uncle might prove to be wide awake and attack the good doctor. A row might erupt and she'd have to come to Dub's aid. She prayed that none of them would come to pass. She prayed for hope. She prayed for sleep, the sort her brother Beau was enjoying right now on the sofa.

But moment after moment reeled by, and nothing happened. There was no noise, no upset, no violent upheaval or ambush. The downstairs hallway where she stood remained still and quiet save for the insistent ticking of the big grandfather clock at its far end and the intermittent creak or subsidence of the old house's framework. She had noticed all those tiny noises before and they'd never struck her as anything but the moans and sighs of an old structure accepting its age. Now, all those tiny sounds set her on edge. The ticking clock, especially. She had half a mind to go stop its big, swaying pendulum herself, just for a measure of peace and quiet.

Something creaked above her. It was not the typical, mouse-small sound that the house made in its everyday affairs. It was a heavy, deliberate sort of sound—a creaking in the floorboards and beams just above her, a telltale sound that she'd heard a thousand times before. She waited a breath, then two, hoping she would not hear any sequel to the creaking, a sound that could only mean one thing—

There it was. Again, the fall of weight and the creaking of the floorboards.

Footsteps.

Someone was upstairs. They moved slowly, even surreptitiously—but they were there. Fralene had lived here long enough to know what footsteps upstairs sounded like from below.

Her breath seemed to freeze in her throat, her ribcage a sudden, constrictive corset around the weak and wavering tissue of her lungs. She opened her mouth to call for Dub, but thought better of it. What if her call for help woke her uncle? What if he attacked Dub and had to be forcibly immobilized again? What if Dub got himself hurt in the process? She couldn't have any of those outcomes on her conscience.

There, *again*. One footfall, followed by another. It sounded like someone moving slowly and deliberately, as though blind or lost in the dark. Was she hearing things? Was the house simply playing tricks on her now that she was sleepless and frightened?

She once more considered calling to Dub, but knew that wouldn't do. He should be left to his work. Likewise, she could wake Beau—but she wanted him to go to school today, no excuses, so he needed the last few minutes of sleep she could give him before she had to roust him out and shove him out the door. No, if she wanted to know what was happening, she needed to check it out herself. That thought gave her little comfort—but what else could she do?

So, Fralene Farnes moved slowly, cautiously, to the stairs. When she heard the hollow clump as her heel fell on the stair, she decided she needed some advantage over the intruder. She bent, slipped off both her shoes, then continued up the stairs in her bare feet.

At the top of the stairs, she peered down the length of the upstairs hall. The footfalls had been almost directly above her, perhaps a little to her left. They had come from one of the street-side bedrooms—her own, or her uncle's. When a cursory glance down the hallway showed her nothing, she resolved to carry on, and willed her stocking feet to carry her forward. They moved sluggishly, as though in a dream. When she reached the door to her uncle's room, she set her hand on the knob and waited, listening.

Again, she heard the footfalls. Or, more rightly, she heard the after-effects of the footfalls, but not the cause. It struck her as terribly strange: she heard the floorboards buckling a little beneath the weight of a passing body, heard the beams beneath creaking—but there was no sound of actual, physical contact. No slough of a boot-sole, no thump of a heel or toe. She wanted to burst into the room and see what it was she thought she heard, but all of the sudden, she could not move. She was rooted where she stood in the hallway, one hand on the doorknob, the other clutching the lapels of her jacket.

There it was again. The groan and creak of weighted passage, with no other indicator of physical contact. And if she was not mistaken, those last two steps had come closer to her, nearer the door.

Suddenly, the doorknob trembled in her hands, as if someone else grasped it from the other side. Before she could let go of it, something even stranger happened: in just a breath, the doorknob turned cold as a church-bell on a January morn. It became so frigid, her skin burned against it. Fralene snatched her hand away and took a hasty step away from the door.

The floorboards creaked again—the stranger on the far side of the door preparing to open the door and step through. Fralene watched, breathless and silent, as the doorknob turned and the door swung inward with a sudden heave. The sudden thwack of the door against the inner wall of her uncle's bedroom drew a tiny scream out of her and she shrank against the balustrade.

But there was no one in the doorway—not a soul in sight.

She blinked. Stared. Was she going crazy? She'd felt it, hadn't she?

Something had drawn it open with terrible force—something that was now completely, utterly invisible to her.

Then she noticed something else—something almost as strange and unnerving as the door opening by itself. She moved forward and stood in the doorway, studying the scene before her.

Her uncle's bedroom was a frenzied mess—ransacked. Drawers were half-open. Clothes lay strewn about. Cologne and tonic bottles littered the floor in front of his bureau. His bedclothes were loose, rumpled, half-torn from the mattress and coiled about the floor. Fralene studied the mess. This was most assuredly not her uncle's work. He'd had no opportunity to come up here last night before his outburst, and she knew him to be a neat and fastidious man under normal circumstances. Was someone searching the place? After something? Just playing a prank or intent on frightening her?

Something squeaked off to her right, and the rodent squeak was followed by a fluid rush. It had come from the bathroom that adjoined her uncle's bedroom. It was the sound of the bathtub faucet being turned on, a gush of water thundering into the old claw foot tub.

Fralene moved forward. Was that where the intruder had disappeared to? The bathroom? Why take refuge there if he'd been discovered? Why turn on the water and make his presence known? The door to the bathroom hung slightly ajar, but she could not clearly see inside, could not discern if someone waited there for her, or if once more she'd find an empty room and think herself mad.

Perhaps this wasn't the wisest course of action. She was alone and unarmed, after all. Dub was downstairs, but maybe he was in danger at the moment, too. Maybe her uncle had slipped his bonds, overcome his sedation. Even now, he could be stalking up the stairs with a knife or a bludgeon in hand, eager to work his mad furies out on her. Should she wait? Should she beg Dub's aid? Should she turn around and walk away, running water in the tub or no?

Too late. Her feet had already brought her to the doorway. She reached out and touched the bathroom door lightly. Without resistance, it swung inward on its hinges, and she saw exactly what she'd expected to see—what she'd hoped and prayed not to see.

The bathroom was empty. There was only the claw foot tub and the gushing stream of hot, steaming water that roiled into it. She knew it was hot water—and only hot water—because steam tumbled off of it in great, white billows, filling the room like a smokehouse.

Fralene bent over the tub and closed the faucet. The little room fell silent and the water slowed to a drip before finally abating.

She only saw the message when she stood and studied her surroundings. Through the murk and haze of the steam, she could see the little medicine cabinet mirror on the far wall, and on that steam-clouded mirror, someone had written words with their fingertip—silver words on an otherwise moisture-clouded surface that dripped like wet sterling paint.

Help me.

That's when she felt a heavy hand fall on her shoulder. Fralene spun on her heels, a scream loud enough to wake the dead leaping from her throat.

Beau, standing behind her, shouted and threw himself backward. For a moment, the two of them stared at one another, speechless, breathless, terrified.

"What are you thinking?" Fralene hissed. "Scaring me like that!"

"Sorry," Beau said, "it's just… I think I heard something."

"Something where?" Fralene asked.

"Down in the basement," Beau said.

XX

He grabbed the loaded hypodermic and drew it out.

Then he heard the scuttling of feet and an inhuman growl from the trussed-up reverend. He had time enough to raise the flashlight. The reverend was rising from a low crouch and lunging toward him, murder in his eyes and a toothy grimace on his lined old face. The *Serpent d'Ogou* didn't hold him at all—it fell away limply as he rose and shot forward—and Dub realized in that instant what a fool he'd been.

Of course! It was day time. Once the Lwa departed, Doc Voodoo and his accouterments had no power. The reverend's resident demon had played him.

He had only a breath or two to realize his mistake and prepare for a fight. He wasn't horsed; he was as vulnerable as any man. With the possessed old man lunging toward him, he did the only sensible thing: he rose to meet him and plunged forward, aiming to close the distance between them and give himself some advantage. He clutched the hypo tightly in his left hand and dropped the flashlight in his right. It went out when it hit the floor. The basement was dark once more.

The reverend met him and their bodies tangled. Though the old man's frame was wiry and ravaged by a full three-score-and-ten, the demon's presence gave it a new strength and suppleness. The reverend tried to get his hands around Dub's neck, but Dub ducked and dodged them, bending low and colliding with the reverend in a haphazard tackle that pinned him against a big, square vertical strut. The reverend blew out a surprised breath as Dub's weight crushed him against the strut, but his claw-like, bony old hands sought purchase without hesitation. He literally clawed—no doubt seeking soft flesh, an ear, Dub's eyes. He got the lapels of Dub's suit coat and tore at them; caught his starched white collar and ripped it loose. Then he found Dub's tie, and his hands sought the knot.

Dear God! Dub thought, wrestling to immobilize the old man. *He'll strangle me!*

The reverend brought one bony knee up suddenly, seeking Dub's nethers but only finding his arched stomach. Dub was lucky that time—one strike to his manhood and he'd be down for the count. If he gave this thing even an inch, it would have him.

"Ain't so tough when you ain't horsed, is you, buck?" the demon laughed, and tried to jab with its knee again. It still missed his manhood, but the knee slammed into Dub's ribcage with considerable force and nearly winded him. Reflexively, his hands sought purchase and he almost dropped the hypo.

No! He couldn't drop the hypo! That was his only salvation at present. If he could just get a straight shot at a bundle of muscle—

Forgive me, Dub thought, then drove one hard fist right into the reverend's solar plexus. The shot did the trick. The demon groaned and snarled and struggled to catch it's breath, winded by the blow. That was Dub's chance. He stabbed the hypodermic into the reverend's scrawny old buttocks and depressed the plunger. The demon shrieked and started bucking like a mad spring colt, limbs flailing every which way, a train of obscenities pouring out of his mouth as foam and spittle flew.

When the hypo was empty, Dub withdrew it and let it fall. With both hands free, he ducked lower, curled both arms around the reverend's kicking legs, and yanked. The old man lost his footing and collapsed, bent awkwardly against the support strut. When he hit the floor, Dub heard a hollow thump, and the old man's body went immediately limp.

Oh dear God, no!

He couldn't let his guard down, not for a moment. The demon might just be stunned or playing possum. It had fooled him once. He couldn't let it play him again.

He shook the old man. "Reverend!" he shouted, slapping his stubbly old cheeks. "Reverend, talk to me! If you're in there, say something!"

The old man mumbled. It sounded like, *Fuck you, buck.*

Well, that was something, at least.

Dub searched the surrounding floor until he laid hands on his fallen flashlight. He played with the switch until the little bulb burned back to life, weak and flickering. The reverend lay unconscious on the basement floor—still breathing, still mumbling. That was a good sign.

But he didn't have long. Dub searched the darkness and immediately found what he needed—a few strands of hemp rope tying up old, bundled *National Geographic* magazines. He fell on the magazine bundles and struggled frantically with the rope, trying to untie it without having to cut it.

The reverend stirred the slightest. Dub got one length loose and tore it off of the pile of moldy old magazines, then went to work on another.

Above, he heard footsteps. They were heavy, steady, purposeful—coming his way.

Fralene?

Dammit, he'd have to gag the old man, to make sure he didn't expose him.

"Where you at, buck?" the old man slurred. His bony hands rose and searched the air weakly, eyes fluttering in search of consciousness.

Dub turned the reverend over with a yank and knelt atop him. He had the old man pinned beneath him now. He went to work tying his hands behind his back at the wrists and the elbows. It wasn't easy, trying to hit the sweet spot between tying the old man tight and making sure he wouldn't totally cut off the circulation in his limbs. At his age, being trussed up for too long, too tightly, could cause him to loose all circulation. He could forfeit a hand or a whole arm to gangrene.

The door at the head of the basement stairs opened. The curvy, petite silhouette above was familiar. Fralene had found them. Dub felt more than a little ashamed of himself, straddling a barely conscious old man and tying his hands behind him.

"Dub?" she asked. "What the hell's going on down there?"

"Just about done," he said, knots tight around the reverend's elbows and wrists. He felt around on the floor in the dark and found the lifeless *Serpent d'Ogou* scarf. He coiled it once around the reverend's skull, gagging him, then tied it tight. The reverend mumbled, all vowels, and Dub was satisfied.

"Dub, there's something strange going on up here! Hurry!"

"No less strange down here, Fralene," he said as he tied the reverend's weakly kicking feet. "Of that, I can assure you…"

XX

They compared notes at the kitchen table while Beau hurriedly got ready for school. Dub could not argue with Fralene's summary of the situation. Phantom noises? Words on a steamy bathroom mirror?

"This is strange," he conceded, realizing that it portended a deeper problem than he'd foreseen. Was the reverend already dead? Calling to them from the other side? No, that didn't exactly make sense. His body would show signs of subsidence and decay if its spirit had already departed for the great beyond. Dub had seen enough true, revenant zombies in his day to know what an ambulatory body without a soul looked like.

Nonetheless, if the noises and the message were some sign from the reverend, where was he? Out of phase with the world around him? Shunted out of his body and consigned to… where?

But of course, Dub could offer none of these explanations to Fralene as she sat before him at the kitchen table and told her story. She'd think he was mad, or having fun with her—or perhaps a little of both.

No, he had to approach this from angles she would understand, and free himself up to approach it from angles only he could understand.

125

As Doc Voodoo.

"Fralene," he began cautiously, "what would you say if I suggested that you acquire an exorcist?"

Fralene stared at him, limpid eyes completely unreadable. She was silent and blank-faced for so long that Dub finally added, "Of course, if you don't go in for that sort of thing—"

"No," she said, shaking her head. "I'm not refusing the idea. I just… I wouldn't have expected such a suggestion from you."

"I remain a man of science," Dub offered, "but I also understand that there are strange things in the world that science is sometimes ill-equipped to explain or even treat. Maybe I've never spoken of it, but I've seen a few things in my time. Strange things—equal to or worse than what you've just described to me, and what I've experienced with your uncle."

She blinked, as though his words were barely discernible. "Strange things? You've never—"

"I don't talk about them," Dub added hastily. "I wouldn't want you to think I'm crazy, or just joshing you for my own amusement. But I mean it, Fralene. I believe that something paranormal is going on here, and I believe that a paranormal solution is the only one for this particular problem. Your uncle was a perfectly healthy man of advanced age just a day or two ago. Fugues that change a victim this radically—and with all their cunning and wherewithal intact—are almost unheard of. Couple that with the strange goings-on you mentioned—"

A plate drying in the kitchen sink suddenly flipped up and over the countertop and smashed to a hundred pieces on the linoleum floor. Fralene missed its first arc, only hearing the loud crash when it shattered on the floor. But Dub saw the whole thing.

Dub and Fralene stared at its remnants, then at one another.

Truth be told, seeing such a manifestation in this house— however humdrum—frightened him a little.

"Beau and I can't stay here," Fralene said, desperation clear.

"I understand," Dub answered, "although I might beg you to give it a try. Though he's doped up fairly well, we can't really leave your uncle alone. Someone's got to guard that barricade on the door and make sure he doesn't get out. And in a few hours, someone will need to go back downstairs and give him another dose of morphine."

"You can't stay?" Fralene asked, and the fragile timbre of her voice, the watery need in her big brown eyes, just about broke his heart.

"No, Fralene. I've got to take care of a few patients in the office. Then, I want to try and help you."

"Help me how?"

"I told you I'd seen strange things," Dub said slowly. "I might be able to employ some folks I know in trying to figure out what's happened here. Folks who won't balk at such a strange request and who won't try to sow phantoms where there aren't any."

Fralene shook her head. "I don't understand—"

"You don't need to," Dub said. "Just trust me. Now, first things first: is there anyone you can call who can keep this quiet while keeping you company?"

Fralene considered, then finally nodded. "I have someone in mind."

"Then you'll call them in just a moment and see if they can join you. Next: can we trust Beau to keep his mouth shut about this if he goes to school?"

Beau appeared in the kitchen doorway, dressed and ready, books belted under one arm. "Trust me to keep my mouth shut about what?" he asked.

Fralene and Dub both laid steely glares upon him.

Beau shrugged. "Heck, Doc… who'd believe me?"

Dub nodded. "Good lad. Keep it zipped." he turned back to Fralene, "I need to know what you and your uncle were doing for the twenty-four hours prior to his… symptoms manifesting. Everything. Leave nothing out, no matter how mundane."

She studied him, giving him a look he'd never seen from her before—a look of inquisitiveness and confusion, but also of shock, even pride. "What are you intending to do?" she asked.

He drew out the little notepad he kept in his coat pocket and the pencil nub that lived beside it. He opened the notepad and licked the tip of the pencil. "I'll get you some answers."

16

Monk was nervous but he tried not to show it. He just sat in the passenger seat next to Toby, smoking a butt. He thought about Rita Mueller and how he'd like to get under her skirt. He thought about a good, fat corned beef sandwich from Katz's slathered in brown mustard. He even thought about how disappointed his papa—a rabbi in the Old Country, dead for almost ten years—would be if he saw his son sitting in a gangster's car waiting to assassinate a nigger preacher. Basically, he tried to think about anything *except* going into the Reverend Barnabus Farnes's house and putting a bullet in him.

But he couldn't really get his mind off it. So he thought he better get it all straight. Monk turned to Toby.

"He live alone? The preacher?"

Toby shook his head the slightest. He'd never once taken his eyes off the house a block ahead of them, not for the whole hour that they'd been sitting here. "He's got a niece and nephew. Niece is in her twenties—swell piece of meat if your into jig dames. The nephew's a kid."

"So they might be home?" Monk asked.

Toby shrugged. "Might be."

"So we might have to do them, too?"

Toby shrugged again. "Might."

"Are we supposed to do that? Do some dame and kid got bupkus to do with the boss's beef?"

Toby turned and studied Monk. Monk knew his answer was in Toby's narrow, dark eyes. "What do you think?" Toby asked.

Monk nodded. Shit. He really needed to find himself another line of work. Driving the boss around and playing bodyguard was one thing—he could throw down on somebody trying to pop the boss, no problem. But he never thought he'd get sent out to clip civvies like this. Guess he should have expected it, what with the boss losing so many guys lately…

The boss sent them uptown in three pairs. Franky and Max would take out the Walker dame, up in Sugar Hill; Spengler and Hantz would go wack Brown, the one who'd been saved on the street by the Cemetery Man; and it fell to Monk and Toby to go after Farnes. The fat jig, Debbs, would have to wait. The boss figured if he was prowling the streets with armed vigilantes, taking him on outright was a bad idea. But those other three do-gooders? Toast.

"What if the Hoodoo Man shows up?" Spengler asked the boss.

"That's why I'm sending all of you in separate pairs," the boss said. "And that's why I want you all to do your business at the same time—seven o' clock. Even if the Hoodoo Man catches wind and comes after a couple of you, he can't be everywhere at once."

"So one of us is bound to run into him?" Franky asked. Monk had been glad Franky asked; he'd been thinking the same thing and he hadn't been too happy about it.

The boss only shrugged. "What do you think I pay you for? Get going."

So they went. Monk and Toby took Toby's Chrysler and they tooled uptown just as the sun was going down. They made it to the Farnes house a little early, so they parked a block away— within sight of the house—and waited. The last light in the sky was the fiery orange of a furnace under a blanket of dark clouds, and that strange, infernal light made all the houses up and down Farnes's street look darker and meaner as the sun fled and the night came up around them.

Toby opened his door. "Let's go."

Before Monk could say another word, Toby was out, slammed the car door, and started striding up the rain-slick street toward their destination. Monk climbed out on his side, pawed under his left arm to make sure his piece was still there, snug in its holster, and scurried to catch up with Toby.

They passed a couple neighborhood jigs out for an evening stroll or coming home from the grocery. Toby looked every one of them right in the eye, even smiled and nodded a little. He'd told Monk that was the way to go unseen before: not to try to be invisible, but to act like you had nothing to hide.

Once they were alone on the sidewalk, Monk leaned closer. "Don't you think they'll remember us?" he asked. "A coupla yids out for an evening stroll in Darktown?"

"Nah," Toby said. "We all look alike to them. They'll remember a couple white guys, and so what if they do? Get ready."

They were almost there. The Farnes house was just ahead. When they reached its lot, Toby ducked into the little driveway that ran beside it and made for the rear of the house. Between the homes on the block, it was dark and quiet. Monk saw lights on in some of the homes around them—directly behind the Farnes house, directly across the street—but the house right next door seemed dark and quiet. Hell, only a single light burned in the parlor of the Farnes place.

"Awful dark," Monk whispered, right on Toby's heels. "Maybe nobody's home?"

"Somebody's home," Toby said, suddenly coming to a stop. He nodded and Monk followed the bob of his head. An old Model A sat in the open garage out back of the house.

"What if it's the kid?" Monk asked. "Maybe the reverend's out? Maybe his niece is in there, all by herself?"

Toby turned toward him. Even in the dark, Monk saw that he spoke around gnashed teeth and that his eyes glittered with menace. "Monk, close your big fat head or I'm gonna lay you out. I mean it."

Monk nodded. He got the message. Toby was thin and wiry and probably weighed half as much as Monk, but he had a mean streak in him and Monk didn't want to get on his bad side. Monk pulled his piece to show he was ready. Toby led the way up the back stoop.

XX

While Toby and Monk were approaching the Farnes house, Ms. Lucille Walker was sitting in her parlor, at her favorite roll-top walnut writing desk, going over an article on the unionization of Pullman Car Porters that her husband had written for *The Messenger*. Why he insisted upon having her read his work and make notes for revisions, she would never know—he was the senior editor of *The Messenger*, after all, so there was no one to tell him his writing wasn't polished enough, or that his argument was too one-sided. Nevertheless, he begged her aid and she gave it, however tedious the task was.

She had just reached the halfway point in the tiresome missive when she heard the ding-dong of their doorbell. Asa, her husband, called out that he would answer it. She heard his heavy footsteps move through the front hall and into the foyer. The door opened with a mild creak.

Then, she heard two loud gunshots, followed by the sound of something heavy hitting the floor.

She dropped Asa's editorial and rose to her feet, nearly knocking over the chair she sat in. Heavy footfalls moved through the front hall. They were coming right toward the doorway to the parlor.

Part of her knew that she should run, should hide, should try to make it to the fire escape and flee. And yet, she also felt a strange sort of serenity. She knew that the distance from the front door to the doorway of the parlor was very short; she knew that the men who had shot her husband would be in the parlor and have her in their sights in a breath, perhaps two; and she knew that she didn't want to leave this world running for her life, screaming, silenced by two slugs in her back. It seemed… undignified.

But I don't want to die, she thought, a little petulantly. *I don't.*

That's when the gunmen appeared in the doorway. They were white men. Smoke still trailed from the muzzles of their shiny black pistols.

"That's her, Ernie," one of the gunmen said. Both pistols rose and she stared down their still-smoking barrels.

She couldn't move, even though part of her wanted to. Was it courage that kept her rooted? Or just plain fear?

Maybe the Cemetery Man will save me again, she thought.

Then the guns spat fire and the world went dark.

I suppose not…

XX

The back door was unlocked—a stroke of luck—so they opened it slowly and slipped in with no trouble. They were in the kitchen, and it was dark. The only light burning—the light Monk had seen in the parlor—bled into a pair of corridors that each stretched forward from a pair of adjacent doors in the kitchen. One hall ran down the center of the house and led to the foyer and the front door. The other led down the north side of the house and gave off onto some side rooms before finally ending up in that front parlor. The house smelled nice, like oleander and warm bread. Monk's stomach rumbled.

"Jesus," Toby snarled. "Shut that thing up."

"Sorry," Monk whispered. "Just realized I'm hungry."

"Then let's get this thing done," Toby hissed, exasperated. "Don't give me any grief and I'll buy you a pastrami on rye when we're done. Now come on—you go left."

He meant they were going to split up, each moving down one of those hallways to see if anyone was home. Monk didn't know why, but he suddenly had a feeling like something bad was about to happen. He didn't know why he should feel that way—the Farnes home was tidy and quiet and smelled good and seemed cozy enough—but the feeling was there nonetheless. Was that what it felt like when the Hoodoo Man came for you? You felt his approach, like goose pimples rising on your arms, or the little hairs on your nape standing at attention, or your nuts sucking up into your groin in search of warmth and safety?

Toby moved away from Monk and stepped into the outer hall. Monk forced himself to breathe again and pressed forward, down the hallway that led to the front door. The floorboards creaked beneath him.

Something brushed the back of his neck. Monk whirled around, gun high. There was no one there—nothing that could have swung into his path and touched him—but he knew that he hadn't imagined it. It'd been firm and cold, but absolutely solid, like a hand falling on his shoulder.

Something clattered out in the hallway. Monk whirled again, gun once more leading the way. A small, cylindrical rack for walking sticks and umbrellas at the foot of the stairs rolled back and forth on the hallway runner, its contents spilled onto the floor. Off to his right, Monk heard heavy, insistent footsteps and knew Toby was on his way.

Where Monk stood in the hallway, just a few steps through the kitchen door, put him right alongside the staircase. He moved outward, away from the stairs and turned, following them upward with his eyes and even searching the landing above. He didn't see anyone—no one could have evaded being seen—and yet...

And yet, that umbrella holder had been knocked over by *someone.*

Or some*thing.*

Could the preacher's house be haunted?

A dark figure sprang out of the parlor. Monk raised his gun and nearly fired before he saw the figure raise its hands and duck a little. It was Toby.

"What the fuck?" Toby hissed.

"I don't think we're alone here," Monk whispered, and pointed to the overturned umbrella stand, a good ten feet ahead of him.

Then, they heard a voice. Toby thought it was coming from a sideboard that stood against the staircase on his left, but then he realized the sideboard was actually blocking a door.

The voice came from behind the door.

"Who is that?" it said. It was deep. A man's voice. "Somebody out there?"

What was that sideboard doing in front of that door?

"Whoever's out there, help me out," the voice said.

Toby was right beside Monk now. Both of them stared at the barricaded door, completely befuddled.

"The reverend?" Monk asked.

Toby just shrugged.

"Look, whoever you are," the voice said, both pleading and impatient, "my kin have gone a little batty on me. Somebody locked me down here and I've been here for hours now. Could you help me out and move whatever's blocking the door?"

Monk had a million questions, not the least of which was why some poor old preacher would get shut up in his own basement by his own family. Could it really be *this* easy? They'd come to find the man and kill him and here he was, locked up in the basement and waiting for them?

"What are you doing down there, sir?" Toby said, speaking forcefully and without hesitation.

"It's a long story," the voice on the other side of the door said. "Who are you?"

"Police officers," Toby said. "Just happened to be passing by and, uh… saw the front door open."

"Saw the front door open, eh?" the voice answered. There was something in the voice that Monk didn't so much care for now. A smile? A sneer?

Toby moved next to the sideboard and leaned against it. He looked to Monk and nodded, making his orders clear without a single word: when the old man came out, Monk should put him down.

Monk stepped back to get a good angle on the door and raised his pistol.

"Hang on," Toby said. "We'll have you out in a jiff."

He leaned against the sideboard and slid it away from the door. Toby turned and reached for the doorknob. "All right, mister. You can come out n—"

The door burst open on its hinges, swung wide, and smashed Toby right in the face. The old jig that came barreling out of there didn't look like a preacher or an easy mark. From where Monk stood—right in his path—he looked like the devil incarnate, eyes alight with lunatic glee and mouth open in a wide, snarling grin.

Monk was so terrified, he forgot to pull the trigger.

The old man was on him in a breath, bulldozing right into him in a flying tackle and sending Monk sprawling backward into the foyer. Monk hit the floor on his back, the old teapot on top of him, and felt the wind knocked right out of his barrel chest. The old man was laughing and growling something—something about being free at last, free at last—but Monk didn't hear it all and couldn't quite make sense of it. He was seeing stars and trying to catch his breath.

The old man punched him square in the face. Monk tasted blood and felt a pillar of white-hot pain shoot up through his brain via his nose. He cried out, vaguely ashamed of himself for doing so, then choked as blood ran down the back of his throat.

"Squeal, fat boy, squeal!!!" the old man sang, lifted himself up, and crashed back down on Monk again with his bent knee aimed right into Monk's belly. That blow stole Monk's breath again and sent a geyser of air and blood sailing up out of Monk's throat.

"Jesus Christ, Monk!" he heard from somewhere far away. Was that Toby? Was Toby back on his feet yet?

The reverend plucked Monk's gun right out of his fat hand, spun, and fired. He emptied three shots and Monk heard Toby give a grunt before something heavy—Toby, he guessed—hit the floor. Monk sure wished he could see something. His vision was all starry nights. He couldn't catch his breath, either, what with the old man on top of him and all that blood running down his throat.

"I said squeal!!!" he heard the reverend say, then something grabbed his nutsack and squeezed. The reverend had a solid grip. Once more, Monk screamed like a girl. He felt sick, too—way down deep in the pit of his stomach. He tried to roll, sure he was going to puke, but the reverend's ironclad hold on his scrotum and the pain in his broken, bleeding nose and his inability to breathe made moving at all hard.

He guessed he wouldn't be getting that pastrami sandwich tonight. Or ever.

The pressure on his balls relented. Something hot and hard pressed against his forehead. He heard a click: a hammer cocked.

"As much fun as this is," the reverend said, "I've got to be on my way, fat man. Thanks for the warm up."

"Please," Monk managed. "Please…"

"No," the reverend said.

Then the front door opened—Monk heard its deadbolt clack and its hinges creak a little. A woman screamed, and a man said, "My God!"

The gun moved away from Monk's forehead. "What the hell…" the reverend said, apparently quite shocked to see anyone in the doorway.

"Back!" someone shouted—the man in the doorway.

Then the reverend screamed and rose off of Monk. The sound he made wasn't a man's scream. It wasn't anything human at all. It was the sound of a legion of voices, all crying out in fright and shame and fury at once, and the suddenness of the reverend's retreat off of him made Monk think that the old man must have been yanked off him by a taut cable. He blinked. His vision was starting to clear now. He could draw breath, barely.

"I order you back in the name of Jesus Christ, the Son of Our Lord! I order you back in the name of God, the Father, God, the Son, and God, the Holy Spirit!"

Monk blinked. He could see now. The sounds that the old reverend made continued. He was shouting in many voices, and they all seemed to be cursing in tongues that Monk didn't understand. The old man was rooted to the floor in the middle of the hallway, writhing and snarling and throwing himself back and forth between the walls and shaking his head and gnashing his teeth and foaming at the mouth.

Monk managed to roll over. He craned his head up to look into the doorway.

A pretty Negro lady stood there, clutching her hands up close to her mouth and looking like she was on the verge of screaming again. On one side of her stood a Negro teenager—gangly and wide-eyed—and on her other side, a man. He was of smaller stature and softer countenance than the Reverend Barnabus Farnes, but he was a holy man too—Monk could tell by the pewter cross he held out before him.

The other preacher looked terrified, but his words and that cross seemed to do the trick.

Thank God for small favors, Monk thought, and wondered when the blood might stop running into his eyes.

17

Jimmy Frame's last act before quitting his shift at Dexter's for the evening and kicking off three straight days of fun and freedom was to take out the garbage. He'd put in almost fourteen hours that day—from opening until just after the early bird dinner rush was done. But he was free now, armed with a pocket full of cash, a line on a rent party down in Philly the following night… and an open invitation to stop by Miss Rae's this evening. *Hot damn!* His luck was in! Maybe he'd play the numbers tomorrow.

He didn't know why Miss Rae had asked him to dust the Reverend Farnes's eggs with that packet of powder this morning and he didn't care. She'd assured him that the old bird might just get a flip-floppy stomach or the trots off it—it wouldn't kill him or anything. More importantly, she'd promised him some *alone time* if he came through for her.

Fella did a favor like this for me, he could call in a favor of his own, she had said as they talked in the alley that morning during one of his smoke breaks from the griddle line. *Maybe I could give that fella a private reading? Or some hot mojo to make sure his weekend in Philly went aces, front to back? I could do that, you know. Make the dice always roll in your favor… make every hand a winner.*

Sounds good, Jimmy had told her, edging nearer so that he could smell the hoodoo lady's rosewater perfume. *Private reading sounds real good. I'd like to know what's waitin' just around the corner for me.*

Mambo Rae Rae was at least ten years older than he was, but that didn't matter. She was still a ripe tomato, as far as he was concerned. He'd tried to pick her up on at least three separate occasions—once here at Dexter's, once at a speak over near Sugar Hill, and once when he'd sold her some bolito slips. Now, he was finally going to get a shot at her, and all he had to do was give some old preacher man the runs. On top of his natural attraction to her, he also thought there was something vaguely exciting and transgressive in the notion of balling a voodoo mambo. Maybe she knew some kind of crazy sex magic or something? Maybe bedding Miss Rae would give him some special shine from here on out, and he could stop being a small time, ex-con fry cook and start making something of himself? Jimmy had always been convinced that good things were just around the corner for him, after all—riches, respect, fame on the streets. He just needed one good, solid streak of luck, and he'd have everything he'd always wanted…

But, for the time being, he was still just a fry cook at Dexter's, ending a long shift by taking out the garbage.

He dragged a trashcan in each hand by their handles. The mothers were heavy—overflowing, in fact—but at least it wasn't raining. That was a blessing. Their appointed places were beside a bunch of other trashcans, twenty feet from Dexter's back door. The only light in the alley came from a lamp bolted high on the brick wall whose bulb flickered in fits and starts. Deeper in the alleyway, Jimmy heard a couple cats rutting, the molly squalling and crying like a baby hungry for milk. It sounded like the animals were killing each other instead of just getting their rocks off.

Maybe he could make Miss Rae squeal like that. Wouldn't that be fine?

And how's this gonna play out? he wondered. *How's she gonna play me when I show up at her hoodoo shop, flash my million-dollar grin, and start laying on the charm with the clear intention of getting* that thing *before the night's done? Is she gonna remember our conversation and cut to the chase? Or am I gonna be playing games with that bitch for hours, talking in circles over a palm reading and some gin in her parlor? She laid her feminine wiles on thick this morning—clearly, she needed the preacher man's eggs dusted, and fast—but so what? Women have a way of forgetting their promises, don't they? Teasing, cooing, urging on—then begging off.*

Jimmy delivered the overflowing trashcans to their place on the alley wall. Huffing from the effort, he drew a cigarette from behind his ear, then lit it with a match popped on the brick wall. He puffed on his cigarette in the dark, the naked light back near the door still fluttering teasingly. The cats were done caterwauling now. It was quiet. He just heard the far away sounds of slow traffic on 140th Street, and the occasional drip-drop of water sweating off the buildings and drainpipes around him.

Yeah… Miss Rae might need some coaxing. Teasers *always* did. True, she wasn't some sweet young thing didn't have a clue as to share her cunny yet—young 'uns were the worst, as far as prick teasing was concerned—but there was still the off-chance that a smart, sexy older lady like Miss Rae might not honor her insinuations and give him what he came for.

Well, then, he'd just have to remind her. *Convince* her. That's what his buck knife was for, right?

Jimmy turned to walk the two dozen steps back to the alley door of Dexter's. His cigarette drooped off his lips, and already he felt his trousers getting tight around his black snake, the promise of some seasoned hoodoo poon exciting him.

Someone stood in his way now, though. Someone big whose frame blocked the stuttering light above Dexter's back door. The stranger wore a coat and top hat.

Shit.

Jimmy turned and bee-lined in the opposite direction—all the way toward the end of the block—before he'd even consciously named the shadow in the alleyway.

Coat and top hat? That's the Cemetery Man! The one everybody's buzzing about!

All Jimmy could think of as he ran—eager to put as much space as possible between he and the Cemetery Man—was that he didn't know what he'd done. He hadn't rolled anybody lately… hadn't cheated at cards or dice in almost three weeks… hadn't been burgling or pulling short cons or even doing truck runs down to Jersey for crates of bootleg hooch for Dexter and his business-owning buddies on the block—not recently, anyway. Sure, he'd been *thinking* about what he might have to do to get Miss Rae to give up the goods when he came to cash in his chips, but what of that? Was he guilty already in the Cemetery Man's eyes for just *thinking* about strong-arming her and making sure he got his due tonight?

Jimmy wheezed, already winded and not even out of the alley yet. His breath was ragged in his chest; his shoes beat time on the rain-slicked pavement; his pulse thrummed in his temples like twin marching drums. He wasn't really paying attention to where he was going—just flying on instinct—so he wasn't too shocked when he ran face-first into a big, dark wall, reeled backward, and went sprawling into a broad puddle of rainwater. After wiping the cold, filthy water from his eyes and sitting upright, he realized he hadn't run into a wall at all.

The Cemetery Man stood in his path, blocking his escape from the alley.

"Aw, hell no," Jimmy whined, and tried to scramble to his feet. His plan was to bolt back in the opposite direction, the way he'd come.

But then the Cemetery Man had him by his shirt-collar. He hauled him up onto his feet, slammed Jimmy into the brick wall like a rag doll, then spun him round. Jimmy tried to touch the ground with cycling feet but found himself lifted right off the ground and pinned to the wall by the Cemetery Man's iron grip. In the faint, guttering light of the alleyway, he could see very little of his attacker's famed skull-face paint and mane of braids. He could only see his eyes, burning under the brim of that top hat like two small jewels with bloody fire smoldering at their centers. Worse, the Cemetery Man smelled like old cigars and hot iron—a smell like the gates of Hell yawning wide.

Jimmy bucked in the Cemetery Man's grip. He begged, pleaded.

"I ain't done nothin'," he insisted. "I swear, no matter what anybody told you! I ain't done nothin'!"

He was doomed.

"Don't lie to me," the Cemetery Man growled. "You lie to me, Jimmy, I'll know."

"I swear—swear on my mama's grave—I ain't lying! I ain't lying about nothin'!"

"You poisoned the Reverend Farnes this morning."

Jimmy shook his head so hard he thought it'd fall right off his shoulders. "No sir! *No!* See, that ain't right! I didn't poison nobody!"

The Cemetery Man shook him. "Then what *did* you do?"

"She gave me a packet is all!" he bawled. Did he just wet himself? It certainly felt like it… "She gave me a packet and told me to dust his eggs with it! Said it was a hex! Just something to put him under the weather! That's all!"

"*Who* did?"

Jimmy's feet pinwheeled in the air, seeking solid ground. His hands squeezed and yanked at the Cemetery Man's grip, but it was no good. The man's grip was ironclad, his stance unshakeable. "Please, mister…"

"*Who?* Give me a name!"

Yep. It was official. He'd wet himself. "It was Miss Rae! The hoodoo lady! She said somebody owed the reverend and she was trying to make it even-steven with the old fart! I had nothin' to do with it! I just done what she asked me!"

The Cemetery Man yanked him closer, burning eyes boring right into the center of him. Jimmy thought the center of his brain might melt like a cream-filled bon bon in the sun under the avenger's dread gaze. God, there were such *depths* in that stare! It was like staring down a black well with no bottom…

"What did she offer you?" the Cemetery Man demanded through gnashed teeth.

Jimmy had to lower his eyes. He couldn't look the Cemetery Man in the face anymore, he was so ashamed of what a fool he'd been. "She offered to be sweet to me… she knows I'm sweet on her… mister, I swear, I wasn't trying to hurt nobody…"

"And what would you say if I told you that you did?" the Cemetery Man asked. "You *did* hurt somebody—*bad*—whether you meant to or not. And there may not be an easy way to *undo* what you did. What would you say then?"

"Aw, hell," Jimmy said. He didn't have any strength left. He felt like a dead, floppy fish in the Cemetery Man's grip. "Aw hell, mister …"

The Cemetery Man pulled him close. He was an inch away now, hot iron breath threatening to blister Jimmy's face, whispered voice like rusty iron in his ears.

"Next time somebody asks you for a favor has to do with a hex," the Cemetery Man began.

"I ain't gonna be part of it!" Jimmy blurted. "No more hexes, no more pranks, no more short cons, no more long cons… *I'm done!* Mister, I'm done doin' wrong, I swear!"

The Cemetery Man snarled like a hungry lion, then let go of him. Jimmy hit the pavement like a sack of yams. His rubbery legs couldn't hold him upright and he fell in a heap, crying and struggling for every breath in his fear and desperation. For a moment, the Cemetery Man lingered over him. Jimmy wondered if he'd get a load of those famous pistols now... or maybe those magic grenades that swaddled their victims in hellfire... or maybe the Witch Doctor would just draw that flaming cane knife and split him like cord-wood...

But the Cemetery Man just studied Jimmy where he lay for a moment or two, while Jimmy sobbed and huffed and tried to get a grip on himself. Finally, the Hoodoo Man reached into his coat pocket, tossed something toward Jimmy, then turned and marched away before it even hit the pavement. Jimmy watched the object arc up into the air and back down again with a combination of puzzlement and fear.

Then it hit the pavement between his spread legs and its ceramic shell broke.

Hellfire consumed his soul.

Jimmy Frame screamed.

XX

Doc Voodoo ran all the way to Rachel Gooden's botanica, traversing the alleyways that ran behind the buildings of Harlem like darker, narrower twins to the city streets they paralleled. He supposed he wasn't surprised to hear that someone who trafficked might be responsible for the reverend's hexing... he was simply surprised that Miss Rachel Gooden had the power and the efficacy to pull it off. Getting horsed for a few short minutes during a vodou ceremony was no great challenge for an experienced *vodouisant*. But drawing down infernal powers for an in-dwelling, powers that took up residence in an unwilling subject and refused to vacate? That was no mean feat.

It was costly too. Such an act meant calling in favors, offering tribute, promising oneself as a sort of future errand-boy or –girl for the *lwa* petitioned. No one in their right mind undertook such operations lightly. While Dr. Dub Corveaux wasn't the best of friends with Mambo Rae Rae, he knew that she was neither an evil schemer nor an adventurous fool. So what had made her willing to do such a thing? Was she out for some personal revenge against the reverend? Or had someone *else* contracted her? The magical equivalent of a paid hit?

Doc didn't know—but he'd have answers, he was sure of that.

Still, something ate at him as he neared her botanica, something just at the back of his mind. It was tender and insistent, like a finger picking at a scar, knowing there was blood to be drawn beneath.

Was it that the reverend was a target?

Not precisely.

Was it that Mambo Rae Rae was willing to compromise herself so dearly for either personal satisfaction or a stranger's money?

No. It wasn't that, either.

No… it was the circumstance itself. Someone laid a hex of terrible power and potency—the sort of thing seldom attempted or achieved outside Haiti. Bizango societies made zombies of their self-marked criminals, outcasts and enemies all the time, the same way the forests of Europe and the bush of Africa were still rife with frightening and potent unseen powers and preternatural dangers that the unwary—or the unlucky—could run afoul of.

But this was Harlem. New York City. The twentieth century. Who'd ever heard of someone calling down such powerful hoodoo hereabouts for criminal purposes?

He had an answer the moment the question bloomed in the center of his brain.

He called on such powers regularly.

And already, he'd had to deal with one gangster using powerful dark magic against another, escalating the weaponry and potential stakes of what should have been a simple money-driven turf war.

Now, here he was again, not just gunning down bootleggers or saving some wayward businessman from his potentially-violent associates, by trying to undo a terrible, *magical* crime, undertaken not for some spiritual or religious slight, but because of the dictates of business. *For money.*

That's when he realized just what troubled him.

It wasn't that anyone in Harlem—or all of New York City—was using magic.

It was that maybe, just *maybe*, they wouldn't be using such powers—might not even *believe* in the efficacy of such powers—if they hadn't seen *him* at work first.

Stop thinking that way, Ogou growled. *You started this thing. Stay focused and finish it.*

"You know I will," Doc said, then stepped out of a dark alleyway onto 131st Street. Mambo Rae Rae's botanica was just across the way.

He wasn't surprised when he found it shut and locked. It was late, after all—getting on eight o' clock—not a time when most privately-owned businesses would be open. Nonetheless, something worried him. Through the front window of the shop, he saw a dim light burning in a back room. Although there were shades that could be drawn down at the end of the day to block the windows, those shades were not presently down. Anyone could meander by and stare in, see the empty shop, and the corridor to the lit room at the rear of it.

He went around back. The back door, though shut, was unlocked.

Not a good sign.

Doc slipped into the building, drew a govi grenade from his pocket with his left hand, then loosed one of his .45s with the right. The back door led into a small, cramped storage room rife with the trappings of Mambo Rae Rae's business—votive candles, powders and potions, little plaster saints, even stranger items like mummified cats, dried out toads and bundles of crow-feathers. There was a Saturday Evening Post calendar on the wall, stuck in December 1924—almost three years old—as well as stacks of old gossip magazines choking the storeroom's dark, dusty corners. Seeing the hoodoo woman nowhere—and more importantly, *feeling* her nowhere—Doc continued into the narrow corridor that led upstairs to her apartment.

He found her in the parlor, slumped in a shabby old wingback chair. She looked peaceful at first glance—as though she might have just fallen asleep. Closer inspection revealed a nearly-empty coffee cup lolling about on the floor under one limp hand, and stains on her blouse, her skirt, the arm of the chair, the floor itself. One of her shoes lay some distance from where her feet rested. Her eyes were half-lidded and already clouding—as though the end had come upon her quickly and unexpectedly.

Or *suddenly*—after a struggle.

Doc knelt, re-pocketed the govi grenade in his hand, and picked up the coffee cup. Its contents—a few drops of chicory coffee—were still damp, as were the arm of the chair and Miss Gooden's blouse. That meant that whatever happened couldn't have happened too long ago. An hour. Two at the outside.

Horsed, his senses were far more acute than when he was merely awake, merely human. He smelled almonds among the bitter smokiness of coffee beans and chicory.

"Arsenic," he said aloud.

Nasty business, forcing that down her throat, Ogou said. *Reasonable men would've just shot her.*

"They've made too much noise," Doc said. "They wanted her out of the way but they also wanted to keep it quiet. So they poisoned her coffee and held her down while they made her drink it. Cops might call it suicide, just because they don't care to look any closer."

Or they've been warned not to, Ogou offered.

Doc felt a fury rising in him. Rae Gooden was no angel, but he never would have wanted an end like this for her. The big question was, why did she believe that dealing with criminals would buy her any other sort of end?

Simple enough, Ogou said, answering the question that the Doc had only posed in his mind. *They offered her something… something she was in dire need of. In her desperation she thought they'd deliver.*

"Well, I can't let this stop me now," Doc said. "We need answers and she had them. Can we still call her back? Even for a moment?"

Ogou was silent for a time. *I ain't Ghede*, he said. *The dead ain't my jurisdiction. You're on your own if you're gonna try necromancy.*

"On my own," Doc growled, not without bitterness. "Don't I know it."

He got to work. He fetched potent sands from the botanica below, along with some herbs and incenses, then created a small ritual space right where Rae Rae's body slumped in her coffee-stained easy chair. With the sand, he drew a summoning *veve* on the floor at her feet, lit candles in a configuration all around her, then immolated his offerings—jasmine, lavender, rosewater, and myrrh—in a little saucer set in the center of the *veve*.

He stitched out a rhythm with an *asson* rattle left lying on a nearby shelf and sang to call her back from beyond.

On his third repetition, Rachel Gooden—Mambo Rae Rae to everyone in the neighborhood—appeared as a diaphanous, non-corporeal form from beyond the grave.

The dead mambo wore a look of stunned surprise. She stared at her own corpse, saddened and frightened by the sight of it. Then, she saw who had summoned her. Her dead eyes grew wide.

The Cemetery Man, she intoned.

"The same," he answered.

The doctor, she added.

"Let's keep that between us," he said, then asked his question. "Who did this?"

It wasn't supposed to turn out this way, she said.

"But it did," he answered. "Who did this to you?"

I didn't think I had a choice, she said, phantasmal eyes still drawn to the body she used to inhabit. Doc imagined that was a terrible place to be—just across the line that separated life from death, filled with terrible regret, like a child who'd done something horrible to a playmate in a moment of awful ignorance realizing that—whatever it was—it could never be taken back.

Mambo Rae Rae had just used up her last chance. She would never have another. Just like she would never have words with a loved one again, never taste boiled crawfish or funnel cake again, never know what a good night's sleep or a good day's work felt like again…

She had choices before. But now, she would never, ever have a choice again.

That was the big difference between living and dying: once you crossed over, you were part of a great, unseen world where everything moved according to need and mandate and power and purpose, where everything and everyone was playing out a role in an enormous cosmic chess game, but where no one and nothing had a choice.

That's why everything and everyone on the other side worked so hard to get mankind under their sway: only living, breathing human beings could make choices. That was a gift that even angels and demons—both slaves to their natures and their divine or infernal mandates—didn't have.

And of course, there was the matter of where she was off to. That was a question above and beyond Doc's own ken. He could only question her now because she was so recently departed. At present, she was like a traveler in a station awaiting the arrival of her train. That train would arrive soon, and after that, she'd never pass this way again.

But he needed answers. Her sadness and regret couldn't be allowed to stop him now.

"I'm sorry it turned out like this for you," he said, trying to snap her back into the moment. "Now tell me who did this so I can make them pay for it."

The ghost kept staring. Without a word, she stepped forward and reached out. Her hand—more or less solid to the eye but completely without corporality—reached out and tried to touch her own dead flesh. Her fingers sank into her cooling body. The ghost seemed troubled that it could not truly feel the body it had been forced from, as though her lack of substance now somehow negated her entire existence.

Then, the ghost raised its head. It heard something. Its eyes were wider now, its mouth hanging open in baleful realization. At first, Doc thought that it became whiter—paler—but then he realized it was a trick of the phantasm in his vision. It didn't grow paler… it *thinned*.

In fear.

I hear them, she said.

"Who do you hear?" Doc asked.

Hounds. Baying. Calling. They're getting closer. Oh God…

Hellhounds. That wasn't good. They'd chase her down then drag her away to her reward. Doc didn't have long now.

"Mambo Rae Rae," he demanded in his best booming, growling avenger's voice. "Tell me, here and now, *who did this to you!*"

Two men, she said. *Oh God… I can hear them coming. They're just up the street now.*

She seemed to search the world around her for an escape of some sort. But of course, on her plane, there was no escape. She saw the same surroundings that he saw—a small apartment, windows, doors, a stairway. But it didn't matter where she went now or how fast. The hounds were on the same etheric plane that she lingered upon. They could find her no matter where she went, or how quickly she went there.

"Who were these men?" Doc demanded. He was starting to think he could hear the hounds now too. They bayed and snarled as they approached, and their feet fell heavily on the paving outside, terrible claws clicking on the asphalt and cement as they bounded nearer. He didn't care for that sound. It almost put such fear in him as to drive him out of the apartment.

But they weren't coming for him. He had to stand his ground.

"Tell me their names!" Doc urged. Their time was short.

Mambo Rae Rae's ghost turned and searched the world around her, seeking signs of her imminent seizure on all sides. She was nothing but smoke and air and a trick of the light, but she was terrified, a woman staring down the barrel of a dark eternity.

I didn't know their names, she said. *Oh God, can't you help me? Can't you get me out of this? I didn't mean it. I didn't mean for things to end like this…*

"Who did they work for?" Doc asked. "You must know. There's no time left and I can't set this right if you don't tell me!"

Even horsed—invulnerable—he felt the tiny hairs on his skin stand on end as gooseflesh pocked the nape of his neck, his back, his arms. The sound was not meant for his ears, true, but he was keyed into it nonetheless, because he could hear what unfolded on the ghost's plane. He heard the hounds below now, bursting the bonds of Rae Rae's magically protected doorway, stalking through the botanica, and tromping up the stairs toward the little apartment.

"Rae Rae," he begged. "Please, talk to me—"

Flood, she said, finally looking right at him, her dead gaze putting an earth-shaking fear into him. *Flood and the Queen Bee. They're the ones who wanted this of me. They're the ones.*

"Now, tell me what you did," he coaxed. "Who did you beg the favor from? Who did you patronize?"

The door to the apartment suddenly burst open on its hinges. Doc saw nothing standing in that empty doorway, but he heard them and smelled them nonetheless: two hungry, snarling black beasts that might have been the size of lions, jaws slavering with pulsing cinders, brimstone smoke puffing from their dilated nostrils. Even though he could not *see* the hellhounds, he *felt* the warm darkness from their seeking gazes sweep through the room, until their fiery, darksome gazes finally fell upon the ghost of Rachel Gooden. She trembled, drew up rigid, screamed as though she were not dead at all, but only now staring down the barrel of her own fragile mortality.

But Doc knew this was worse. She was staring down the barrel of eternity. It terrified him and he wasn't even following her. But being this close… hearing… smelling… *knowing*… that was almost as bad.

It put a great many things in perspective for him.

"Who allowed this?" he demanded a final time, before they sunk in their teeth and claws and dragged her away. "Who did you call on, Rae Rae?"

She turned to face him one last time, her back to the open doorway and the hellhounds that had come to collect her. *Kalfou,* she said, voice drowned in shame. *He's after the reverend—*

Then they had her. The ghost was torn right off the material plane, dragged backward out through the door, erased like a wisp of smoke on a strong breeze. Doc heard the triumphant howling of the hounds and her last, eternal scream sounding into the depths of some deep, dark hole to nowhere.

Then, the room was silent.

Once more, he was alone with a corpse.

Kalfou, Ogou snarled, his voice suggesting both disdain and fear.

"Dear God," Doc said. "Was she mad? Kalfou?"

We can't do a damn thing against that son of a bitch, Ogou said.

"I know, I know," Doc answered. "I'm on my own."

18

The Reverend Adam Clayton Brown, Jr., stood in the doorway of the Farnes home, his old pewter cross held out before him, the words of a prayer tumbling from his mouth like vomit: unbidden, uncontrolled. A fat man lay on the foyer floor, rolling around in apparent agony from a very bloody nose and mouth.

And there was Barney, crouched on the hallway floor, writhing and snarling and jerking about, an infernal, obscene marionette expelling a chorus of voices speaking in many tongues from his single mouth, his eyes rolled back in his head like a couple of white marbles.

This was the moment Brown dreaded after hearing Fralene Farnes's story just a few hours ago. Perhaps this was a moment he'd dreaded all his life.

This was the moment when his faith had to stand firm. This was the moment when he had to stand fast against the ruin of his own fear. His life depended on it, as did Barney's soul.

"Get inside, Reverend," Fralene said beside him. "Go on. Beau, shut the door behind us."

Brown managed to limp forward, the cane he'd been employing since the attack hooked over his left arm. The cross stayed level. Barney remained in his sights, writhing under the weight of its power, no doubt cursing them in all those alien tongues. Behind Brown, Fralene stepped into the foyer. Her brother Beau followed them and shut the door.

Dear God, Brown thought. *What now?*

The Reverend Adam Clayton Brown, Jr's, first thought when he opened his apartment door to find Miss Fralene Farnes on his doorstep was that something terrible had happened. Barney had a heart attack… or a stroke… or had been murdered. Before he even knew what he was saying he spat, "What's wrong? What's happened?"

What Fralene told him proved even stranger that the reverend could have imagined.

He'd been witness to the Reverend Farnes's strange outburst at the HCCB meeting, and Brown himself had wondered just what could be eating at his old friend and fellow man of the cloth. Was it just a temporary madness—a false bitterness brought on by a fever or the sugars? Or perhaps it was simply emotional stress—Barney *had* been working hard of late. One too many sleepless nights, jam-packed days, or pointless meetings with a strutting peacock like Jebediah Debbs could bring the worst out of almost anyone. Brown himself had been at odds with his own life or everyone around him at one time or another, and usually took such realizations as cues to slow down, to get extra rest, and to spend more hours in meditation with the Word of God. Usually, a week of low-key living and doubled Biblical study did the trick, and equilibrium returned.

That hadn't worked for him lately, though. Since his run-in with those gunmen and being saved by the vigilante that everyone called the Dread Baron or the Cemetery Man, the Reverend Adam Clayton Brown, Jr., had found himself quite out of sorts. Distracted… anxious… fearful.

Even ashamed, mostly of himself.

But here was Fralene Farnes, on his doorstep, begging his aid with frightened eyes. Then, in his parlor, telling him a tale he could barely fathom and preferred not to hear at all.

Brown had been silent for a long time when Fralene finished her story.

"What do you want from me?" he asked, fearing he already knew.

"The Cemetery Man said we needed a holy man," Fralene answered. "Someone to cast the demon out."

"Fralene, I can't," Brown answered, too quickly and perhaps too forcefully.

"There's no one else," she insisted. "You're his oldest friend, reverend. I can't let anyone else see him like this! What would it do to his reputation? His ministry? Think about that!"

Brown thought about it. He knew it. If Barney was to come through this, his deliverance had to be affected secretly, otherwise this one possession could taint his reputation and all his public undertakings. Could Brown really surrender Barney to that sort of humiliation? That sort of persecution?

He could not.

But that still didn't change the fact that he was terrified. He wasn't just terrified of the things he would see and hear when he was in Barney's presence, or that the thing in Barney might be too hard to drive out—he was must terrified of simply not being good enough; of learning that his faith was weak, his courage a sham, his life's work and very title were all meaningless.

In the long silence that followed Fralene's petition and his consideration of it, he almost began to pray that the cup should pass from him. Hadn't Jesus prayed the same prayer, in the garden?

God didn't let that cup pass from his own son, Brown thought then. *Why would He let it pass from me?*

And so, with a strangled voice that sounded like little more than a croak, the Reverend Adam Clayton Brown, Jr. agreed to accompany Fralene back to her house and do his best to deliver her uncle—Brown's oldest, dearest, and closest friend—from the Devil's bonds.

All the way along their seemingly endless walk, even after they had stopped and picked up Beau at school, he fought the urge to turn and run.

They heard gunshots when they were mere steps away from the house. The three of them hurried up the walk—Brown's limp and cane not aiding his attempt at haste—then Fralene had unlocked the door and thrown it open.

A bloodied fat man lay in the foyer, and the Reverend Barnabus Farnes—Barney, dear Barney—crouched atop the fat man, a pistol leveled at his sweaty, bloodied brow, hammer cocked. Then they saw the dead man further back in the hall.

Brown was so horrified by that scene—so disgusted by this use of his old friend's body and spirit—that he acted without thinking. He drew the big pewter cross that he'd brought along from his coat pocket, leveled it before him like a flashlight, and started shouting the first holy words that leapt into his brain.

"Stay where you are!" he shouted. "Stay right where you are in the name of the Lord God Jehovah and in the name of Jesus Christ!"

The demon's answer was immediate. It dropped the gun in its hand as though it had been burned. It's whole long, thin frame shook like a rickety scaffold. Its eyes rolled back in its head, white and blank and horrible to behold. Its mouth—Barney's mouth—fell open wide and out came a chorus of voices and animal sounds, all cursing and shouting in tongues completely alien to Brown's ears. Even stranger was the multiplicity of voices—the sense that many, many voices spoke from Barney's solitary mouth.

But the cross… his words… *they worked!*

Brown forced himself to step forward into the foyer. The bloody fat man rolled around before him, moaning and distracted. Brown decided that formal words—praying words—were now required. He summoned up a psalm.

"Save me, O God, for the waters are come in unto my soul. I sink in deep mire, where there is no standing; I am come into deep waters, where the floods overflow me."

The Barney-thing continued to writhe and struggle under the weight of the words and the shadow of the cross. Behind Brown, Fralene and Beau edged into the foyer and shut the door.

Fralene hit the light switch beside the door.

The chandelier that came to life, hanging above the foyer, swung crazily from its chain above, making all the shadows that it cast in the foyer and front hall veer crazily back and forth, shifting and dancing all around them like a troupe of slate gray ghosts. As Brown kept praying and limping forward and the beast in his old friend kept writhing and screaming, more objects in the immediate vicinity began to tremble and dance, as though the demon's defiance infected them.

Some umbrellas and a walking stick strewn on the foyer floor all jittered like broken sticks in a gathering gale.

A mirror hanging on the wall parallel to the staircase trembled on its nail, threatening to dismount and fall.

In the parlor, off to their left, a series of small, porcelain figurines on the fireplace mantle came leaping off, one after the other, to shatter with shotgun-like explosiveness on the stone hearth.

"I am weary of my crying, my throat is dried," Brown continued. "Mine eyes fail while I wait for my God—"

"You coward," the demon snarled from the depths of its gullet, amid the continuous and insane cackle of all the other voices it spewed forth, "You fool! Come closer and I'll tear you limb from limb, you sickening little fairy—"

Another voice suddenly joined Brown's, calling out the psalm in unison with him. "They that hate me without cause are more than the hairs of mine head," that voice said, "they that would destroy me, being mine enemies wrongfully, are mighty!"

It was Fralene. She was right at Brown's elbow, praying along with him. As he took his next few halting limps forward, she stood beside him, assuring him silently, with a squeeze of her hand on his arm, that she would not abandon him or let him fall. Beau joined in a moment later, taking his sister's hand and reciting the psalm along with her.

Brown anticipated the words to come. They had new meaning for him that he'd never understood—never truly felt before. "O God, thou knowest my foolishness; and my sins are not hid from thee. Let not them that wait on thee, O Lord God of hosts, be ashamed for my sake; let not those that seek thee be confounded for my sake, O God of Israel."

They were right up on the demon now. It threw itself back and forth between the narrow walls of that front corridor, as though it could physically throw off the holy chains that their psalm and the power of that cross laid on it. Its shoulders and arms and legs all twisted and gnarled and contorted in the strangest and most inhuman ways. Barney's head seemed to whip and tremble back and forth, the frayed end to the jittering live wire of his body.

"To the basement," Fralene whispered in the momentary pause that each took for breath between verses. "Drive it back."

Brown nodded. He kept praying. The beast kept struggling. The basement door was just a few feet away.

The front door suddenly burst open. The sound yanked Brown, Fralene and Beau right out of their prayer and both spun on their heels toward the thunder.

The front door gaped wide, and in the portal stood that frightening apparition that had saved Brown's life just the other night—the dark avenger the people of Harlem called the Cemetery Man.

Then Brown realized that they'd turned their backs on the beast. He turned again and saw Barney's evil doppelganger lunging toward them, grasping talons outstretched, mouth in a furious rictus, eyes alight with fury and madness and bloodlust.

Brown threw himself back, taking Fralene with him. Both tumbled to the floor. Only Beau managed to throw himself clear and stay on his feet.

The Cemetery Man whistled, loud and shrill—a signal of some sort.

Before the beast in Barnabus Farnes could reach them, some long, thin, crimson serpent came slithering with blinding speed up out of the open cellar door. It raced right across the carpet, coiled and sprang, then wrapped itself around Barney and brought him crashing to the ground like a roped steer.

The demon cursed and bucked against its bonds.

The Cemetery Man shut the door behind him. He looked down at Brown and Fralene, bundled in a heap on the foyer floor.

"What took you so long?" Fralene asked.

The Cemetery Man just huffed, stepped over the bound-up Reverend Farnes, and yanked him to his feet.

XX

This time, the possessed Reverend Farnes was removed to his bedroom. He struggled against his bonds and cursed them, but the crimson scarf that acted like a snake at the Cemetery Man's command held him fast while the Cemetery Man and Beau tied the old preacher to his four-poster bed with rope from the basement. In the end, the Reverend Barnabus Farnes was incapable of escape. The Cemetery Man knew knots that made Brown shudder at their tying. Beau looked shell-shocked, but he took orders well. Clearly, the boy was not afraid of the man that Harlem called Doc Voodoo.

Finally, with all four limbs tied, the Cemetery Man used the last of the rope to tie the reverend's torso to the bed, coiling it over top of him and under the old oak frame. He was well-trussed, and going nowhere, despite the terrifying sounds that issued from his snapping mouth, or the struggles of his energized old body.

A storm was brewing outside—dark clouds, thunder and rain that approached with an unyielding slowness indicating that it would probably settle upon them and drench Harlem all through the night. Big storms had a way of doing that, in the Reverend Brown's experience.

Who knows? Brown thought idly, still feeling a serpentine coil of fear in his belly, *it might not be a natural storm at all.*

The Cemetery Man waved Beau off, then stepped back to admire his handiwork. He nodded, satisfied, then looked to Brown and Fralene. Before anyone could say anything, the creature on the bed bucked, cackled, and spat a long litany of curses in a chorus of foreign tongues that Brown himself couldn't claim to understand.

Beau stared at the obstreperous old man. "He'd hide me six ways to Sunday if he heard me talkin' that way!"

"Rude," the Cemetery Man snarled. "I think you need to apologize."

"Go spit," the thing said. At least, that's what Brown *thought* he heard. The many voices all seemed to have different answers.

How could it speak like that? So many voices all at once? All of those voices spewing up out of Barney's familiar old mouth? The same mouth that delivered Sunday sermons and blessings and prayers to the sick and infirm?

You know well, he reminded himself. *Just remember scripture. For all of Jesus's good and benevolent miracles, he had his seasons of doing battle with evil as well. The first account was in the Gospel of Mark, wasn't it?*

And Jesus asked the man possessed, "What is thy name?" and he answered saying, "My name is Legion, for we are many…"

The Cemetery Man moved away from the bed to where Brown, Beau and Fralene stood, all huddled in the doorway. "Are we ready?" he asked.

"I don't know," Fralene said. "Are we?"

"That one," the demon said with Barney's mouth, staring right at Brown, "will never be ready. *Never*. The bloody, blithering, goddamned coward…"

Brown felt his guts turn to water and slosh around inside him. He turned and stepped out of the room, into the upstairs hallway. There, vision aswarm with darkness and fireflies, he leaned against the wall and drew deep breaths. A moment later, Fralene, Beau and the Cemetery Man appeared beside him. They half-closed the bedroom door, allowing the four of them some small measure of privacy from the gaze of the trussed-up demon.

"Are you ready?" the Cemetery Man asked.

Brown tried to answer but couldn't find words. He shook his head.

"He's ready," Fralene said.

"I didn't ask you," the Cemetery Man growled.

"You're ready," she said to the Reverend Brown, ignoring the Cemetary Man.

"Reverend Brown," Beau said with surprising tenderness for such a young man, "you can do this."

Brown's throat felt dry as the Sahara. Outside, thunder rolled and the first rains began to patter on the rooftops of Harlem. "Fralene, Beau… I don't—"

"That's Uncle Barnabus in there!" Fralene hissed. "He's waiting for you to deliver him!"

A picture hanging just a few feet from them suddenly leapt off its nail and crashed to the floor, then went sliding down the runner in the hallway, right past the three of them, as though someone had kicked it. As Brown and Fralene turned toward the sound and watched the picture slide across the carpet, they suddenly heard the thumping of footsteps, as though someone was hurrying right toward them across the floor. The footsteps came right up to them: fast, heavy, determined.

Then a terrible cold enwrapped them. Fralene threw herself into the Reverend Brown's arms, trembling. The Reverend Brown felt it, too—a cold that penetrated him right to the bone. He shook in Fralene's embrace.

The Cemetery Man stood by and watched the whole strange series of unfolding events with scientific curiosity. His black eyes narrowed and he seemed to growl deep in his throat, a sub-sonic sound like the purr of a lion.

"I think I'm starting to understand," he said.

"Understand what?" Brown asked, trying to stop his own shaking. The cold was gone now, but its memory still lay on him like a wet blanket.

"Don't you worry about it," the Cemetery Man replied. "It'll be my cross to bear when the time comes. First things first—we need to do something about the fat man downstairs. Let's get that taken care of before we start. Beau, help me out."

Brown liked the sound of that. The Cemetery Man swept past them. Beau followed and both went thumping down the stairs. Brown and Fralene trailed behind them. Outside, the wind moaned under the eaves of the old house and rain rattled against the window panes like a thousand tiny claws scrabbling for ingress.

The Cemetery Man stopped before he'd even reached the foyer below. He was staring at the spot where they'd left the fat man, bleeding and unconscious.

"What the hell…?" Beau said.

Brown blinked. Fralene drew breath beside him.

The front door stood open, swinging idly on its hinges in the gathering wind from the rising spring storm outside.

The fat man was gone. Apparently, he'd had enough life left in him to get on his feet and go stumbling out into the rainy night.

"Are you going after him?" Beau asked.

"Where could he have gone?" Fralene added.

The Cemetery Man descended to the foyer, marched to the door, and slammed it shut. He tripped the deadbolt and the main lock. "Doesn't matter," he said. "Let's get started."

19

The rain actually helped Monk regain his wits. While the preacher—the one that wasn't crazy—and the young Negro lady and the kid and the Hoodoo Man did whatever the hell they were doing upstairs with crazy old Farnes, Monk managed to regain his senses, get back on his feet, and scurry out into the night. He was limping, since it seemed that the old preacher had maybe sprained one of Monk's ankles while giving him his beating, and there was still blood in Monk's eyes and a terrible sense of displacement from the pounding in his head and the scrambling of his senses, but at least he could see and he could move. That would do. He could make it at least a block or two on sheer willpower.

Then the winds kicked up, and the rains started, and Monk actually welcomed the cold little droplets of water as they skirled down out of the sky and beat down on his hat brim and covered his face and refreshed him and washed some of the blood away. He had to breathe through his mouth—his nose was broken—but that didn't matter. He just wanted to be out of that house. He needed a phone. He'd call the boss, and tell him what happened, and hopefully the boss would send a car to come pick him up and take him home. He couldn't ride a train looking like he did, and he didn't have the money for a taxi.

He'll kill you, he thought. *You know that, don't you, Monk? The boss ain't gonna be forgiving.*

But it wasn't his fault, was it? He and Toby came and tried to do what it was they were supposed to do. It wasn't their fault that the old man was loony and got the drop on them, or that he shot Toby and almost beat Monk to death, was it?

Nah. It wasn't his fault. They couldn't have seen this coming. And truth be told, Monk didn't give a flying fart at present if the boss iced him or not. With the way his head and nose throbbed like a couple of hot boils, ready to burst, he might welcome it. But he had to get out of Jigtown. He was alone up here—exposed, wounded and scared. He saw disgust and confusion and shock on the faces of all the darkies he passed as he lumbered down the street. He had to be a frightful sight, blinking rainwater and blood from his eyes, wiping blood and snot from his nose and mouth. Shit, what if the cops picked him up? Or some uptown nigger gunmen who ran with the Queen Bee?

He needed a phone. He needed a ride home. Whatever came after that really wasn't his problem.

The rain was falling hard and fast now, and thunder rolled over the rooftops like a Heavenly censure. Maybe that was Monk's old dad, the rabbi, rumbling his disapproval from on high. That figured. The old man never had understood that Monk didn't want to be a rabbi. For one thing, he hated reading. For another, he just didn't like having to be so goddamned upright all the time. What did it get his dad, after all, except a lifetime of scraping to get by and the same plot of earth that everybody else got?

The thunder rumbled.

Dad didn't approve of such thoughts.

A car horn honked and Monk suddenly found himself face to face with the glaring headlights of a chugging Ford. He saw a shiny front grill and some dark faces behind a rain-streaked windshield and the twin suns of the lamps, like glaring eyes, but he could see little else. He was in the middle of the road. How did he get out here? Did he really stumble that way? Right off the sidewalk?

He thumped against the hood of the Ford but kept moving. "Sorry!" he said, probably looking like some bloody demon to the startled driver. He hobbled on, finding the sidewalk and tottering toward it before another car came along to plaster him on the street. He thought he raised his feet to climb up onto the sidewalk, but apparently he didn't raise them high enough because he still tripped and fell. He landed on the rain-slicked cement face-down, thumping his nose again. More warm blood came gushing forth and he cried out at the pain.

Monk didn't know how long he laid there, face-down on the wet pavement. He knew he was crying, he knew he was bleeding, and he knew he probably sounded like a dying animal. He didn't really care anymore, though. He just wanted it all to stop. The rain, so refreshing a few moments ago, now lashed him mercilessly, eager to keep him down, intent on stealing his last warmth. His raincoat didn't seem to be doing its job of keeping him warm and dry. He was cold. He was lonely. He wanted his mom.

But he'd settle for the boss.

He lifted his head and blinked. A bright and welcoming light shone out of the darkness, a beacon in the night. It was just a few yards away, calling to him like an old friend.

Ferguson's Pharmacy and Tobacconist, the sign said. *Open late!*

Pharmacies had phones. Even in his addled state, Monk knew that much. He struggled to his feet, tried to focus on the pharmacy door in the middle of the three shifting apparitions he saw, and trudged forward. The first door he tried ended up being a wall, but the second one felt like an actual door, so he seized the knob and yanked. A little bell tinkled as he lumbered in out of the rain, water dripping off of him and pooling around his feet.

The sound of the rain stopped once the door shut behind him. Monk saw two men—both black—sitting at a short soda fountain talking to a third—a wiry old shine in a white smock with thick, coke-bottle glasses. That must be the pharmacist. There was a kid hanging around the counter, too—probably not much older than ten or eleven.

Monk sniffed, trying to keep a fresh rope of blood and snot from dropping out of his schnoz and worming down his upper lip. He drew breath and squared his shoulders.

"Pardon me, sir," he said, his mouth tasting like it was full of pennies, "would you happen to have a telephone?"

The pharmacist—clearly just as stunned as his two patrons—pointed down the center aisle. Monk followed the line of the old man's brown finger and thought he saw a booth of stained wood and glass awaiting him on the back wall.

"Thank you kindly," Monk said, and headed toward it. Once again, he saw three phone booths—not just one—but he figured finding the right one, the *real* one, was just a numbers game. Sooner or later, he'd find a door to open, a hook to tap, and a horn to speak into. It was just a matter of eliminating all the false options, wasn't it?

20

The rain beat the roof like a chorus of tiny drums and rattled against the windows in susurrating sheets. After gathering some accouterments—a vial of blessed oil from the Reverend Farnes's own study, as well as his favorite, dog-eared reading Bible—the four of them gathered in the Reverend Farnes's bedroom. The demon was still immobilized, still glaring, cursing at them as it thrashed and tried to free itself.

The Cemetery Man surprised the reverend with his gentle insistence that Fralene and Beau need not witness what was about to unfold. Nonetheless, the Farnes siblings would not be talked out of it. Their uncle's welfare was of great concern to them. They would be present, they would bear witness, until they could stand to do so no longer.

The Reverend Brown silently commended them. He had to fight the urge to withdraw and keep his feet firmly planted in the bedroom from the very first moment. He was afraid the demon knew it, too.

As they were about to begin, the demon seemed to sense something in the room—to silently read each of them, to take stock. It's appraisal brought a smug grin to its face.

"Lordy lordy lawes…" the thing that was Barnabus Farnes croaked from the bed. "Here come the crusaders to free this poor, sad holy man from his bondage. What surprises I have in store for you!"

"Don't listen to it," the Cemetery Man said.

"Him," Brown said, trying to convince himself as much as the Cemetery Man. "That's my friend, sir. He's not an *it.*"

The Cemetery Man glared back at the reverend. "The Reverend Farnes is a *him…* the thing inside him is an *it.*

Remember that even though they're in the same body, they're not the same. Not by a long shot."

"Listen to him," the thing in the bed said. "Takes one to know one, eh, buck?"

The door to the Reverend Farnes's bathroom suddenly slammed shut with such force that it rebounded and swung back and forth on its hinges. All of them—the demon included—stared at it.

The demon's own surprise wasn't lost on the Reverend Brown. For just a moment, the reverend closed his eyes. He tried his best to not concentrate on anything in particular, to simply let his ears and his skin and his congregate senses help him to read the room, to feel it, at an instinctual, gut level.

Finally, he opened his eyes. The demon's eyes were darting all about, as though it was afraid of something. Something *nearby*.

"We're not alone here, are we?" Brown asked the thing.

"Oh, you're *all* alone," the demon answered. "More alone than you know. It doesn't matter if the four of you stand shoulder to shoulder, or if you call in an army—"

"No, you're right," Fralene said. "I feel it, too. There's something else here."

"Well, what is it?" Beau asked. "And how do we get rid of it?"

The Cemetery Man was making a strange sound in his throat: a thoughtful, purring growl. "I understand…"

"Understand what?" Brown asked.

"Never mind," the Cemetery Man said. "Get to work."

Brown accepted he was about to do the most terrifying thing he'd ever done. He stood directly before the trussed-up Reverend Farnes while the Cemetery Man withdrew to the inner corner of the room, off to Brown's right. Fralene and Beau lingered in the doorway, holding a lamp so that they need not view the demon in the Reverend Farnes under harsh electric light.

The demon smiled—no, sneered—where he sat, looking up at the three of them and surveying them like they were the shoddiest trio of fools and pilgrims he'd ever encountered. That withering gaze—alien though it might be—made the Reverend Brown feel like a frightened, incompetent child. He was only a few years younger than the Reverend Farnes, true… but there was still something in the man—even possessed by a demonic outsider—that withered Brown's own estimation of himself and filled him with trepidation.

They stood like that for a time—exorcists and possessed. No one said a word.

The demon thrust its chin out like a petulant child. "I ain't goin' anywhere," he said. "You'll have to kill him to pry me out of him."

Fralene drew a breath but managed not to say a word. The Reverend Brown looked to the Cemetery Man, as if for verification. Would it come to that? *Could it?*

"Get started," the Cemetery Man commanded, standing sentinel.

Brown did as he was told.

"You're a fool," the demon said through the Reverend Farnes's mouth. "Worse. You're a hypocrite. You're in over your head, parson."

The Reverend Brown's throat suddenly felt like Lennox Avenue blacktop on a thirsty summer afternoon. He stared at the bound simulacrum of his old friend, Barney; stared into the dark and glaring eyes; at the sneering mouth.

The demon strained suddenly against its bonds. Though the ropes held, the sudden movement was enough to put Brown on guard and send him reeling backward in fear. The Cemetery Man caught him and shoved him forward again with one hand.

"This isn't play time!" the Cemetery Man snarled. "The reverend's mind and body are under siege and you're the only one that can set him free! *Now, do what you know how to do!*"

Reverend Brown, the scourge of fear and doubt assailing him from his very core to the tips of his fingers, turned and stared the Cemetery Man in the eye. He'd never been so scared. It shamed him to say it—especially when Barney needed him—but what could he do? He was just one man. Suddenly, he felt not half so righteous as he thought himself to be. He felt like a fool and a hypocrite. In his mind, he could not summon a picture of himself saying the words he needed to say, summoning the holy spirit that he needed to summon to see Barney delivered. All he could see were his failures. The tiny moral shortcuts. The little white lies. The moments of soft self indulgence. Even his moment of apparent bravery downstairs, at the door—it came reflexively, without conscious thought or courageous effort.

Just like that night that he and Ms. Walker had nearly been murdered…

"I can't," Brown told the glowering apparition with the skull face and top hat. "I can't do it. I… I… I…"

"Cause he's a sham as a holy man, that's why!" the demon said from the bed and chuckled from deep down in its old belly. "Hypocrite! Liar! Fraud!"

The Cemetery Man reached out, snatched up the Reverend Brown's lapels in a single fist, and lifted him bodily off the floor. Fralene screamed and dove forward, lantern still in one hand, tugging on the Cemetery Man's muscular arm with the other. Beau tried to hold her back, but he didn't have much strength left in him. He was too busy being scared.

"Put him down!" she commanded.

"Leave him be!" Beau begged his sister.

"We haven't got time for your fear," the Cemetery Man said. "Or your doubt. The Reverend Farnes needs you, Reverend Brown."

"But—but—but—"

The demon laughed at all of it. It seemed to find Brown's fear and the Dread Baron's fury great fun.

"Put him down, right now!" Fralene demanded.

"Your fear means *nothing*," the Cemetery Man snarled, eyes boring right into Brown's own, convicting him, tearing him down, and building him up all at once. "His need is *everything*. If you're his friend—a shepherd, a man of God—*this* is where you're needed! Right here, right now! Don't turn your back on this moment, reverend! Face it! Meet it! *Seize it!*"

Brown felt something strange overtaking him as he stared down the barrel of the Cemetery Man's black and smoldering gaze. Whether the feeling invaded him from the outside or bloomed entirely from within, he could not say. But it seemed to bleed inward from his extremities and gather in the center of him, like iron filings drawn to a magnet. It was warm and strong; dense as iron, yet light as a favorite coat.

Was that courage?

Maybe it was simple necessity; the blind understanding that Barney *needed* him, and that it was his job—*his alone*—to deliver him. That's why the Lord had put him here. That was the work the Lord had for him to do this night: his whole life leading up to it, the rest leading away from it.

"Put me down," he said. "I'm ready."

The Cemetery Man obliged.

"You ain't ready for shit," the demon croaked.

The Reverend Brown reached into his coat pocket and drew something out: the long, purple stole that he often wore upon his shoulders on Sunday mornings, when he stood at the pulpit to preach. It was rolled up at the moment, nothing but a thick bundle of cloth the size of two fists. When he had it loose from his coat pocket, he let it unravel, straightened it in both hands, then bent forward.

"Don't you dare!" the demon snarled.

The Reverend Brown draped the mantle over the demon's shoulders. In an effort to keep it on him, he even flipped it rakishly round the demon's throat, like a scarf. The moment the purple mantle lay on his shoulders, the demon began to scream and writhe and growl like a rabid beast in a cage being prodded with dull pikes.

Fralene let a small shriek escape her—involuntary, pitiful. The Cemetery Man swept her back with one arm, urging her toward the bedroom door, then turned and spoke to her.

"Turn your back if you have to," the Cemetery Man said. "Say prayers if need be. It'll help."

Brown saw that Fralene struggled mightily in that instant to compose herself. She stared right back into the Cemetery Man's eyes. "I won't look away. I *never* look away."

The Cemetery Man seemed to smile. "Yes, ma'am. I've heard that about you."

Beau put his arms around his sister. "It's okay," the boy said. "I'm here."

The Reverend Brown, having been encouraged by this exchange , now found the page he was after in his Bible. He flexed the spine of the book open so that he could see it more clearly. The demon writhed and bucked against its bonds on the bed, howling and snarling and hurling obscene epithets at them.

"In the name of the Father, the Son, and the Holy Spirit," the Reverend Brown began, barely believing that the voice he heard in his ears was his own, "I call you, liar, you deceiver, you lurker in the shadow to show yourself!"

XX

Monk was just finishing his chocolate soda when he saw the big Bentley pull up outside the pharmacy. Even through the rain and darkness he recognized its long, lean lines; its shiny black paint; the glare of its two eye-like headlamps. That was the boss's car. Monk was finally going to get the hell out of here.

He reached into his coat, pulled out two bits, and left the coin on the counter.

The old pharmacist and his two customers were still there, staring at Monk like they expected trouble from him. The kid had run off while Monk was on the phone. Monk felt strangely embarrassed—bloody and messy as he was, soaked to the bone. He was glad the old jig had given him the chocolate soda. That calmed him and helped pass the time until the boss arrived.

The front door bell jingled as two big figures stepped inside: Benji, one of the boss's junior gunmen, and the boss himself. Both shook the water off themselves in the doorway. It was cats and dogs out there. Monk couldn't remember the last time he'd seen such a nasty storm.

The boss got a good look at Monk's swollen, blood-caked face. "Jesus, kid, what happened to you?"

Monk shuffled closer. The old pharmacist and his customers were listening. He didn't really want to discuss it in front of them. He leaned close to the boss.

"It was the old man," he said. "He aired out Toby."

The boss looked at him like he was speaking Chinese. Monk knew Dolph Storms to be capable of almost Biblical rages, but there seemed to be no rage in him at the moment, just complete confusion.

"Wait a minute," the boss said. "You're tellin' me old Farnes did this? Beat you silly and capped Toby to boot?"

Monk nodded.

"Can I help you gentlemen?" the pharmacist asked.

"Yeah," the boss shot back, "you can shut the fuck up and keep your jig pals on their soda stools. We're engaged in a conversation here, if you didn't notice."

The pharmacist swallowed. "Yes, sir, I see. It's just that… we're gettin' ready to close."

The boss rolled his eyes, stepped up to the counter, and yanked a buck out of his pocket. He tossed the crumpled bill on the counter. "Here, Sambo—make me a goddamned root bear float. How 'bout that. Not gonna close with paying customers, right?"

The pharmacist seemed to stare at the bill as though it were paper poison. His two patrons stared at it as well, silently daring him to take it. But he took it. Then, he went about making the float.

The boss turned back to Monk. "Now, explain yourself. You're tellin' me that the Reverend Farnes, who is seventy goddamned years old, shot Toby and beat you black and blue."

"I ain't makin' it up, boss," Monk said.

"Bullshit," Benji huffed from his place by the door.

"Shut your trap!" Storms barked at Benji. "Monk here's senior on this crew, you little punk, and that means he doesn't have to put up with incredulity from the likes of you!"

Benji seemed to shrink at the boss's rebuke.

The boss then hauled off and smacked Monk a good one, open-handed, right across the face. Monk felt all the subsided pain in his ruined face return in an instant.

"As for you," the boss said, "I expect a better story than the one you just gave me."

"It ain't a story," Monk said. "Swear to God, boss, it ain't! When we got there, he was locked in the cellar—"

"Shut it," Storms snapped. "Just shut your mouth. I mean it. Where's that float?"

The pharmacist put it on the counter. Storms snapped it up. He displayed it for Monk. "You got until I finish this thing to come up with another story, or I'm gonna leave you here for Uncle Remus to take out with the garbage."

Storms began to drink his root beer float in large gulps. Steams of brown soda and melting ice cream tumbled out from either side of the glass and trickled onto his collar.

The door bell tinkled as someone suddenly burst in. It was Irving, the boss's driver. He'd left the Bentley idling at the curb. His eyes were wide and startled.

Monk felt a sinking in the pit of his stomach. He saw the kid who'd run off standing outside in the rain. He was pointing at the pharmacy, directing someone that Monk couldn't see.

Jesus! The cops?

The boss turned and lowered his soda. "What the fuck is this?"

"You gotta see this, boss," Irving said.

"See what?" Storms asked. "I got a root beer float here."

"Niggers with guns, boss," Irving said. "Lots of 'em."

21

Doc Voodoo watched in silence as the Reverend Farnes's body stiffened, bending board-straight for an instant before flopping down again onto the bed and convulsing under the weight of the spiritual forces the Reverend Brown invoked. The demon seemed to laugh and mumble worriedly at the same time, in a multitude of voices. Near the bedroom door, Fralene's lantern flared and flickered, as though unnatural air currents swirled in and around it as the object of the exorcism rocked and the exorcist himself—the Reverend Adam Clayton Brown, Jr.—carried on in a strong, clear voice.

"Barnabus Farnes," the reverend declared, "the law of the Spirit of life in Christ Jesus hath made you free from the law of sin and death! Slip all your bonds and come out from your prison! Your jailer cannot bind you! Your oppressors cannot keep you in chains! Your persecutor will be swept aside—"

The demon roared, straining against its bonds. Outside, the wind howled in answer, groaning against the eves and rattling the windows in their sashes. The whole house seemed to contract and flex around them, as though threatening to tear itself to pieces.

And through it all, Doc held vigil, feeling the near-undeniable force of the Reverend Brown's prayers threatening to chase Ogou from his own body every time they were recited. It was like trying to stand fast in the face of a hurricane wind, or stay afloat in a stormy sea.

You know this could get out of hand, Ogou said to him. *You realize that if we get caught in the crossfire of this man's prayers and the demons struggles, I could be forced right out of you?*

"Just stay with me, Ogou," Doc whispered to himself, to his patron. "No matter how hard the spirit winds blow, you just hang on to me."

Dub Corveaux knew he was taking a terrible chance, standing here horsed as a holy man sought to cast the demon out of the Reverend Barnabus Farnes. In spiritual terms, after all, there was little difference between the demon in Farnes and the strong and ancient *lwa* that horsed the Dread Baron. The Reverend Brown's prayers could end up driving one out while leaving the other intact—and it could very easily be Ogou, and not the demon in Farnes, that was forced to flee.

"Tell me your name!" Brown cried.

The demon in Farnes cursed him in a hundred different tongues at once.

"I command you to tell me your name!" Brown cried. "In Jesus' name! In the name of the Father, the Son, and the Holy—"

Then, Doc smelled it. Heat. Smoke. Something burning. He looked to the bed.

Somehow, the demon was radiating heat from its host body, and that heat was burning right through the cords that held it to the bed. It happened in an instant: the rope on its wrists blackened and snapped, then the bonds on its ankles, and finally, the fat coil that wrapped around its middle, keeping it bound to the bed itself.

"Oh dear," Brown breathed, seeing this, knowing what it meant.

"Keep going!" Doc shouted, and dove toward the bed.

The last ropes sizzled, blackened and snapped. With a howl of triumph, the demon was free. It shot upright on the bed, shifted to get its legs under it, and prepared to spring. It had murder in its eyes and ropes of drool cascaded down from its borrowed mouth.

Then Doc landed hard atop it, a flying tackle that drove the demon back onto the bed. An instant later, demon and Baron were rolling around, a tangle of locked arms and kicking legs, Doc struggling to hold the beast at bay, the demon doing its damnedest to scurry free.

Doc saw from the corner of his eye that the Reverend Brown very nearly screamed and ran—but something in him kept him rooted. Doc didn't know if it was courage or foolishness or plain shock, but either way, Brown stayed right where he was. Behind him, Fralene Farnes screamed and stumbled against the tightly-shut bedroom door. She shrank and she drew the lantern up close to her, but to her credit, she didn't flee.

But Beau was the one that most surprised him. The boy had left his sister's side. He was hurrying to help Doc hold the demon down.

"No!" Doc roared. "Stay back, boy! I've got him!"

Doc's strong, coat-clad arms jostled for a good grip on the wiry, long-bodied Reverend Farnes, who snarled and snickered as he struggled to get free. The thing might have been in the body of an old man, but it was supple and strong nonetheless, a clear match for even the magically-enhanced Baron. The demon jerked to the right. Doc yanked back toward the left. The two of them went tumbling onto the floor with a room-shaking thump.

For one instant, the demon was free. It leapt to its feet, turned toward its quarry—

—then Doc had it again, bolting his arms around it from behind and lifting it bodily off the floor. The spindly old legs wheeled in the air. The long, lithe body bucked and squirmed.

"Do it!" Doc barked.

"Do what?" Reverend Brown asked.

"Drive it out!" Doc shouted back, still struggling. "I'll hold it!"

"The hell you will!" the demon growled. "Two for one, reverend! See if you can drive us both out! This sum-bitch's horsed too, you know!"

The Reverend Adam Clayton Brown, Jr., stared at the thing before him—the thing that looked like his old friend and mentor, Barney, but that seemed to have a hellish light in its eyes and terrible misdeeds on its mind. Amid his struggles to hold the demon, Doc Voodoo saw the confusion and the sudden realization on Brown's face—that the only thing standing between Brown and the beast was a man who looked like Doc, a man invoking infernal powers and paying homage to the darkness—an apparition in a skull face and top hat and ropy, whipping braids. Brown probably never imagined that he would find himself in such a situation.

Truth be told, Doc hadn't imagined it either.

But that didn't matter right now.

"Do it!" Doc commanded. "Don't stop until its gone!"

This could get bad, Ogou said in the center of his brain. *Very bad.*

"Just hold on," Doc growled, and braced himself.

Brown's words came loud and strong. He held the Bible before him. The demon writhed and made its terrible, other-dimensional sounds—the sounds of many voices crying from the same mouth, cursing and pleading and assuring him they were going nowhere—*nowhere*—that his prayers would all amount to nothing.

The Dread Baron held the thing. The two of them jerked back and forth. They slammed against the far wall of the bedroom, pirouetted back toward the bed, bounced off the bed and rolled across the floor, lurched once more to their feet and whirled like belligerent dancers through the room. All the while, Brown kept reading, invoking, commanding, demanding a name. At the bedroom door, Fralene prayed as well. When the demon seemed to grow too powerful, Brown took out a vial of Holy Water that he had stowed in his pocket and began anointing the thing.

When the droplets hit the demon's skin, they drew smoke. They did the same when they hit Doc. Both of them cried out in their distress.

Brown hesitated.

"Don't stop!" Doc shouted. Holding the demon while also holding the threatening-to-bolt Ogou within himself felt like trying to cling to an umbrella that had been snatched by a powerful wind.

Brown went on, his voice reaching a high, wavering crescendo. Doc felt the older man's struggle to gather all of his strength, all of his faith, all of his will and to channel them all through the sound of his voice as he shouted the words from the Psalms he read. The storm outside was raging and every board, window pane and piece of furniture in the bedroom shook, ready to tear itself apart. As Brown's voice grew louder, Doc saw that he drew nearer as well. With all the Holy Water gone, Brown had no other recourse but to return to the pewter cross in his coat pocket. He drew it out and leveled it before him. The pewter bauble hovered just inches from the demon's face.

Doc had to avert his own gaze and strain against the force radiating from it. It was like a heat storm in the middle of cold winter wind—hot, bright, pure kinesis. He dug in his heels, gritted his teeth, and sought to hold Ogou inwardly while still holding the demon-possessed Reverend Farnes in the physical world.

When the demon in Farnes saw that cross—so close, so bright—it let out a multitudinous howl that seemed to fill the upper floors of the Farnes home and threatened to lift the house off its very foundations. This was the moment—the wave Brown had been riding had reached its crest and Brown could only press forward and ride it toward the shore, even if it destroyed him upon impact. Brown stabbed the cross forward, planting its cross-bars right on the demon's face. Barnabus Farnes's eyes rolled, turning white. His mouth threatened to snap right off its hinge as his mouth opened wide and a thousand infernal screams came thundering out.

The Reverand's body went taut.

An invisible force lifted Doc and threw him backward, blasting his grip on the struggling Reverend Farnes and driving him right against the outer wall of the bedroom. He hit that wall with bomb-blast force and landed in a heap on the floor. The whole room filled with light and heat and a roaring sound not unlike a great pillar of wind rising out of a deep abyss, although Doc could not swear that the light and heat and roaring existed anywhere other than in his own fevered brain.

Doc lifted his gaze. Blinked. He saw Brown press the cross against Barnabus Farnes's forehead. Smoke and flame rose—from Barney's flesh or the cross itself, Doc couldn't tell—and behind that haze the demon gave one last electric convulsion—one last, long wailing from the deepest pits of Hell—then went silent and collapsed.

Barnabus Farnes hit the floor like a dead man, a heap of old bones and dark flesh.

A terrible silence fell. There was only the sound of three people breathing, the light rattling of the rain against the wind panes, and a gentle, jostling wind skirling up under the eaves of the old house.

The Dread Baron looked inward. *Ogou?*

Let's not do that again, eh? Ogou answered.

"Not anytime soon," Doc said aloud.

Brown stared at the heap before him.

"Did it work?" Fralene asked in a small, quailing, little girl's voice.

"Is he dead?" Beau breathed, voice strangled in his own throat.

Doc found his feet again. He replaced his fallen hat atop his nest of thick, black braids.

Fralene and Beau lunged forward from the doorway, shouting their uncle's name. She fell upon him, shaking him, turning him onto his back. Beau took the old man's bony hand.

"Stay back!" Brown said.

"Don't!" Doc warned.

Neither Fralene nor Beau listened. And to their mutual relief, nothing came of it. Once they had Barnabus on his back and more or less laid out straight, they could all see clearly that he was unconscious—veritably comatose—but still breathing.

Breathing. Alive.

Tears sprang to Fralene's eyes, rolled over Beau's smooth cheeks, cut tracks down the Reverend Brown's soft, lined old face.

Doc stepped forward, looming over the fallen Farnes. Fralene and Beau each bent over him, as though they intended to protect their uncle from the vigilante's depredations.

"Don't worry," Doc said. "I just want to put him back in his bed."

Fralene stared for a moment, as though she didn't believe him. Beau was the one who finally convinced her, with a single touch of his hand, that the Cemetary Man meant what he said. Fralene looked to Brown and Brown nodded too. The man had proved a friend so far, frightening countenance or no. They had no reason to stop trusting him now.

Fralene stood and backed away.

Doc lifted her uncle with Beau's unnecessary help, swung round, and laid him gently upon his bed. Fralene straightened the now-tangled sheets and drew off the charred ropes that had been holding him. Brown moved to the Reverend Farnes's side and checked his pulse.

"Still with us?" Doc asked.

Brown nodded, looking more than a little disturbed. "It's there, but it's weak."

Fralene leaned forward, prying her uncle's eyelids open and staring into them. "Uncle Barnabus! Uncle Barnabus, we're here! Talk to us!"

"Could be he'll need time to recover," Doc said.

Could be I will, too, he thought.

But then he felt something new and realized there would be no time for him to recover. Not tonight. With all the psychic and spiritual turbulence in the bedroom subsiding, the Dread Baron could once again feel the vibrations that ran along the great psychic web that he was the center of… the web that told him where danger could be found, and who needed his assistance.

He was used to hearing the moaning of distressed webstrands in the center of his brain like a slow, low note bowed on the strings of some invisible cello, the note gradually rising as he neared the location of the distress. Now, though, he heard a storm of bows on a great convocation of strings, like some lunatic's orchestra tuning all at once and making a terrible botch of it.

The web was groaning, crying, screaming under the weight of soon-to-explode mischief.

And he was the only one who could do anything about it.

He made for the door.

"Where are you going?" Fralene asked.

"We need you," Beau added.

"Not anymore," Doc answered. "There's something else nearby. It can't be ignored."

"Will you be back?" Brown asked.

Doc bounded down the stairs and out into the raining night without answering him.

Truth be told, after the paces he'd been put through, he really couldn't say.

22

Dolph Storms couldn't believe his eyes. He couldn't chalk it up to just being a rain mirage or some kind of hallucination, either: it was right in front of him, big as life and twice as ugly. He was starting to think that maybe—just maybe—he should've let Monk find his own way back downtown.

Stretched out across 134th Street was a platoon of darkies in hats and raincoats. They filled the street from one side to the other, so there had to be at least twenty or thirty of them, all standing shoulder to shoulder. And goddamned if they weren't armed to the teeth.

He saw scatterguns, he saw Tommies, he saw Springfield rifles left over from the Great War, and he saw big, black Smith & Wesson pistols. Every one of the men in the street held his rifle like he knew what to do with it—well-practiced, comfortable, ready for action. At the center of the big, broad skirmish line that stretched across the street stood a fat man with little round glasses whose wire frames hugged his broad, dark face like golden thread.

Jebediah Goddamned Debbs, Dolph thought.

Storms took stock. He had four guys, including the still bloody-faced, half-dazed Monk. They were outnumbered five to one.

He glanced over his shoulder. Maybe, just maybe, they could hop in the Bentley, gun the engine, whip around in the street, and flee in the opposite direction… but the vigilantes looked like they had itchy trigger fingers. They'd open fire the minute they moved for the auto, and with all that firepower, they were likely to hit something, even if they were lousy shots. If they got caught in that car with a flat tire or a busted engine block, they were screwed. There was no way out for them at that point.

Dolph Storms didn't mind fighting tooth and nail, down to the last little spark of life in his body and the last drop of blood—hell, he'd always figured he'd go out that way—but he just didn't plan on going out that way tonight. He didn't care to die in Harlem on a rainy April evening, and he sure as shit wasn't eager to be aired out by a bunch of Sambos strapped with Army surplus. It struck him as akin to a big, tough bull terrier getting torn to shreds by a bevy of rats.

He wouldn't lay down for rats.

The fat man as the center of the broad line, Debbs, spoke, his voice low and booming like a preacher on Sunday. "What's your business here?" he demanded, having to shout to be heard about the rattle of the falling rain.

"Just out for a drive," Dolph answered. "Picking up my associate here." He suggested Monk with his bloody and broken face.

"And what's your associate's business uptown?" the fat man asked.

"Last I checked, it's a free country," Storms countered. "This fella wants to come up to Jigtown, chase darkie tail and swill nigger booze… well, it ain't for you and yours to tell him otherwise. But, apparently, somebody hereabouts didn't like him and made it known. Brought it to fisticuffs. Uncivilized, you ask me."

The fat man smiled a little. He wasn't buying the story, but he could appreciate that Storms was trying to defuse the situation.

Truth was, Dolph didn't think he could defuse the situation. At the very least, he just thought he could unravel that fuse and keep it from finally reaching the powder keg just a few minutes longer, until he could formulate a plan.

The pharmacy, he suddenly thought. *I could duck back in there. It's a nigger business. These assholes won't go blood simple on one of their own. They might try to box us in and storm the place, but they won't just blast away.*

Will they?

If I can make them hesitate… force them to reformulate… shit, I could slip out the back, skin out through the alleys, and grab a train over on Lenox. The boys can hold these assholes off long enough for me to get away.

It occurred to him that the boys probably wouldn't make it out along with him—but that's what he paid them for, right?

And wasn't the price of doing business in Harlem rising? If he lost these guys tonight, in addition to the half dozen lost so far… shit, Harlem would owe him a whole new crew. Dolph Storms didn't think he could let an insult like that pass. He thought if he made it out of Harlem alive tonight, he just might have to come back up here at a later time and level the place. A little Old Testament blood and thunder was just what the doctor ordered.

"I know who you are," the fat man suddenly said.

"Yeah?" Dolph asked. "And who is that?"

"You're the one called Storms. You're a beer baron and a killer. You're not welcome here. Ever."

"Well, isn't that something," Storms countered. He felt a rage rising in him. "My reputation precedes me. Tell me, Sambo—if I make it my personal mission to stalk Harlem after dark and fuck every jungle bunny dame who crosses my path and bust every nigger melon head that looks at me sideways, just what the fuck do you think you're gonna do about it?"

"Boss?" Irving asked.

"Get ready to skin it," Dolph whispered.

"Gentlemen!" the fat man shouted in answer to Dolph's taunt, addressing his fellow vigilantes, "Take aim!"

All those hungry black gun muzzles swung up and gaped for Dolph and his crew. For just a moment, Dolph's rage was cut through by a cold, hard spike of fear.

"Back inside!" Dolph barked, and ducked for the pharmacy door. The boys followed.

The guns roared.

Dolph dove through the pharmacy door first, followed by Benji and Irving. Dolph threw himself down onto the linoleum floor and went scurrying into the aisles as Benji and Irving flanked either side of the door. Outside, the night lit up with muzzle flashes and the thundering music of thirty or forty guns all roaring at once. Bullets and buckshot tore through the Bentley, shattering its windshield and headlamps, peeling off coins of paint and punching deep, dark holes in the steel body. Stuffing wafted out of the open windows as hot lead ripped through the seat cushions. The tires popped and the whole car rocked back and forth on its empty tubes.

Dolph watched as his favorite car was blasted apart, right there in the street. Benji and Irving had their pieces out, but they were still cowering under the forward wall of the pharmacy, trying to keep their heads below the big picture windows that fronted the place. Monk dove for safety too soon and landed half in and half out the door, head in the pharmacy, feet in the street. He had both hands clamped over his melon head and he lay flat as could be, face down, trembling as slugs cris-crossed the air above him.

Dolph reached into his coat and pulled out his Webley. He cracked it, checked the cylinder. He only had five shots. He wasn't carrying any more.

The gunfire subsided. Rain beat down on Dolph's ruined touring car. Dark bodies in wet coats started to fan out in front of the pharmacy, taking up safe positions behind parked cars, trashcans, fire hydrants and mail boxes. They moved with almost military speed and precision.

Meanwhile, Dolph's men cowered, not sure whether they should lift their heads and risk a shot.

Something moved off to the right. It was the old pharmacist, hurrying toward the front door. He was stripped down to his undershirt and bracers, waving his white smock like a flag of truce. When he reached the front door, he stepped right on Monk and kept going out into the rainy night.

"Hold up!" the old pharmacist shouted. "If you're gonna air these fellas out, you're gonna do it when I'm good and clear!"

"What about us?" one of the unlucky Negro customers cowering beneath the soda counter called.

Dolph heard a shotgun rack a new shell into its chamber. The old pharmacist stopped where he stood on the sidewalk. He wasn't waving the smock anymore.

"Get back inside with your wicked associates, sir!" the fat man boomed. "Any man that would take a Hebe gangster's coin is no friend to the good people of this Negro Metropolis!"

"They just came in!" the pharmacist countered. "I didn't even know what for—"

The shotgun barked. Buckshot shattered one of the front windows. The pharmacist turned and dove right back through the front door, landing on top of the sprawled Monk and scurrying over him. He crawled all the way back to the soda counter and cowered beside his customers.

"Is that Debbs?" one of the customers hissed. "That gum-flapper from Liberty Hall?"

"Think so," the pharmacist growled. "He's off his nut."

"Hey," Dolph hissed at the pharmacist. "You packin', old man?"

"A plague on both your houses," the pharmacist answered.

"Listen here!" Debbs said from the street. "I have it on good authority that this pharmacy fronts for a bolito bank, and makes illicit coin from the trade of bathtub gin and soul-stealing narcotics! So far as this vigilance committee is concerned, the proprietor and customers present in such a den of vice are no better than the gangsters they serve! Therefore, I decree—"

"He decrees," Storms muttered. "Get a load of this guy…"

"—that all persons on the premises are hereby named enemies of the good people of Harlem, and subject to prosecution! You have ten seconds to throw out your guns, raise your hands, and surrender yourselves for manumission to the authorities, elsewise we open fire!"

Dolph looked to the pharmacist. "There a back way out?"

The pharmacist nodded.

Dolph looked to his men. "Cover me, boys."

They didn't look too happy about that order.

Just as Dolph scrambled up onto his feet and went dashing down the aisle, bent double to keep his head low, the guns started barking again. The whole pharmacy seemed to come crashing down around him. Cotton wadding and bottles of iodine exploded on their shelves and filled the air with whirling clouds of thread and the tang of disinfectant. Newspapers leapt up from their racks like gray ghosts covered in tiny printed tattoos and were shredded in the air by flying lead. Behind the soda fountain, fluted glasses and syrup bottles shattered and made crystalline music amid the gun-song.

Dolph kept running. The back door that led (he presumed) to the storeroom and the rear entrance was less than ten feet away. He heard the buzz of slugs passing uncomfortably close to him; felt the warm wind of bullets that just might have had his name on them; caught more than a few flying shards of glass on his face and uplifted hands; but no matter—he kept running.

When he finally made it through the door, and plowed right into a big desk and shelf unit, placed smack-dab in the center of the room. The desk blocked his path and he bent right over it, almost doing a full somersault and landing on the floor on its far side. Although it was quieter back here, he could still here the chatter and thunder of gunfire from out front, and more than once hot lead punched right through the back wall of the pharmacy and cut the air of the storeroom. He wasn't out of the woods yet.

So, still bent double, he rounded the big desk and shelf unit, searched the darkness, and found the door that he presumed would lead him into the alley. He made for it, desperate to feel the open air on his face again and get out of the line of fire. When he got there, he had to struggle to open the two dead bolts that held the door shut. A couple more slugs punched into the doorframe, throwing splinters in his face.

Finally, he had it. Dolph tripped the dead bolts and threw open the door. For just a moment, he saw a broad empty alley veiled by falling rain, deep puddles, some trashcans. The gunfire seemed far away now, all the way on the far side of the building, fronting the street. Dolph stepped out into the night, not even caring that he'd be soaked by the rain in seconds.

"There's one!" somebody yelled.

Dolph turned toward the voice.

There were men at each end of the alley. The vigilance committee had outmaneuvered him. The minute he stepped out the back door, they opened fire. Holes appeared in the swinging door and splinters skirled off the doorframe as it caught stray shots. He cursed and ducked back inside.

Dolph wanted to lock the door again, but they were still blasting away and it was out of his hands. He quickly backed into the darkened storeroom, readying his Webley six shooter in his right hand. He ran into the shelves behind the big desk. Outside in the alley, the gunfire stopped. He heard the click of shoes on pavement, nearing. The two parties of men guarding each end of the alley were converging on the back door.

"Go on in!" someone shouted. "We'll cover you!"

"The hell with that!" another answered. "You go first! We'll cover you!"

Son of a bitch. The assholes were going to storm Dolph's little back room redoubt. He swung around behind the big shelf, putting it between himself and the back door. Although the shelves were littered with all sorts of junk and old jars and bottles of retired pharmaceutical powders and chemicals, there was no back on it; it was just a wooden framework subdivided into cells. Dolph realized it wouldn't provide much cover, so he rounded the desk, then lurched against it and slid it right up against the shelves. That might at least give him some shielding over the lower half of his body, not to mention clearing his retreat path to the door that led back into the pharmacy.

The back door was thrown aside. Three men crowded into the doorway, one after the other, weapons raised. Before Dolph could even study them or figure out just what they were packing, the first man through the door blasted away with his shotgun. Dolph dove down behind the desk as one, two, three shotgun shells filled the air about him with a storm of buckshot that shattered the bottles and jars on the shelves and sent the loose papers and invoices on the desk flying like oversized confetti. A moment later, someone else joined in. Dolph could tell from the way the thunder of gunfire spread wide across the room, by the flight of the junk on the shelves and desk, that the gunmen were spreading out right and left, flanking him.

He didn't have much time.

Without raising his head, Dolph lifted his pistol above the desk. He fired first off to his left, then off to his right. The gunman on the left cried out in surprise and stumbled for cover, making an enormous racket. The gunman on the right cried out and fell with a thump.

Dolph had hit him.

"Son of a bitch!" the right-hand gunman cried. "That kike piece of shit shot me, Fergie!"

The third gunman in the doorway must have ducked toward his wounded friend to check on him, because no gunfire answered. Dolph saw his chance. He dove back through the door into the pharmacy. Just as he cleared the swinging door in the portal, his assailants recovered from their shock and started shooting again.

He found the boys where he left them, cowering down below the front windows amid a litter of shattered glass and shredded magazines. The pharmacist and his customers still hid beneath the soda counter, covered in flavored syrups. His boys and the goons in the street still traded lead, but the rate of fire had slowed, now more of a tennis match instead of a full tilt firestorm.

"Thought you were makin' a break?" Benji asked as Dolph crawled up to him.

"Jigs out the back, boys," Dolph said. "They're gonna be coming through that door any minute."

What happened next happened very fast, so fast that Dolph almost didn't realize what was happening until it had played out.

Out in the street, he heard a series of incredulous cries. For just a moment, the gunfire stopped and silence reigned, broken only by the sound of the falling rain.

Then, he heard the voice of the fat man, the leader of the vigilante band: "And just who is this, crashing our party in his spook show raiment?"

Dolph dared a peak above the lip of the front window. Someone stood out in the middle of the street, between his own ruined Bentley and the brood semi-circle of gunmen that surrounded the pharmacy's main entrance.

It was that Halloween spook—the Cemetery Man.

Dolph didn't even think. He rose up on his knees, leveled his Webley, and started pulling the trigger. He'd never have a better chance. He roared like an angry bull as three shots blasted out of his six shooter, aimed right at the Cemetery Man's back.

Every shot hit home.

Dolph's hammer clicked on dead slugs. He was dry.

The Cemetery Man didn't fall. He just turned to glare at Dolph, as though annoyed by the slugs that now lived in his broad, strong shoulders.

Then the door from the pharmacy storeroom burst open and the raiding party from the alley rushed through. They had their shotguns up, they gave rebel yells as they came, and they managed to pop off one shot apiece as they fanned out on the ruined pharmacy aisles for a final charge.

The Cemetery Man whirled and opened fire with his twin pistols. The slugs tore the air right over Dolph's head, sought each of the three raiders from the back room, and downed them where they stood.

"Boys!" the fat man in the street shouted. "Air this demon out!"

Dolph heard bolts being drawn and ammo being reloaded on all sides. The Cemetery Man whirled again, sweeping his gaze—and his guns—over the gathered throng. "This stops now!" he roared. "Every one of you, drop your weapons and throw up your hands!"

The fat man stepped forward, leveling an accusatory finger. "You're outnumbered, friend, and outgunned. What say you throw down your weapons and throw up your hands?"

The Cemetery Man leveled one of his automatics at the fat man, Debbs. He thumbed back the hammer. "Try me," he said.

"Boss," Irving said beside Dolph, "what the hell is all this? What'd we stumble into?"

"A swamp of shit," Dolph grumbled, then looked to Monk, with his wide eyes and slack jaw and ruined face. "Thanks a heap, you dumb lummox."

Monk's lip trembled. "Sorry, boss. How could I know?"

Dolph turned back to Irving. "Irving, you got shots left?"

"A couple," Irving said.

"Gimme," Dolph ordered.

Irving put his automatic in Dolph's hand.

Dolph shot Monk in the face.

Out in the street, someone heard that shot and thought it was the Cemetery Man; or the Cemetery Man thought it was one of the vigilantes. Regardless, Dolph's single shot, putting down one of his own men, set off a fierce volley of gunfire. Irving and Benji took cover. Dolph threw his own head down and waited.

It seemed to go on forever: a deafening, rattling, roaring storm of chilly rain and damp air cris-crossed by hot slugs spraying every which way in an apocalyptic storm. Dolph heard men take fire and fall, the not-quite-dead ones crying out as they did. Little by little, the gunfire subsided, slowly replaced by the sound of men exhorting their comrades to lam it, then by the beating of feet in all directions, usually accompanied by the clatter of weapons thrown down before said retreat was made.

Then, finally, it was all quiet. There was only the sound of the falling rain and the wail of police sirens drawing near.

Dolph cautiously raised his head above the lip of the front pharmacy window. At least a half-dozen dead men lay in the street, along with twice as many wounded. The rest of Debbs's vigilantes had made a run for it.

The Cemetery Man stood where he had before, smack dab in the middle of the street, a big, blue .45 in each hand trailing ribbons of smoke. He surveyed the carnage. Dolph couldn't see his face, so he couldn't really tell if the spook was pleased with his bloody handiwork or not.

On the far side of the street, someone moved. It was one of the vigilantes, bleeding but still kicking. He was trying to crawl away.

The Cemetery Man marched up to him. He kicked the crawler onto his back, planted one boot on the guy's chest, and leveled one of his pistol's right into the scared jig's face.

"Who's in charge here?" the Cemetery Man snarled. Dolph heard it clearly, even though he was a good thirty feet away. His voice was like two pieces of broken concrete heaving up on one another.

The scared fellow on the ground threw up his hands. "I threw down my guns, mister!" he shouted. "Look! I got nothing! Wasn't even me shot you! Those fellas—"

"Who was he?" the Cemetery Man barked. "The man in charge? The man who gave you all this iron and told you Harlem needed gunslingers instead of cops on the streets?"

"Mister Debbs, sir!" the guy crowed. "It was Mister Jebediah Debbs, sir! He said this is what the neighborhood needed.... said the cops couldn't be trusted… said the rackets ran everything!"

Dolph smiled. Yeah. It'd be nice if they *did* run everything.

And then it occurred to him: he was still holding Irving's gun, a single live round in the chamber.

The Cemetery Man was busy questioning the guy in the street, his back to Dolph.

This was Dolph's chance.

"Boss," Irving said, head still covered with his hands, afraid to look up.

Dolph shushed him.

Then he took aim over the lip of the pharmacy window.

"You're done with this, aren't you?" the Cemetery Man asked the scared fellow under his boot.

"Yessir," he said, nodding like a loon. "Yessir! All done!"

The Cemetery Man removed his boot. "Drag yourself to Harlem Hospital. That isn't a fatal wound."

The scared fellow tried to shuffle himself upright, stumbled, then managed to find his feet. He went limping away.

Dolph pulled back the hammer. He had the Cemetery Man in his sights, dead center, right on that broad, black coat of his.

"That goes for every one of you still breathing out here!" the spook roared. "The boys in blue are the law in Harlem! And only crooks and thugs keep order with fear, at the point of a gun!"

One of the shifting bodies in the street spat. "Hah! What about you, Hoodoo Man?"

Pull the trigger, Dolph told himself. *Why don't you pull the trigger?*

The Hoodoo Man wheeled on the wounded vigilante, leveling his gun again. He didn't have his back to Dolph anymore—

although Dolph didn't think that the spook saw him. He was too busy glaring down at the smart mouthed bastard that just challenged him.

"Crooks and cops answer to me," the Hoodoo Man snarled. "Now, where's Debbs?"

Dolph thought he saw fire in his black eyes beneath the brim of that top hat and all those crazy braids.

Pull the trigger, you lummox!

"He's over there," the mouthy jig said, not so mouthy any more. "Hidin' under them dead men! I see him plain, the fat bastard!"

Dolph watched as the Cemetery Man strode over to a pile of dead men. He kicked two bodies aside and there lay fat, cowering Jebediah Debbs, stained red and cowering in the rain.

"I'll not have any spawn of Satan laying hands on me!" Debbs boomed, terrified but still putting on a show.

"Shut up," the Cemetery Man said. "You're coming with me." With that, he yanked Debbs up off his feet. Dolph's jaw dropped when the scarf around the vigilante's neck slithered off like a serpent and wrapped around Debbs, binding him fast. The Cemetery Man hoisted the fat man with one hand.

That's when the distant sirens stopped being distant. Their whine split the night from either direction. Dolph heard the squeal of brakes. Headlights cut cross paths from either end of the block and the Cemetery Man was caught between them.

The Cemetery Man saw Dolph.

Dolph looked into the Cemetery Man's eyes.

I'm not pulling the trigger, Dolph suddenly realized, *because that son of a bitch already took a fusillade of lead. One shot from me won't do shit.*

Not tonight anyway.

Dolph dropped his gun and threw up his hands.

"Drop the heater!" one of the newly-arrived cops shouted.

The Cemetery Man seemed to give Dolph a sneer—a promise that they'd finish their business later—then, in a series of snake-fast moves, he holstered his remaining pistol, heaved Jebediah Debbs over his shoulder, got a running start, and leapt right up onto a second floor brownstone ledge from the street.

"Hey!" one of the cops yelled.

The Cemetery Man crawled up the façade of the brownstone, carrying Debbs along with him. He made the roof in ten seconds, heaved himself up and over the coping, then disappeared into the rainy night.

Irving and Benji were up now. They both looked to Dolph.

"Come on, boys," Dolph said. "Out the back."

They went.

23

Fralene, Beau and the Reverend Brown stood vigil at Uncle Barnabus's bedside. He lay peacefully, his breathing slow and steady but shallow. Since the apparent expulsion of the thing that possessed him, he hadn't moved or shown any sign of life or consciousness. Fralene had tried to call Dr. Corveaux, but Dub wasn't answering his phone. He'd promised to get her answers. She hoped to God that nothing had happened to him. If he'd put himself in a tight spot to try and figure out what was wrong with her uncle and her uncle ended up a comatose shell anyway… she wasn't sure she could bear both losses.

Worse, ever since the demon had departed his body, it seemed to have taken up residence in the house—disembodied, but still making noise. As she and Beau and the Reverend Brown attended to her grandfather— removing all the accouterments and artifacts of the exorcism, giving him a quick bathing with a warm cloth, changing him into a set of clean pajamas—strange forces continued to assail the house around them. Fralene felt a cold hand on her shoulder when she ran downstairs to dispose of the frayed and charred binding ropes. Reverend Brown told her when she returned that he'd felt something similar—cold hands, breath on the nape of his neck, the ghost of a voice in his ear. While the three of them tried to carry on with getting her uncle clean and comfortable, a caddy containing her uncle's cuff-links, clean handkerchiefs and pocket change had flown off the bureau, catapulted by some unseen force.

And then, after almost an hour of oppressive silence, broken only by the beating rain on the roof and some distant, indistinct sounds like the backfiring of a bevy of automobiles, there was the familiar message.

Fralene was alone with her uncle, the Reverend Brown and Beau having both gone downstairs to make some coffee, eggs and toast. As she sat there in a chair beside his immobile, unresponsive body, the bathroom door suddenly slammed shut behind her. It was so sudden, so loud, that it shot her right up out of her chair. She was on her feet, spinning toward the sound in an instant.

Behind the door, she heard the tub faucets turn. Water thumped into the tub.

"Oh God," she muttered. "Not again."

She thought that, perhaps, she should wait for the Reverend Brown to return. But after a few minutes of standing there, staring at the closed door and listening to water rumble into the claw foot tub, Fralene decided she couldn't stand it any longer.

So she marched to the door and threw it open.

She stared into a roiling mist now thick in the little washroom because only the hot water had been turned on.

Just like before, there was a message scrawled, as if by fingertip, on the surface of the steamed-over mirror.

Still here, it said.

Fralene shut off the water, fled the room, and moved her chair from the left side of her uncle's bed—where her back was to the washroom door—to the far right side. That's where she'd been sitting now for fifteen minutes, staring straight at the washroom door, awaiting another manifestation.

None came.

Would they have to exorcise the whole house now?

Beau and the Reverend Brown arrived, carrying steaming cups of coffee and a platter of eggs and toast. When they saw Fralene's straight-backed, nervous posture they instantly knew something was wrong.

"What is it?" Beau asked.

She took one of the coffee cups and pointed toward the washroom. "Go see," she said.

Beau, still carrying the plate of toast and eggs, ducked into the washroom and stared at the steamed-over mirror. He turned back to Fralene. There was a look of terrible fear on his young face.

"No way," he said.

"You see the message," she said. "It's still here!"

One of the bedroom windows suddenly rattled, as if beaten by a fist. Fralene cried out and dropped her coffee cup. The

Reverend Brown managed to hold onto his. Uncle Barnabus lay on the bed, breathing, but as good as dead.

The rapping at the window came again.

Fralene hurried to the Reverend Brown's side and they both peered through the window out into the dark, rainy night. Rainwater poured down the pane in sheets, but they could clearly see a bulky black shadow outside.

The shadow knocked again.

It was the Cemetery Man.

Fralene lunged for the window and threw up the sash. The Cemetery Man crouched on the porch roof outside. The rain beat down on him and rolled off in thick rivulets, but he didn't seem to care. He made no move to come in through the window.

"How is he?" he asked, nodding toward Uncle Barnabus.

Fralene shook her head. "He hasn't opened his eyes… hasn't stirred once."

"Does there seem to be a problem?" he asked.

"No," the Reverend Brown answered. "He just lays there. Responds to nothing. The body keeps on operating but it's like… well, it's like no one's home."

"Come in," Fralene said. "You have to see something."

The Cemetery Man hesitated. "I'll make a mess," he said.

"I'll clean it up," Fralene insisted. "Just hurry, before it's gone."

Moments later, the Cemetery Man was leaving puddles on her uncle's bedroom floor, tracking cold wet footprints across the boards and the rug as Fralene led him into the washroom. The steam was long-dissipated, but the message on the mirror was still clear. The Cemetery Man studied it, turned to study the comatose reverend, then studied the message again.

"Is it the demon?" Fralene asked. "Is it really still here?"

"No," the Cemetery Man said. "Not the demon."

XX

Doc Voodoo had suspicions as to just what that message on the washroom mirror suggested, but he didn't want to share them with Fralene. He knew he had to get back to his sanctum, to have a quick palaver with Erzulie and Legba and Ogou, and to take action as quickly as he could.

After disposing of the dead gunman in the downstairs hall and recovering the trussed-up Jebediah Debbs from the rooftop where he'd been left, Doc hurried back to his private sanctum. He deposited Debbs on the earth floor, the fat man's arms, hands and eyes bound by the *Serpent d'Ogou*.

"Where am I?" Debbs boomed. "I demand to know, you demon from—"

Doc snapped his fingers. His serpentine scarf tightened its coils and added gag to its list of duties. Debbs spoke only in vowels after that.

Finally, Doc summoned Erzulie and Legba so that he could speak to the two of them along with Ogou. Outside, the rain still didn't let up.

He offered his own theory on the strange messages in the steamed up mirror, as well as the poltergeist activity.

"Is it true?" he demanded. "It's the only explanation I can think of."

Sounds about right, Legba answered. *If some low-end Ghede in Kalfou's employ took up residence in the reverend's body for a time, he might have shunted the reverend's soul right out of its body into the borderlands beyond the Guinee Door.*

On the other side of the Guinee Door lay the borderlands to the world of the dead.

And if that is the case, Erzulie added, *then the reverend's attempts at communication from beyond that door could look at awful lot like a haunting to someone who didn't know any better. He'd be in an Otherworld that bore some resemblance to his everyday plane, but where time and space were all topsy-turvy. He'd be out of phase with the people and events around him. Given that, he could've resorted to trying to communicate by knocking down random objects and writing messages on steamy mirrors.*

"Is there any way to draw him back?" Doc asked,

There was a long, uncomfortable silence in the center of his mind.

Short of passing through the door yourself and drawing him out? Legba asked. *No. No way that I know.*

"Then I'm going through the Guinee Door," Doc said, "and draw him out myself."

No, Ogou said.

I wouldn't recommend it, Erzulie added.

We can't protect you there, boy, Legba argued. *If you go through horsed, then we're trespassing on some other lwa's turf. We're breaking rules we swore not to break in the most ancient of days.*

"This is non-negotiable," Doc assured them. "I can't leave the man over there indefinitely."

It's not indefinite, Legba said. *All the dead pass through there on their way to the Far Side, like a giant train station.*

"The reverend's not dead," Doc countered. "He was forced out of his body by a trespasser."

But he can't dwell in the borderlands forever, Legba answered. *There's only two ways out: he either finds his own way back to his body and wakes, or he gets drawn by the Realms of the Dead and passes on, beyond the veil, to the Far Side. No spirit can dwell in the borderlands indefinitely.*

"So how long might it take to draw him back to his body?"

Years, Erzulie said. *And by that time, his body itself could have wasted away and died—in which case his spirit would have nowhere to return to—or his spirit and consciousness could have been driven mad by their time beyond the doorway, so he'd be back in his own body, but he'd be crazy as a loon for the rest of his life.*

"We're back to non-negotiable."

You go after him, Ogou said, *and you're inviting a war on the higher plane. And what if the reverend's not just lost on the other side? What if Kalfou's actually holding him?*

Legba hummed thoughtfully. *Hard to pry an offering out of a lwa's greedy fingers.*

"I take it you speak from experience," Doc cut in. "What about a trade? Debbs there for the reverend?"

Debbs made an inquisitive sound. Doc ignored him.

It could work, Erzulie said. *In currency terms, flesh is flesh.*

I still don't like it, Ogou grumbled.

"This is a good man—a man with plenty of years left in him! If Rae Gooden summoned that ghede from beyond the door, then Kalfou already broke that truce. You're setting things straight, not trespassing—"

Kalfou won't see it that way, Erzulie assured him.

Debbs was back to struggling against his bonds where he lay. He couldn't hear the voices of the lwa—those were only in Dub Corveaux's head. All he heard was the Cemetery Man, apparently talking to himself, and only having one side of a conversation at that.

"Enough of this," Doc snarled. He hurried to his altar and went rooting among the litter of offerings and ritual implements. In moments, he found what he needed. Chalk in hand, he moved to the nearest outer wall of the peristyle—brick, solid, two feet thick. He drew a large, upright rectangle on the brick, taller than himself, and finished it with a small, chalky circle set about halfway up its length, on the far left.

"There," he said, throwing down the chalk. "There's my door. One of you better open it."

He knocked three times on the brick, three more, then three more. After the ninth knock, he reached down and touched the small circle. It had become a dry, chalky, three-dimensional doorknob. His peristyle was already charged and his rituals completed at the night's opening: such simple magic—a door to the other side—was easily undertaken in such a charged space.

But his magic could only *create* the door. He needed one of his patrons to unlock it, to allow him access, to shuttle him through.

"Well?" he asked.

This is a bad idea, Ogou snarled.

Your power may not be as potent on the other side, Legba warned. *Even if the three of us ride along.*

Doc Voodoo hove Jebediah Debbs onto one shoulder like a stack of fertilizer. Even with his super strength, the man was heavy.

"Are you opening this door, or aren't you?" Doc demanded.

There was a low, scuffling shift in the wall of bricks. The door had suddenly leapt forth, three-dimensional, its attendant bricks standing out from their fellows on either side or above. It sounded like a stone tomb opening after centuries of lying in wait.

Doc grasped the door knob and pulled. Slowly, heavily, the brick door opened, revealing a misty blue mirror image of the room behind him.

Then, he felt his patrons settle upon him, like layers of clothing for an explorer stepping into some cold and polar regions. Ogou wasn't his only rider now; Erzulie and Legba had joined the party as well.

"Lead me to him," Doc said. "The faster I find him, the faster we leave."

I still say this is a bad idea, Ogou growled.

But they all followed him when he stepped through to brave the other side.

24

Doc Voodoo studied his surroundings. He was in a simulacrum of his peristyle, although herein bright blue light flooded in through the high windows and there was a strange, low roaring sound in the air, like a steady wind in one's ears on a vast, empty prairie. It was his sanctum, yet it wasn't. Looking behind him, he could still see back through the door that he'd used to access this plane. His own peristyle was on the far side—dark, shadowy, lit only by candles. Here, it seemed bright enough to be daytime… except that the bright light pouring in through the windows was not precisely daylight. It was, rather, as if someone had cranked up the moon to five or ten times its normal brightness.

He had only been here once before, and that was after being so wounded as Dr. Dub Corveaux that he was literally shuttled here, to Death's Door. He didn't care for it. He needed to find the reverend and get the hell out.

At least Debbs was a lighter load on this side. The fat man bucked. Doc gave him a low-powered cuff to the ribs.

Still with me? he asked his patrons. Although he commanded his mouth to move and his voice to come forth, he did not hear himself speak. Instead, his voice sounded in the middle of his brain like a poor radio signal, muffled and indistinct, so distant it was as if someone else spoke.

Here, Erzulie said.

Here, Legba said.

Wish I wasn't, Ogou said.

Doc was satisfied. He found the stairway, descended, and eventually emerged onto the street outside the Otherworld's doppelganger of his brownstone on 136th Street.

Going through the Guinee Door was like going through the Looking Glass. The world on the other side was not so unlike the world that Doc hailed from—except that it was completely different. Time and space were collapsed, so that seemingly large spaces could be covered in moments, while passage across seemingly short distances could feel like a long, slow slog through a swamp. The colors of the bricks, the walls, the streets, the buildings, the sky… they all seemed muted and dulled, like an old, faded painting or photograph. Nonetheless, amid those faded colors and darkened shadows, there were strange pools of light or color that seemed to bleed-through from the world of the living: a puddle of light below a certain streetlamp; the lamp glow and moving silhouettes behind a certain curtained window; a specific shopkeeper's sign; a lone car parked on the Otherworldly streets.

But the strangest addition were the strollers. Spirits moved up and down these twilit streets, spirits that had forms and faces, but no substance, like the spirit of Mambo Rae Rae. They wandered like towers of vapor loosed from a sewer grate or a subway vent, appearing only as wispy apparitions without form or feature one moment, as ghostly people with sorrowful faces and wide, staring eyes the next. Most, he knew, would wander here in the borderlands for a time before they were naturally drawn to the last gateway between this pocket plane and the next, to return to the Source or to be cast into the Abyss. What went on beyond those borders, Doc could not say. No one ever moved beyond those borders and returned. These apparitions that surrounded him—they were just the last remnants of the dead. When their essence passed on, some measure of their ectoplasmic forms would remain here, like the warm spot a hand left after long idling on a cold table, or an old box of precious artifacts stored in an attic, awaiting discovery.

Okay, then, Doc said, once again chilled by the distance of his own voice in his ears, *where do we begin?*

Draw out your pendants, Legba suggested.

Doc did so. He held up the neck chain and let the knot of *veve* pendants dangle freely. For a moment, they seemed to hang still, straight down, but after a time, the pendants began to rise up, gently tugging on the chain they hung from, drawn away from Doc as if by a magnet.

On the other side, Legba said, *their polarity shifts and they're drawn to life-force—the kind possessed by a living being.*

It's not reading me? Doc asked. *Or Debbs here?*

You're both at the center of the veves' power, Legba said. *They'll never read you.*

Doc nodded and followed the angle of the dangling *veve* pendants.

The projection of Harlem that lay beyond the Guinee Door was like the one he knew from the other side, yet different as well. The wrong streets crossed the wrong avenues. Distances were alternately longer than their real-world counterparts, or shorter. Straight streets curved. Flat streets rose like hills or fell like valleys. Sometimes, the buildings on either side of the street seemed to loom, as though they were in danger of toppling and falling right on top of him.

All the while as he followed the gentle tug of the pendants, he passed the denizens of this Otherworldly way station: disembodied spirits, personified hopes and fears wandering like stray or abandoned animals, fonts of etheric energy that would manifest in the real world as thin membranes in the fabric of reality; low-level *lwa*, locative spirits and demons lingering in the doorways, on the stoops of the strange, otherworldly brownstones, or in the shadows. He was truly in another neighborhood here. On someone else's turf.

He didn't care for it.

Then, someone or something laughed. It was a low, rumbling, throaty sound, and it came not to Doc's ears but sounded right in the center of his brain and even seemed to pass through the strange silver and indigo night clouds that tumbled across the etheric sky above him. It was laughter, but a laughter manifested as thunder, and when that sound filled his own mortal mind and rolled across the sky, all the spirits and demons in his vicinity, large and small, scattered and ran for cover like scared mice.

The Dread Baron froze where he stood.

Even Debbs stopped grunting and struggling.

What was that? he asked.

I don't think you want to know, Ogou said.

Why would he be here? Erzulie asked. *Just waiting for us?*

Why would who *be here?* Doc demanded.

Could be this is his turf, Legba offered. *It's the ultimate crossroads, after all. Butts right up against his Big Black plane.*

Or it could be we've gotten on his bad side, Ogou added, *seeing as we hustled his soldier out of that Holy Man and all.*

Who are we talking about here? Doc asked. *Kalfou?*

The laughter came again, the sound of a storm approaching—a storm that was malevolent, and sentient, and eager to shower its rage and hatred and vitriol upon the world.

He haunts the crossroads, Legba said.

I thought you *haunted the crossroads?* Doc asked.

I facilitate crossings, Legba corrected. *I give aid to those at places of determination, places of chance and opportunity. I point the way at the crossroads, to see the petitioner safely guided to a good end… but Kalfou, he* owns *the crossroad. He owns the random disaster, the one bad choice, the obsession that leads to total damnation.*

But it's more than that, Ogou said. *This isn't just about Kalfou being on the make. This is about the fact that you—that we— deliberately crossed him and undid his plans. Kalfou doesn't take kindly to such interference.*

We can stand against him, right? Doc asked. *I'm a living man, so I've got more potency here than some lost soul or low-level infernal. Hell, I even brought an offering. And the three of you—*

We're on Kalfou's turf, Erzulie said sternly. *That means we're stuck playing by Kalfou's rules.*

Find the reverend, Ogou ordered.

Get us out of here, Legba added.

The Dread Baron drew a deep, shuddering breath. *Fine. Let's do this.*

He studied the bend of the pendant chain and followed it around a corner.

The street unraveled before them, bending and undulating in ways that its worldly counterpart never would or could, but still providing a more or less clear view down its wobbly length into the distance. The forced perspective of the misaligned, looming buildings focused Doc's sight on what lay far ahead. He squinted under the harsh blue light of the big, bilious moon that hung in the sky above and thought that what he saw in the distance was the Park Avenue Bridge… or rather, a twin of the Park Avenue Bridge that only resembled its real world counterpart in the most superficial ways. For one thing, it seemed to arc across the Harlem River instead of lying flat. For another, that arc seemed much longer than the length of the real bridge. There seemed to be another strange factor at work, but from this distance and with his senses scrambled, Doc couldn't be sure of just what it was.

Somewhere, a hound bayed. The sounds echoed down the canyons of the ghost plane around him, weaving this way and that like winds shaped by the lay of the land and the walls of architecture hemming them in. In the midst of the first bay still sounding, Doc heard another hound bay in answer. They were both off to his right, one further uptown, one seemingly downtown. But, as he stood and listened and the bays wove and sparred and tumbled around one another in the fetid air, he realized something.

They were getting closer.

Move, Ogou snarled.

The Dread Baron broke into a run. It wasn't easy, with Debbs's bulk perched on his shoulder. With his free hand he still held the pendant chain out before him, and he still let them determine his path. Their gentle tug led him onward up the strange and winding Park Avenue that he moved upon, noting how the ground would rise and fall in soft, curved waves like a frozen concrete ocean, how the empty, dark windows of the buildings around him seemed to glower and stare, or even how lights would sometimes switch on in those dark windows, like eyes opening to assay his passage and glare their disapproval. Doc did his best to push these realizations aside. All he was interested in now was the reverend. Retrieving him, guiding him, seeing him safely back on the other side of the Guinee Door.

The hounds bayed again. They were close now… closer than Doc dared imagine.

I know those sounds, Doc offered. *Those are the same sounds I heard when I conjured Mambo Rae Rae's spirit and the hellhounds came for her.*

They're common as curs on this side, Legba said. *Although they don't tend to hunt the living when the living move here.*

Not unless they belong to someone, Ogou said, *and someone set them on us.*

Doc realized what Ogou was suggesting: the hounds he heard baying might be a brace owned by Kalfou. If so, they'd been set loose specifically to hunt him down or flush him out.

Doc did his best to shut out the noises that assailed him from all sides, but it wasn't easy. He was vulnerable here… trapped…

isolated. One wrong move, one enemy stronger than the *maji* supporting him, and he'd be done for. And who knew—dying while trespassing in the borderlands could have a stiffer penalty than dying on the material plane. Maybe here, your spirit couldn't be loosed to its final rest at all, and you just sat out eternity, floating aimless and free like all the apparitions that Doc had seen upon his first arrival. Worse, maybe over here one never truly died at all if one came in his physical body. He shuddered to think what could happen to him if his patrons were forced to unhorse him… if he ended up mortal, but stranded on this in-between plane.

On he ran. Like a dream, the street stretched out before him and frustrated his forward progress. The faster he went, the farther away the bridge and his quarry seemed to get.

Debbs bucked and made a guttural, insistent sound.

Hold still, Doc growled. *I'll deal with you soon enough.*

The bays sounded again, followed by the low sound of throaty snarls. Doc thought he could hear the panting of great beasts rising in his ears now; the sound of their obsidian claws scraping the pavement as they hurried on; smell the brimstone on their breath and the feel the ambient temperature of the air around him rise, increment by increment.

I need a plan, Doc said, stopping in the middle of an intersection. The fat man bucked again but the scarf still held fast on his eyes, mouth and hands. The Dread Baron scanned all sides, dropped the pendant chain back around his neck to free his hands.

No plan, Legba countered. *On the other side, we could offer suggestions, but here—*

We don't know what'll work on this side, Ogou interrupted. *You best keep moving.*

The hounds bayed. The sound was close and shot infernal cold through Doc's being like a subcutaneous injection of frozen silver.

Debbs huffed and mumbled. He bucked like a fish drowning in air.

Stay quiet, Doc growled, *and they might ignore you.*

Debbs didn't seem to get the message. Doc resolved to ignore him.

If he walked, the street stretched. If he ran, it stretched farther and faster.

So I won't run, Doc decided. *Hell, I won't even walk.*

He stopped where he stood. The bridge still seemed to be at least a mile away.

What's this about? Ogou asked.

Playing a hunch, Doc replied, and closed his eyes.

He waited. He wasn't precisely sure what he was waiting for. All he knew was that he would stand for a time, eyes closed, and just wait. The baying of the hounds grew uncomfortably close, their throaty snarls now as little as a block away.

Doc struggled to keep his eyes shut, to will himself where he wanted to go. This wasn't real, physical space, after all. There wasn't real movement on this side, only will… intent. A fast march hadn't gotten him where he was going; neither had a hearty sprint. Maybe just standing here, eyes shut, and expecting that bridge to be right in front of him when he opened his eyes would work.

He opened his eyes.

It had worked. He was right at the entrance to the bridge—right where he'd willed himself to be.

Then he heard the hellhounds and turned.

It was a good plan, Legba said. *Just a moment too late, is all.*

Shit, Doc said.

There were two of them—big as horses—and they were so black that they almost looked like wells of shadow punched right out of the world around them—pockets of nothingness shaped like hounds, with only two fiery pin-pricks for eyes. Their snarling was deep and guttural—the sound of bull alligators mating or lions preparing for a kill.

They each stood less than a block away, and they were closing.

Their fire-ball eyes settled on Doc. For the first time since he'd been taken under the wing of his three *lwa* patrons—for the first time since discovering that the old gods still held power in the world—he knew the fear of death.

So the Dread Baron did what he always did when Death stared him down: he threw Jebediah Debbs off his shoulder to free his hands and went for his guns. In a breath, the twin .45s were ready to spark and bark when his fingers tensed on their triggers.

The hounds charged.

Doc opened fire. Flossy tongues of flame spat from the pistol muzzles and shells flew from the ejection ports, but the shots were muffled in his ears and sounded like little more than firecrackers popping under cotton wadding. Still the hellhounds charged. They'd be on him in moments.

Not working, Ogou said.

No shit, Doc countered. Though it flew in the face of logic and defied his instincts, he did the only thing he imagined that could save him. He holstered his pistols, reached under the length of his coat, and drew out the *Machette d'Ogou*. When the blade was freed, it burst into flame and he held it in two hands before him like a fairy tale knight on guard with his sword against a charging dragon.

Although in this case, there were *two* dragons.

The hellhounds leapt.

Doc lunged.

The flaming machete split the air in a long, fierce arc, biting deep into the flank of one of the leaping hounds, then smoothly rising on his trajectory to slash crosswise over the belly of the other.

Doc's lunge carried him forward. Both hounds screamed, roared and thrashed as they hit the pavement where he'd been standing just moments before. They bent against their wounds, both slashes smoking and hissing, bleeding soot and flame and cinders instead of blood or entrails. Each turned their lamplight eyes on him, snarled, and rounded for another pounce.

Don't wait, Ogou barked. *Take the fight to them! Now!*

Doc did as he was told.

The hellhounds may have looked like a pair of shadows punched out of a starless sky, but they had a terrifying mass and weight when they pounced, just as they spat noxious fumes redolent of burning flesh and brimstone when they snapped and snarled and slashed with their stony black claws. The Dread Baron sparred and grappled with them. More than once he felt their teeth—burning, charring, like red hot brands against his flesh. Once or twice they got in deep slashes with their claws—burning, smoldering, like a quartet of cigarette burns that cut right through his clothing and raked across his skin. Little matter. Doc gave as good as he got and better. He slashed and hacked and thrust with the flaming *Machette d'Ogou*, reveling in how deep it bit into the infernal beasts as they tried to double-team him and take him down.

But he wouldn't go down. He just kept fighting, eager to see if the machete could spill whatever guts these nasty curs from the depths of Hell might have, eager to kill them both or die trying.

Finally, he had them. One went down, a torn and discorporated mess, bleeding sulfurous smoke and cinders as its fellow turned and ran, howling and snarling as it went, trailing an Orcal vapor and a trail of swirling cinders in its wake.

Doc struggled for breath. His clothes were burned and torn, as though he'd passed through a fire. Here and there his bare, brown flesh showed through, replete with cauterized slash-marks and gouges and dried rivulets of blood.

Well done, Ogou said.

Doc didn't even answer. He looked to Debbs's trussed-up bulk on the sidewalk. The demagogue was still grunting and thrashing.

Let's get this done, Doc said, *and get the hell out of here.*

He turned. There before him was the Otherworld's reflection of the Park Avenue Bridge, arcing and stretching across a vast gulf of windy darkness that bordered this phantasmal Harlem just as the Harlem River did, but that seemed to be no river at all. The Dread Baron, finding himself in the intersection of Park Avenue and Harlem River Drive, moved forward to the shoulder of the road, where there would normally be a slope and some bare stone and dying grass and a lot of detritus and garbage in a broad carpet all the way down to where the river lapped at the bank. But here, there was no river. There was just a deep, abyssal darkness that seemed to having no source and no bottom.

He looked left. He looked right. The void occupied the river's space, as far as his eye could see, and far off to his right, where the East River would normally separate Manhattan from Brooklyn, he saw just another gulf of darkness, and nothing on the far side. If there was a phantom Brooklyn over there, he couldn't see it.

Doc reached into his shirt and lifted out his *veve* pendants. He held them up, let them dangle. The chain slowly bent sideward, lifted by invisible hands. They now bent backward, to a point just over his left shoulder. Had he passed his quarry?

He turned.

The man he sought—and the beast he didn't—waited in an empty lot veiled in mist and shadows behind the last looming brownstone on the corner of Park Avenue. When Doc saw the

Reverend Barnabus Farnes—and the thing that held him—he felt a fear deeper, surer, and more unendurable than he had ever known. It shot right to the core of his being, seeming to freeze his beating heart in his chest and turn the blood in his veins to winter currents from the Hudson locked beneath glacial, wintery ice.

Kalfou held the Reverend Barnabus Farnes in his his arms like a doll, the old man's mouth covered and his cries choked by one great skeletal hand. The reverend bucked and struggled in Kalfou's grip, and his eyes were wide and frightened, but there was still life in him—still fight.

What can you do for me? Doc asked, planting his feet wide, letting go the pendants.

His patrons didn't answer.

Kalfou stepped from the shadows and Doc got a better look at him. He was vaguely human in shape, but stood over ten feet tall and was skeletally thin, like some titanic scarecrow meant for prehistoric birds. The clothes that the great apparition wore were a ragged patchwork made from old clothes and the flayed skins of men, and ended well short of the creature's long, thin forearms and tapering, bony calves and ankles. A slouching, wide-brimmed hat lay askew on the *lwa*'s large, leathery, rotten-apple head and shadowed the upper part of its face save for the deeply recessed glitter of its eyes.

Doc stared. He knew that some *lwa* had terrible true forms. He also knew that those true forms were often more terrible when viewed up close, on a crossover plane like this one, as opposed to viewing via visions, dreams, or ceremonial possession. But this thing that towered above him now, that slouched and lurched from its shadowy hiding place between the looming brownstones of this half-dead otherworld, that held the frightened, struggling Reverend Barnabus Farnes in its big skeletal hands like a child … this thing was more frightening and malign than anything that Dub Corveaux could have ever imagined.

And worse: there was a deep, malign *vitality* to it. This was no mindless beast of sulfur and smoke like the hellhounds, no meandering whisp of cold and memory like the ghosts that haunted this other Harlem's streets… this thing, this Kalfou, was alive and intent and sneering and eager to end him—after torturing him and seeing his hopes first utterly dashed.

Kalfou smiled. It had pickets of rotten, misaligned teeth in a wide scar of a mouth hiding a serpentine purple tongue behind them. The smile was a sign of its evil intent. It held up the Reverend Farnes.

Lose something, horse? the Haunter of the Crossroads asked. Its voice was like a night wind howling through the eves of a haunted old house.

Terrified, Doc rolled Debbs off his shoulders and dropped him on the pavement. *I'm here to offer a trade*, he said, *my prisoner for yours.*

He whistled and the *Serpent d'Ogou* scarf uncoiled from Debbs and slithered back across the pavement to climb Doc's staunch form and settle once more on his shoulders. Free at last, Debbs got a look at Kalfou and his eyes grew big as saucers. His mouth fell open, he screamed to wake the dead, then he turned and ran off deeper into the phantom city around them.

For just a moment, Doc felt sorry for the fat demagogue and the fate that awaited him here.

But only for a moment.

He ain't nothing to me, Kalfou said. *I got me a holy man.*

Draw the Machette d'Ogou, Ogou said in Doc's mind. *Let me take over.*

But—

Now!

The Dread Baron drew the blade. The *Machette d'Ogou* flared, the flames that dressed its blade roiling and brightening in intensity as if dipped in petrol.

Doc wasn't sure he wanted to defer to Ogou entirely. True, the *lwa* was his patron and protector and was always, in some sense, with him. But to totally surrender his body to the *lwa*—to become a vessel for an in-dwelling instead of a mere horse—it was a terrible risk.

For one thing, Ogou might decide he liked having a body, and refuse to give it up. If Dub Corveaux willingly surrendered his body to Ogou, even Reverand Brown might not drive the *lwa* back out of him.

We don't have time for this, Ogou snarled. *You've got to trust me!*

Doc wasn't sure he trusted any creature of the aether—even his own patrons—with his own body. But what choice did he have? Staring down Kalfou filled him with a fear he hadn't known since fighting in the trenches of the Great War. If he didn't take the strength that Ogou offered, what else did he have to fight with?

Kalfou took a step toward him.

I'm all yours, Dub Corveaux said, his fear of the beast before him overcoming his distrust of a full-on possession.

He felt Ogou step forward. What had been a vague presence just over his shoulder became part of his own consciousness, his body, his spirit. All of the sudden, in a mad, roaring, rush, Dr. Dub Corveaux's fear fled. He felt Ogou's fire fill him from top to toe, from his tingling fingers down to his trembling toes. In that instant, he became righteous rage, fearless indignation, the strength that came from purpose and the surety that came with passion.

In answer to his newfound power and the dissolution of his fear, the *Machette d'Ogou* flared up in his grip, the flames billowing forth brighter and hotter than before, as though its thirst had been quenched with white hot magnesium.

Now! Ogou snarled. *Let's take this bastard's feet right out from under him!*

They charged Kalfou and brought the *Machette d'Ogou* sweeping round in a wide flaming arc. Kalfou saw the lunge and the blade and took a single step backward in anticipation of it.

But Ogou closed the distance between them in a breath and his blade bit deep. He chopped right through the rotten, corded meat that covered Kalfou's bones and the beast above him howled and shuddered, rocking against the pain. As it threw its arms out in fury and terror, the Reverend Farnes braced himself, apparently sure that he was about to be thrown.

Ogou didn't waste another moment. Seeing how deeply his blade bit, the agony that it caused Kalfou, however fleeting, he spun on his heels, letting the force of his strike carry his whole body round, and struck again at Kalfou's opposite calf. Once more, the *lwa's* rotten flesh sizzled when kissed by the flames and the iron. The giant rocked and roared.

This time, the Reverend Farnes fell free. He tumbled through the air and hit the pavement hard, but managed to roll himself sideward out of Kalfou's reach. Seeing this little piece of fortune, Ogou wove around Kalfou's bare and shifting feet and charged. As Kalfou bent to snap up the reverend again, Ogou brought his flaming machete down once more. He sliced off two of the dread lord's fingers. The bony protrusions turned to ash and cinder the moment they were separated from Kalfou's body and disappeared on a skirl of wind.

Run! Ogou shouted at the reverend, though the strange acoustics on this plane still made his voice sound faint and far away, like someone else's voice, spoken in some other room beyond a wall.

The Reverend Barnabus Farnes scrambled to his feet, and scurried for freedom, out beyond Kalfou's reach.

They turned just in time to see the big *lwa* bending toward them, both enormous skeletal hands spreading above him and falling like striking spiders. They hacked and slashed with his flaming machete, taking pieces of Kalfou with every savage swipe of the flame-licked blade, but Kalfou still managed to get them in his grip. The big *lwa* yanked them up off the pavement and drew them toward his rotten mouth, like a giant from a child's fairy tale. Drawn toward that terrible, shriveled face, those burning, deep-set eyes and that yawning, rotten-toothed mouth, Dub knew fear again.

Trespasser! Kalfou snarled as he drew him near, then shook him. *Burglar! Thief! I'll toss you into the hell of my own gut and let you roast and roil for all eternity in the brimstone fires that fill my belly! Even your precious patrons won't be able to save you once I've made a meal of you!*

He lifted them right up to his mouth and opened wide. His rotten jaw seemed to come unhinged and his maw yawned deep and wide like the mouth of some enormous snake. A great black gulf rife with the stench of rot and hellfires yawned beneath them as they were up-ended in preparation for being tossed down the hungry god's hatch.

Kalfou's hands crammed him into his rotten mouth.

Ogou shoved his flaming machete right into Kalfou's gaping maw. He slashed the *lwa's* throat, its whipping tongue, its rotten, worm-ridden gums. Smoke bellowed up and out of the open mouth and rotten flesh sizzled and popped and blistered.

Kalfou screamed and dropped his morsel.

Doc landed hard on the warped pavement and rolled clear. The *Machette d'Ogou* clattered on the pavement beside him, its fires doused. Doc felt weaker, less potent and less fearless than he had when Ogou had been in control of him.

That's it, Ogou said in the center of Doc's brain. *That's all I've got to give. Run for it.*

Doc looked to the Reverend Barnabus Farnes. The old man already had a good head start. He was still looking back over his shoulder, waiting for the Cemetery Man to follow, amazed at Kalfou's apparent agony as it bent and spat black blood and brimstone smoke from its slashed and ruined gullet. The Dread Baron shouted at the old man again.

Run! he commanded. *I'm right behind you!*

The reverend ran. Doc snatched up the flamed-out *Machette d 'Ogou* and followed.

In moments, he had reached the reverend's side. For just a moment, he marveled at how quickly the old man moved—how spry and healthy he seemed for a man of seventy. Then he remembered that this wasn't really the reverend at all: it was the reverend's living soul, separated from its body and isolated here on the Guinee plane. No doubt, this shadow of the reverend—this shuttle for his consciousness and intellect—could do a great many things that the real, fleshly reverend could not.

Where are we running to? the reverend asked, his voice having that same faraway, muffled quality as Doc's own.

Behind them, Kalfou came stomping down the street, roaring like a summer storm, howling like a hurricane wind, his long, skeletal legs taking impossible strides that closed the distance between he and his quarry with terrifying speed. As he cried out, all the looming brownstones seemed to alternately quail and loom closer, as though they were minions of the Haunter of the Crossroads, felt his pain and his fury, and sought to harry and slow Doc's escape. Worse, his fury seemed to be empowering him somehow. Doc thought at first it might just be a trick of perspective, but soon enough saw the truth: as Kalfou stomped after them, he grew larger and larger.

He rage was making him more powerful.

Doc ran faster. He clamped one hand on the reverend's arm and drew him along. The street warped and wobbled beneath them, like a barrel bridge floating on unquiet waters. The whole of the spectral world around them trembled and rearranged itself in answer to Kalfou's fury. The distance ahead of them stretched out, further and further with each sprinting stride they took. Behind them, Kalfou seemed to close without even straining.

Have you forgot what you learned already? Legba said in the center of Doc's mind.

Forgotten what? Doc asked, still running, still dragging the reverend along beside him. He threw a glance back and saw Kalfou gaining, his long strides carrying him closer and closer by the moment.

Running will get you nowhere on this side, Erzulie said.

Close your eyes, Legba urged. *Picture where you're going.*

He's right behind us! Doc snapped in answer.

A moment's peace and concentration is all that'll get you out of this, Erzulie countered. *Do it! And tell the reverend to do the same!*

They were right and he knew it. It had worked before. It should work again.

I want you to think of One Hundred and Thirty-Sixth Street, Doc shouted at the reverend. *Right at the corner of Seventh Avenue! Can you?*

What do you mean, think of—

Picture it in your mind! Doc commanded. *Think of the buildings. Think of the view. Most of all, think of those two street signs, one mounted atop the other on the corner street light.*

The reverend nodded. He was still keeping pace. No matter— the faster they ran, the farther their destination seemed to be from them, and the closer Kalfou seemed to get.

Just do it! Paint that picture! Tell me when you've got it!

The reverend looked perplexed for a moment, then seemed to concentrate.

I think I've got it, he said.

Close your eyes, Doc said.

The reverend looked at him like he was insane. *I won't be able to see—*

Paint the picture and close your goddamned eyes! Doc roared.

The reverend did as he was told.

Doc did the same.

A moment later, their blind flight took them right into a brick wall. Each man slammed into the barrier with incredible force. Nonetheless, there was no pain, no lost breath or dazed collapse. There was just the sudden shock of realizing that they had hit an impenetrable barrier, and the recoil from it.

As they stumbled backward from the wall, each opened their eyes. They stood on the corner of 136th Street and 7th Avenue. They had run into a brownstone that stood on the northwest corner. There were spirits swarming the streets, and Kalfou was nowhere in sight.

Come on, Doc urged, dragging the reverend bodily toward the alley that ran behind the building. *We're almost there.*

Where are you taking me? the reverend demanded.

Doc ushered him on into the long, deep, dark alley that ran parallel to 136th Street. It was even more shadowy and isolated than its real world counterpart. Shadows in the shape of stray cats skulked at the edge of his vision and drifting ghosts wheeled above steaming sewer grates like pillars of smoke. Doc pointed toward a fire escape that ran up the backside of the second building along.

Climb, he said. *Fast.*

Before the reverend could open his mouth to ask just where they were going, something large and vaguely human appeared at the far end of the alley, off toward 8th Avenue.

It was Kalfou.

Move! Doc shouted, and all but threw the reverend up onto the lowest rung of the fire escape ladder. The old man climbed steadily and surely, as nimbly as a child. Nonetheless, he still seemed to move too slowly.

At the far end of the alley, Kalfou bounded nearer, his long, skeletal legs dancing crazily, his tall, gnarled form seeming to fill the alley from side to side like some bizarre, upright spider.

Doc clambored up the ladder beneath the reverend. *All the way to the top!* he shouted. *Climb into one of those attic windows when you reach them! You should see the door just inside!*

What door? The reverend called back down.

The door that'll take you home! Doc answered. He looked toward Kalfou. The *lwa* was nearly upon them, rotten-toothed grin looming in Doc's vision like an oncoming nightmare.

Doc stopped on the second landing of the fire escape, reached into his coat, and drew out his pistols. He blasted away, centering his fire right on Kalfou's shriveled, rotten face. The dead flesh and rotten skull beneath crumbled under the weight of that onslaught of pummeling, hammering, white hot lead... but Kalfou didn't stop. He was only slowed, stunned, momentarily blinded. He reeled back, ambling crazily from side to side in the alley as he tried to shake off the weight of the gunfire.

Doc kept climbing.

Up above, the Reverend had almost reached the top landing. He stopped, glancing back down at Doc as if to ask directions.

Don't stop! Doc roared. *You're almost there! Through that window!*

The window won't open! the reverend answered.

Then break it! Doc answered. *That's where we're going.*

Then the whole fire escape seemed to shudder beneath Doc and he swiveled his gaze. Kalfou was just beneath him, climbing up the building, using the fire escape for hand and foot-holds. The rotten head beneath its floppy, wide-brimmed hat leered up at them.

The Dread Baron reached into his coat, drew out a pair of govi grenades, and dropped them right into Kalfou's grinning face. They shattered on impact. A storm of red and blue spectral flames engulfed Kalfou's terrifying countenance and once again, the *lwa* roared and shook with rage—yet another annoyance in the path to his prey.

Doc climbed.

Above, the reverend had done as told and shattered the window. His shoes were just disappearing over the sill as Doc clambered onto the highest landing, launched himself upward, caught the lip of the sill with his gloved hands, and scrambled up and over the brick of the building's outer walls.

Below, Kalfou climbed, hand over hand, the last of the govi flames trailing off of him like the last drops of rain falling from a clearing sky.

The Dread Baron was helped through the window by the reverend, whose apparent strength once more reminded Doc that they weren't on the material plane anymore. When Doc had wriggled through the window and collapsed on the earthen floor of the big, wide attic, the reverend took a moment to study their surroundings. He didn't seem pleased by the vodou accouterments and sandy *veves* painted on the earthen floor.

What is this place? he asked.

Never mind, Doc said, scurrying to his feet and shoving the reverend so hard he almost knocked the old man off his. *Over there! That door in the outer wall!*

The reverend saw it but couldn't believe it—a door made of bricks opening right out of a wall that, by rights, should have had nothing but empty air and a four story drop on the other side. But looking through that strange portal, what the reverend saw on the other side was… a mirror image of the attic chamber they stood in.

Where will this take me? he asked.

Home, Doc said, and shoved him through.

He didn't wait to see if the reverend seemed to arrive in the peristyle on the far side, or if he simply disappeared upon crossing the barrier. Instead, Doc spun round, once more drawing his pistols from beneath his coat.

Kalfou's enormous, demonic face filled the window, his skeletal fingers creeping through on either side. He was trying to wriggle his entire enormous bulk through the window like a huge, misshapen baby trying to force its way into an unwelcoming world.

Then, Kalfou seemed to compose himself. His snarl turned to a sly grin. His head and body started to shudder… and shrink. In moments, he'd be able to scurry right through that window, and then there would be nothing keeping his hands from Doc's throat.

Doc opened fire, once more pumping round after round right into Kalfou's huge, hideous face and the gaping maw of his mouth.

Kalfou's head and shoulders wriggled through the open window. One long, skeletal arm reached out toward Doc.

Doc threw himself backward, hoping he was aligned with the open Guinee Door.

When he hit the earthen floor of his peristyle flat on his back and saw nothing but a brick wall above him, he knew that he'd made it.

25

His patrons assured him that Kalfou could not follow him back through the Guinee Door. Mortals who ventured through could return, and lost souls with living bodies awaiting them could do so as well, but the creatures that dwelt on the far side had to remain there, and could only take their vengeance or follow their quarry if someone on this side opened another door for them, invited them through, and gave them a horse to ride to see their reckoning accomplished.

That might be coming. Kalfou would not forget this insult. Nonetheless, the Haunter of the Crossroads was almost never invoked by sensible vodouisants. Dr. Dub Corveaux could breathe a sigh of relief. It might be some time before Dread Kalfou found someone on this side to facilitate his vengeance, and by then, the good doctor's three patrons—Legba, Erzulie, and Ogou—would have gathered their energies, warded their charge's sanctum, and prepared themselves and he—their champion—for the retaliation to come.

They assured him of this just as they left him with the sunrise. Unhorsed, the Dread Baron slept and Dr. Dub Corveaux descended his secret staircase to wash the night's terror off of him. Once he was clean and dressed, he skipped breakfast and hurried out, knowing that he had a patient to attend to.

XX

Dr. Dub Corveaux found a smiling, teary-eyed Fralene Farnes awaiting him at the Reverend Barnabus Farnes's house. He opened his eyes just before sunrise, she said, going from comatose unconsciousness to wide-eyed, staring disbelief in the blink of an eye. The old man woke in a fright, panting as though he'd just run a race, and his eyes darted all around the room as though he were shocked as could be that he found himself there.

According to Fralene, the reverend's first words were, "Where's the Hoodoo Man?"

"Is that right?" Dub asked, doing his best to feign disbelief.

Fralene insisted that it was so as she led him up the stairs to her uncle's bedroom. "It's true. He said that the Cemetery Man found him on the other side. He showed him the way back home."

Dub only offered a little incredulity. After all, they had all been through a great deal in the past few days. Why should he still disbelieve now that evidence incontrovertibly supported the existence of a potent spirit world and the availability of magic for use or misuse by any interested party?

Fralene stopped him just outside the Reverend Farnes's bedroom. "It's been a long night," she said, looking into the doctor's eyes. "I'm glad he's safe—so, so glad—but I think seeing you again does me good. More good than I can say."

"I learned some things," Dr. Corveaux said. "I've been out all night, following some very tenuous leads that finally led me to a very unfortunate realization."

"What did you find?" Fralene asked.

"Let's discuss it together," the doctor said, nodding toward the reverend's bedroom. "So I only have to go over it once."

Fralene agreed and led him into her uncle's bedroom. The Reverend Brown, sat in a chair at the Reverend Farnes's bedside. Beau at the Reverend Farnes's opposite elbow. The two old men, Farnes and Brown, had their hands clasped and tears shone in their eyes. It was clear to Dr. Dub Corveaux in that moment that the two old men were the very best of friends—the closest and most precious sort—and that their separation had been hard on both of them.

The reverend gave Dr. Corveaux a strange look when he saw him. "Good morning," the old pastor said with a crooked smile and a strange pause, "doctor."

Dub didn't know what to make of that.

He pulled up a chair and they pieced it all together, bit by bit.

XX

The doctor had backtracked over the reverend's footsteps on the day of the onset of his 'fugue state' as he jokingly referred to it. At Dexter's, where Fralene and the reverend had breakfast, the doctor had gotten a sense that one of the fry cooks, Jimmy, was hiding something. He had cornered the young man in the alley, in the dark, and urged some cooperation. Young Jim had admitted that the hoodoo lady, Mambo Rae Rae, had given him some strange packet of powder to put in the reverend's food and promised the young man some love and affection in return for his cooperation.

"So what did the powder do?" Fralene asked.

Dr. Corveaux explained that—based on what little he knew of vodou and its practice—such powders were often used to plant a curse, or 'prepare the way.' The spirit (a practicioner might say) was already summoned, but the reverend's body needed to be weakened, its natural defenses subverted so that the spirit summoned could take up residence.

"Hence your flu-like symptoms," the doctor offered in summation. "That was part of the curse. The precursor."

"Did you learn all this from that Gooden woman?" the Reverend Brown asked.

"No, sir, I did not," Dr. Corveaux answered. "Because she was dead."

He told them of what he'd found and reached the same conclusions. He simply left out the part about summoning her spirit or bearing witness to her final surrender to the hellhounds. "The way I figure it," the doctor surmised, "based on finding her dead like that, she was hired to give you that powder and get you possessed. Then, whoever hired her offed her so that she couldn't talk."

"That poor woman," the Reverend Brown said.

"She played with fire," Beau muttered, almost to himself.

"She got what she deserved," Fralene said coldly.

"So, who was it?" the Reverend Farnes asked. "Who hired her?"

Dr. Dub Corveaux shrugged. "That part, I don't know. But I think it's safe to assume it's the same gangsters who tried to disband the HCCB." He paused then, not sure how the news to follow would affect them. "There's more. Apparently, the gunmen who came here last night weren't the only gunmen loose in Harlem last evening. I saw in the paper this morning that someone gunned down Ms. Walker and her husband. And word on the street is Mr. Debbs is now missing."

"My God," the Reverend Farnes said. He and Brown shared grief-stricken looks. Dub Corveaux knew those looks well. They were the gazes of two men who had survived a charge across No Man's Land or an artillery bombardment—but who also realized that some of their closest friends had not.

A long, unpleasant silence fell as they all absorbed what had happened.

Reverend Brown was the one to finally break it. "But, to hire a voodoo priestess to put a curse on Barney," he said. "That's positively insane."

"It worked, didn't it?" Beau asked.

"But where would they even get such a notion?" the Reverend Brown asked. "Don't misunderstand, none of us can deny that the supernatural exists after the things we've seen. But, surely, most people don't take such things for granted, do they?"

"Criminals are a superstitious and cowardly lot," Fralene said, and her voice still had that bitter coldness in it, as though her hatred didn't know where to go. "Why shouldn't they try to put a curse on my uncle, if killing him outright didn't work?"

"Maybe something gave them the idea," the Reverend Farnes said. "Something they saw. Someone who's been giving them trouble."

He looked right at Dr. Corveaux as he made these statements.

Dr. Dub Corveaux rose from his chair, suddenly very uncomfortable. "Fralene, I need a little privacy to examine your uncle. And I think we could all use some coffee. What say you go brew some?"

"And breakfast," the Reverend Brown said, also rising. "Come on, Beau. Let's help your sister and leave the doctor with his patient for a bit."

"I'll be here," the doctor said. "I just want to give your uncle the once-over. Make sure he's all right."

Fralene, Beau and the Reverend Brown all nodded and left and went downstairs. Dr. Dub Corveaux was left alone with the Reverend Farnes. For a long time, the two stared at each other.

"Thank you," the Reverend Farnes said.

"My part in this was very small," the doctor answered.

"Hardly," the reverend answered. "Coming all the way to the other side to drag me back?"

The doctor was speechless. The reverend smiled a little, but it was a sad, suspicious smile, not a joyful one.

It was being on the other side, the doctor thought. *It gave him the sight. It allowed him to see through a great many things, including my disguise.*

Dr. Dub Corveaux lowered his eyes. Suddenly, he felt very ashamed under the Reverend Barnabus Farnes's stern gaze.

"It was the very least I could do," the doctor said.

"Let's make this quick and easy," the reverend said, staring up at him from the bed but still seeming to look down on him like a schoolmaster. "You're both of age, so I can't tell either of you to keep away from the other. Likewise, I don't think I can tell her the truth, nor do I think you would. Not yet, anyway."

Dub nodded, but kept his eyes down. "Those are true statements."

"I just want to know that she'll be safe," the reverend said. "She and Beau."

Dub raised his eyes. He wanted the reverend to see that he meant what he was about to say.

"I love her," he said.

"I know," the reverend answered. "But you're also in danger… constantly. So everyone around you is in danger, too. As a loud-mouthed crusader, I ought to know."

Dub nodded. "I know. But let me remind you that you got yourself into this mess. I had nothing to do with it."

"Half true," the reverend said. "I got myself into this mess. And henceforth, I can assure you, good doctor, I'll pick my battles. Can you say the same?"

Dub didn't answer.

"Likewise," the reverend continued, "I wasn't kidding when I said that those men who wanted me dead got their notions about curses and hexes from something they'd seen. That other fellow—the one who yanked me back from the other side—he strikes fear into them and he wages his war with powers I don't understand, but the very fact of his being—the things he does—proves to all those that he's fighting against that there are more potent powers in this world than dynamite and machine guns. If you can use them, so can they."

Dub couldn't argue with that. The reverend was right.

"So those are the only two warnings I'm going to give you," the reverend said. "You do whatever you have to do to keep her safe. And you never, ever forget that, sooner or later. As you sow, so you shall reap."

Dub nodded. He couldn't honestly say the thought hadn't occurred to him before. He just didn't want to admit it.

He thought he was fighting crime and corruption.

But he was just inspiring them… showing them the way to new tools, new weapons.

"All that being said," the reverend finally added, "I want to thank you."

He took the doctor's hand. Squeezed it. When Dub looked into the old man's eyes, he saw the glint of tears.

"Thank you," the reverend said.

Dub squeezed his hand in return. "I don't do this for thank yous," he said with a sad smile, then turned and left the room.

XXX

ACKNOWLEDGMENTS

Doc Voodoo: Crossfire was nursed through domestic upheaval, a speedy cross-country move, a difficult pregnancy, a premature birth and a lot of sleepless nights by the faith and support of my publisher, editor and friend, Matt Peters, so he gets kudos from the get-go.

Warm words of encouragement from Charles R. Saunders regarding Doc Voodoo's first outing and the promise of his future also kept me going when the going was tough.

Finally, a special thanks to Keith Gouveia, whose insightful criticism and boundless enthusiasm helped me hone and polish Doc's newest outing to razor sharpness.

And for all the friends, family and fans who have thrilled to Doc's adventures, written reviews, and driven me on by clamoring for more, rest assured: Doc Voodoo will return…

NO SURRENDER

A novella inspired by HP Lovecraft's Cthulhu Mythos.

In the wake of the American Civil War, Union Army Lieutenant Nathan Kenning commands a detachment of peacekeeping troops in Tampa, Florida. Their mandate: to police the area, assist the harried Freedmen's Bureau and defend the thousands of emancipated slaves in the region from Confederate reprisal. Then, one fateful evening, a ragged madman stumbles into town ranting about mass murder and black magic in an adjacent county. War-weary but determined, Lieutenant Kenning leads a small detachment into the swampy countryside to investigate the madman's reports of disgruntled Confederate soldiers running a brutal campaign of terror and murder… and, just possibly, awakening an ancient evil beyond mankind's influence or understanding…

ABOUT THE AUTHOR

Dale Lucas is a novelist, screenwriter, civil servant, and armchair historian. He is the author of the *Doc Voodoo* book series, the novella *No Surrender* and the story collection *Right Behind You.* His short stories have appeared in *Futuredaze: An Anthology of YA Science Fiction, Samsara: The Magazine of Suffering* and *Horror Garage.*

He lives in St. Petersburg, Florida.

Find him online at:

www.facebook.com/AuthorDaleLucas

www.AuthorDaleLucas.Wordpress.com

@DaleLucas114 (Twitter)